"Kitsap County Sheriff Detective Marcus Jefferson investigates cases no one else appreciates, but his current case is personal. Something about his Uncle Jerry's suicide just isn't right. *Jerry's Motives* spirals through a series of twists and turns to the surprising end that left me nodding my head in admiration at its cleverness."

~ ROBERT DUGONI, *#1 Amazon and New York Times bestselling author of* My Sister's Grave

"Relentlessly mysterious."

~ TOVI ANDREWS

"So many twists, it's a compelling story to the end."

~ SHEILA CURWEN, *editor*

"Couldn't put it down."

~ SANDRA BEALL

"*Jerry's Motives* was engaging from the beginning. When you believe you know how the story ends a surprise twist develops... This is a brilliant story that is hard to put down."

~ RJ BAUER, *author*

"Peter Stockwell is an author who spends time and energy on developing his talent for writing. The results are pronounced in his latest book, *Jerry's Motives*. The storytelling is tighter and more compelling. I look forward to more books from him."

~ ML SCOTT

Published by
Westridge Art
PO Box 3847
Silverdale, WA 98383

First Printing 2015

20 15 10 9 8 7 6 5 4 3 2 1

ISBN 978-0-9886471-2-1

Printed in the United States of America

Publisher's Note
This book is a work of fiction. Names, characters, places, and
incidents either are the product of the author's imagination or are
used fictionally, and any resemblance to actual persons, living or
dead, business establishments, events, or locales is entirely coincidental.

Cover by Peter Stockwell
Graphics from Shutterstock.com
Interior design by Marsha Slomowitz

Distributed by
Epicenter Press Inc. / Aftershocks Media
6524 Northeast 181st Street Suite #2
Kenmore, WA 98028

JERRY'S MOTIVES

THE STORY OF MARCUS JEFFERSON'S UNCLE

PETER STOCKWELL

Peter Stockwell
PO Box 3847
Silverdale, WA 98383

HOME: 360 697-4099 ~ CELL: 360 509-3651

STOCKWELLPA@WAVECABLE.COM

DEDICATION

This book is dedicated to readers of books everywhere,
who find escaping into created worlds of fiction
cathartic and emotionally enhancing to their lives.

*"Sometimes even to live
is an act of courage."*

————

SENECA

CHAPTER ONE

Kitsap County Sheriff Detective, Marcus Jefferson, sat at his desk reviewing the two year old report about his Uncle Jerry's death. Jeremais Jefferson had committed suicide.

He had doubted the results of the investigation then, and nothing since had changed his mind. How could a decorated law enforcement officer fall so far in such a short period of time?

"Are you reading about your uncle's death?" Marc looked up to find his partner and friend, Tom Knudson, standing in front of his desk. "Does Joan know?"

"Know what?" Marc scowled, realizing Tom was right. His tolerant wife, Joan Jefferson, had accepted the last investigation but made it clear his affinity for criminal examinations interfered with their lives as a couple. They had patched up their marriage because family was important; he believed it. Family stuck together and sacrificed.

Marcus had finished uncovering who caused the death of Mary Waite over three months ago. Now was the time to unravel his uncle's mystery. Suicide was not an option.

"You're looking into your uncle's suicide. I'm not sure she's interested in losing you to a fantasy." He sat in the chair next to Marc's desk. "She was pretty clear last time."

Marc frowned. "I don't have to let her in on this, and you can keep quiet. It shouldn't take long to find out the truth."

"Maybe. But if you're asking Snohomish County for help, they're probably less interested in changing their findings than you are."

Marcus stared at the document. "Do you believe in fate?" He looked at Tom.

"No, not really."

"Could it be fate to prove my uncle died at the hands of some perp? Fate to show my family is innocent? Fate to chance destroying everything I love and care about to confirm he was blameless?" The silence deafened the space between them.

Tom stood. "I hope you know what you're doing." He walked away leaving Marc thinking. *Had Uncle Jerry become involved in an impossible case?*

Enough vacation time, accumulated over the last few years, provided freedom for a family cruise to Alaska. He and Joan had saved for years to live their dream. Would Joan be upset if he allocated some of his time to prove his theory correct? No secrets. He had to tell her.

First, he made a call to Seattle Police connecting with his father, Tiberius Jefferson, a sergeant in the North Precinct. "Dad, when you get this, call me. I need some information about Uncle Jerry's death." His father had scrutinized the Snohomish report as a politeness to his sister-in-law. He never revealed his true feelings about it. Professional courtesy? Marc didn't know.

"I'm headed home," he informed the desk sergeant. "If you need me for anything, call." As he left, Sheriff Glenmore Fellington beckoned him into his office.

"Marc, I understand you want to investigate your uncle's suicide."

"Tom talk to you?"

"Yes, he's worried about you mixing it up with fellow officers. I agree with him. We don't need to open a closed case."

"If my uncle was investigating illegal drug trafficking, it may have been a reason to eliminate him, make it look like a suicide. I knew my uncle. He wasn't weak."

"Suicide is not necessarily an act of weakness. And he wouldn't be the first cop wanting to end a miserable life." Fellington sat down in his large leather office chair which creaked as his weight pressed into it. "Let it go."

"Is that an order or just your sage advice?" Marc glowered at his boss, knowing he'd be left to do what he wanted. As he turned to leave, he thought of one more thing. "If I'm right, we can help Snohomish with their drug problem."

"It's not our jurisdiction. We have enough problems right here."

"What if they're related? What if the same group of people supplying Snohomish are supplying Kitsap? What if we uncover who they are and take down their network? It could make you look like the best cop in western Washington."

"I don't need to be the best cop anywhere. You need to think this through before anyone gets hurt." Marcus nodded leaving his boss to finish whatever the pile of folders on the desk contained.

Sitting in his car, he reread the final verdict. Disgraced because of a drug investigation which went south. Asked to retire or be indicted for corruption. Depressed about the situation. Put an end to his suffering with his own hand. End of story.

He started the car, heading for a confrontation he wished to avoid and believed was inevitable. Joan was a beautiful, talented, intelligent woman, tolerant beyond tolerant. Now he wanted to present her with a scenario defying logic. A scenario which more than ever could create unbearable stress.

At the senior resident center for dementia patients, Joan's home away from home, he approached the front door with trepidation. His promise to be a more involved at home person challenged his desire to clear Jerry's character.

At the front desk, the receptionist acknowledged Marcus. "Is Joan expecting you?" He shook his head. She punched in a number on her phone set. Marc waited. "She'll be out in five minutes. She's finishing with a patient." He nodded and sat in a blue armchair to await fate's intention. A magazine advertised solutions to personal addictions. *Ironic*, he thought. A check of his watch showed less time passing than his imagination fashioned. Looking around the reception area, the colors on walls and floor offered a calming influence, tolerable for the moment to come.

A door opened and an angel emerged, offering assurance all was well. Joan's smile softened any strain on his face. He returned the expression. "What a nice surprise. Is something up?" Straight to the point.

"I came to ask you a serious question." The smile melted from her face. "Can we go somewhere?"

She led him through the angel portal to a staff lounge. "Alright, what's on your mind?"

"I've been reading the report about Uncle Jerry's suicide." He paused as if pausing would ease her response. "I want to delve deeper into the outcome and find out if anything needs changing."

"You want me to agree to use our vacation time for you to prove the Snohomish County Sheriff's Office is incompetent." The glare of her eyes could blind Medusa. "You promised to be more interested in our family." She sat in a vinyl seat next to a breakfast table. The glare darkened as he contemplated what to say. She was right and he knew what he asked was more than she might accept.

"I don't think it will be a big deal. I just want to clear up some questions I have and then we can take our vacation. I know the kids are excited, so I need to be there."

"If you want me to condone this, I can't, or better, I won't. Tom can look into it and report his findings to you while we're away."

"Okay, I'll call Aunt Lydia to let her know I'll look into this later."

The glare returned. "Did you call her about this?"

"No, she called me and e-mailed a report to me. Something about Jerry wanting her to contact me if anything happened to him."

She folded her arms across her chest. "She's setting you up. She knows you never believed the truth, and now she's going to have you put everything on hold just to satisfy her."

"Uncle Jerry left instructions to wait two years before getting in touch with me. She never said anything to me about this until now. She's kept his secret even when we gathered the family. I owe her this, but it can wait."

"Damn you. If she waited this long, there's more to her request than she's admitting. Check with her and find out what's going on." She stood. "I have to get back to work." He watched her depart; his heart hollow. Why had Aunt Lydia kept this secret?

After returning to his car he pondered the fate of investigating a case two and a half years old and colder than a Cascade Mountain lodge in winter. He opened his door and sat in the driver seat. As he pushed the key into the ignition, his cell phone sang. Looking at the caller, he smiled.

'Hi, Dad. Thanks for calling back."

"Why do you want information about Jerry?"

"Aunt Lydia contacted me about investigating his death. She said Uncle Jerry made her promise if anything happened to him, but she had to wait two years."

"That doesn't make any sense. You've seen her several times since my brother died. She could've asked you at any one of the gatherings. What did she say?" Marc switched his phone from one ear to the other to free his hand for opening the e-mail received early in the morning on his computer.

"I got this letter from her asking me to investigate because Jerry said he was sure something bad was about to happen and I was to look into his death. His instructions to her were to wait two years."

"Investigate what? The final report said he committed suicide. His personal service revolver was right next to him." Marc picked up the report, read many times during the day.

"The report has some discrepancies."

"It's not our jurisdiction and we shouldn't be questioning the finding of another agency. Does she have any reasons for pursuing this?"

"She asked me to come to Everett and meet with her. Will you come with me? I'd feel more comfortable with you there."

"Do the kids know?"

"Cammie and JJ? I don't think so. JJ might be of some help, though."

"He's not been with Snohomish Sheriff long enough to have any pull. They may even release him before his probationary period is finished, if he involves himself in this harebrained plan of Jerry's. Let me make a couple of inquiries and I'll get back to you. By the way, does Joan know about this?"

"Yeah, I just left her. She's not too keen on another convoluted wild goose chase, but I don't think this is one. Aunt Lydia isn't much for false premises or hair brain plans. Something's not right." They concluded the call with a promise for Marcus to wait. His vacation started in a month. A cruise to Alaska and Glacier Bay for ten days. All could be resolved by then, couldn't it? He was sure it could.

At home Marc opened his computer and Googled news reports about his uncle's death. Each account iterated the same information. Snohomish County Sheriff sergeant, Jeremais Jefferson was found by his wife, Lydia, dead of a gunshot wound to the head. After investigation by the Agency and an independent study by the Washington State Patrol, a report concluded the wound was self-inflicted. Jefferson had been involved in an undercover action against drug traffickers working in the county. When the operation collapsed due to the incompetent engagements of the sergeant, he retired after a 28 year career. Five months later he was dead.

Marc closed his browser. Nothing convinced him to drop pursuing his aunt's request. Waiting for a call from his father was difficult. He wanted conclusive evidence of foul play on the part of someone.

Pulling out a pad of paper he wrote questions about the conclusions from Everett, Washington. Does the drug investigation have any connection to the suicide? Who was the reporting officer? Where were the undercover operations conducted? Who were the officers involved in the undercover work? Why did the operation fail? How did Uncle Jerry fail? Or did he?

As he finished his last question, the phone rang. "Hello." He had what he wanted.

"Marc, I'm going up to Everett tomorrow to get a copy of the official findings from the State Patrol office. Come with me. We'll stop by the Snohomish Sheriff's office and get their report. I spoke with Sheriff Granger Collins. He's an old friend of mine and willing to help relieve Lydia's concerns."

"Good, I'll call Fellington and ask for the morning. Not much happens in Kitsap until evening. I can meet you at the ferry terminal. What time?"

"Walk on the 8:45 from Wendlesburg."

"Thanks, Dad. See you in the morning."

Studying the few pieces of his puzzle, with key parts of the picture missing, he put them aside when the back door opened. He left his home office to meet Joan in the kitchen. "Hello, my love. How was your afternoon?"

"Fine. Are the children home?"

"No."

"Then tell me what you want to do about your Aunt? And I want the truth." The glare of her expression revealed an internal angst.

"Fair enough. Aunt Lydia contacted me about Uncle Jerry, a request he made of her before he died. As far as I know he figured his life was finished because of the case he was working."

Joan sat in a chair, placing her purse on the table, her coat remained on. "Maybe he was so depressed, he knew he was going to die at his own hand and that's why he wanted her to wait. He wanted her to forget about what he did."

Marc sat next to her. "I don't think so. Her message indicated she had something for me which I have to get from her. I'll finish this up before we go on the cruise." She reached for his hands which he gave to her.

"If you need to help your aunt, do so. Remember your family, though. Be attentive to us, to me. And stay out of trouble." Marcus leaned in and kissed her. He understood.

"Dad's picking me up at the ferry in Seattle tomorrow. I have to call Fellington and let him know I won't be in until the afternoon." He rose from the table. "I'll be back to help with dinner."

In the office his call produced the usual clatter about following protocol. He promised a full report regarding the sojourn to Snohomish County. Another sort of clatter arose in the hallway. Marc investigated to find his three children placing coats in the closet and dropping bags on the bamboo floor.

"Where have you been?" Guiltless questions sometimes cause fear in the hearts of the guilty. Sarah, their middle child, answered first, "I was at my friend Maddie's house. I don't know what these two were doing."

James spoke, "Marcus and I were playing soccer with some other guys at the park."

"Thank you, but I want you to all keep us informed of your whereabouts from now on." Marc scratched his neck sensing a foreboding future attributable to Jerry's request. "I mean it, kids. I have an important case I'm about to start and it could invoke the wrath of some bad people." Three sets of eyes flitted from father to siblings and back. He had never warned them of any danger.

Joan stood in the doorway of the kitchen listening. "Go upstairs and get washed up for dinner." As the children ascended the steps, she approached her husband. "Why did you say those things to the children and not to me? Is there more to this than you're telling me?"

"I don't know. But if Uncle Jerry was concerned enough to let time pass and have his case go cold, I fear something worse may be in store for me. And that may mean you and the kids. I'll know more after I speak with my aunt." He entered the kitchen to help finish dinner's preparation.

After a silent meal filled with unspoken queries and a clean-up completed by the children, Marc and Joan retired to the master bedroom.

"Marc, what's bothering you?"

"My uncle was a fair man who worked hard to protect his community and raise a family he could be proud of. He never exhibited any trace of fear until that stupid undercover investigation they involved him in." Marc, slow and steady, removed articles of clothing as he continued. "As I grew up, I watched him tackle all kinds of difficult jobs and not once do I remember him slinking away from a challenge."

Joan remained dressed in her nurse's uniform. "Is this quest enough to come between us? Again?"

Marc watched her for a sign showing him how to answer. He wanted to be the type of man who was always available, but he had his duty to the community. What had she said before? You care more for your police buddies than you do your family. Was she right? But he did love his family and would protect them at all costs. How much was the price of this investigation?

CHAPTER 2

"Jefferson, come in here." Assistant Sheriff Captain Daniel Kopinski of Snohomish County called out for his favorite sergeant, Jeremais Jefferson.

"Yes, sir," he said as he entered his boss's office. He had been with the department for twenty seven years, earning praise from fellow officers and public officials. Already assigned to work the Charles 1 division, he took on special investigations, as needed. He stood by the desk awaiting another set of distinctive orders.

"Close the door and have a seat." He complied and waited as the captain shuffled folders. Pulling one out, he tossed it across the desk. "Read that."

Opening it he scanned the information and looked up. "Is this current?"

"As current as yesterday." Jerry perused more closely. "We want to set up an undercover with you in charge." Closing the folder he placed it on the desk.

"What are you thinking of setting up?"

The captain pulled another folder from a drawer. "You will act as the lead investigator organizing a group to go out and gather evidence. To make this work, though, we have to get a person into the organization so they think they control our office. I want you to oversee that person."

Captain Kopinski waited as he opened the folder and read. Closing it and looking up, he said, "I don't think this is a good idea.

It may be better to have me stay in charge and become the corrupt person. It wouldn't be easy, but it may have better results if the target in charge of this thinks they have me on the payroll."

"That could be dangerous for you. I still think a person on the inside is best."

"Who do you think can pull this off?" Jerry stood as he spoke. He look out the interior windows at the officers conducting interviews, writing reports, and generally being busy.

"Vice sent a list." He accepted it from Kopinski and read. Three of the names were in his precinct. Two were fairly new recruits in the north precinct.

"How do you propose we get someone into the operation?" Jerry returned the list.

"We need someone who is not known in the county and can be seen as a person wanting to get involved. Maybe an addict or a person with a history of drug involvement."

Jerry sat again not sure about the possibility of success. "I hope you have some insight I'm missing, because this is real sketchy."

"I know. We'll set up a plan before we go in, but we must limit the number who are informed of what's happening."

"I agree, but who do we bring in?"

Kopinski wrote three names on a paper and passed it to Jerry. "Pick two and then we'll do background work and see which one fits the profile we're creating."

Jerry studied the names and wrote a circle around his choices. He handed the paper back to his captain, who nodded. He stood to leave. "I hope this works."

"I do, as well. We don't need this business in our county."

"Let me know when we start." Jerry left, returning to his desk. He wasn't sure he wanted to be involved, but the criminal activity was escalating and had to be curtailed. Finding the head and cutting it off became a prime target in his mind.

CHAPTER 3

After parking at the Wendlesburg police station near the ferry, Marc trudged to the terminal and walked on the boat to an unsure fate. He and his father were headed out to gather information about a case which may have killed Jerry.

Although he doubted suicide resulted, he kept an open mind. In his line of work nothing surprised him. Human dynamics, as diverse and intricate as any physics problem he studied in college, created challenges in investigations.

When the ferry landed at Colman Dock in Seattle, he walked down the ramp from the second floor waiting area and saw his father's patrol car on the other side of Alaska Way.

"Thanks for doing this. Dad. I'm not sure what we'll find, but we can clear up any questions and close it." Marc climbed into the front passenger seat and they headed out.

"Son, you and I have been on the same page about this since it happened. I've not said anything because I didn't have the evidence to confront the findings. Let's uncover what your aunt has for us and compare it to the records we get from WSP and Snohomish."

"Do you think she has documents related to his case?"

"Knowing my brother, he kept his own files secreted away from official records so he had a trail to follow if anything went wrong. And wrong it went. Do not under any circumstances mention any evidence we uncover at your aunt's. We'll gather all we can and determine if there is anything to follow."

"Sounds good." The drive to the State Patrol office in Marysville had the usual crowd of cars as they approached Everett. Road construction continued to be a way of life as if employment opportunities were satisfied by never ending road work.

After procuring copies of the records from WSP, they returned to Everett and Charles 1 Division in the South Precinct of the Snohomish County Sheriff's office. Finding Granger Collins waiting for them, they sat in his office while he retrieved copies of the files regarding Jerry.

"I wish this meeting was under better circumstances. Your brother was a fine officer, until his final operation." Granger displayed genuine concern about Jerry, but when asked about the case, the sheriff clammed up.

Tiberius confronted him. "Granger, what was Jerry working on when he was asked to retire? What prompted him to leave?"

"I'm afraid I cannot discuss any cases we still have pending."

"So his undercover work is an open case. I thought it had been finished." Marc sat silent absorbing the emotional environment of the assistant sheriff.

"The group of people we were after have not been identified and apprehended so I cannot discuss it with you."

Marc entered the conversation. "We have a similar problem with drug trafficking in Kitsap. If the two are related, we may be able to shut down their operations, if we work together on this."

"I don't see how our investigation relates to anything in Kitsap. We still have no connection or anyone inside helping to break them. Jerry was supposed to be the one who gathered what was needed and he failed."

A secretary knocked and entered when directed. She handed a folder to Captain Collins and left. He gave it to Tiberius without opening it.

"Thanks, Granger, I know we can alleviate my sister-in-law's sorrow with this." They shook hands and left for Aunt Lydia's house.

"Is he always so cool to old friends?" Marcus asked. He held the folders from the two agencies, waiting to read them when he was alone.

"He can be, but I think this may have been more of a reluctance to share what happened. He was the one who came when Lydia called. They were close, although he was not part of the investigation."

At Lydia's house they parked in the driveway and were met as they came up the walkway. "How are two of my favorite men?" She acted upbeat, relaxed, as if she had no cares.

"Good morning, Lydia. Marc and I are here to find out what you have." They hugged each other and Marcus in turn hugged his aunt.

"I don't know what to do. Your brother was tight lipped about what happened. I miss him. Would you care for some coffee?"

"Thanks, I would." Tiberius sat on the sofa.

"Would you like some, also?" Marcus nodded and sat in a side chair. She left for the kitchen. Silence held the time before she returned with two mugs. "I know you are in somewhat of a time constraint." She handed them the mugs.

Marcus spoke, "When you called, you said you had something for me. That Uncle Jerry asked you to wait two years before contacting me. Do you have any idea why?"

"No, but he was adamant about not involving either of you. He was sure something bad was going to happen, and then he killed himself. I still don't understand his reasoning." Tears filled her eyes, spilling over the lids.

"Listen, Sis, maybe Marcus and I can clear up some of this confusion about what happened." He motioned for her to sit next to him. "Now, what is it Jerry has for us?"

"He left me a key to keep on my house key ring and I was not to let anyone have it. When they investigated his death, they scoured the house looking for something. I thought it was related to the shooting, but now I'm not so sure. This key is the only thing he left for me with instructions to contact Marcus if anything happened to him."

"But he asked you to wait two years. That's the part which makes no sense to me," Marcus said. "Anyway, do you have the key?" She reached into her pocket and pulled out a set of keys. She removed one from the ring.

"Here." She placed it in Tiberius's hand. It was a small key for a padlock or similar security device.

"Do you know what it fits?" he asked. She shook her head.

"Well, Dad, I guess we have some investigating to do." Tiberius handed him the object. A number on it indicated it belonged with a storage place, but not where.

"One more thing," Aunt Lydia said, "he asked me to mail you a letter which he had in our bank safety deposit box. I didn't send it." She pulled a small envelope from her other pocket. "I went to the bank yesterday and retrieved it." Marc accepted it. "Please find out what happened." Tears returned.

"We will." Marc unsealed the letter and removed a piece of paper. As he read he looked at the key and then back at the letter. He nodded.

"What's it say?" His father leaned toward him.

"We have the place this key fits and it's not here in Everett." He handed the letter to his father. "When did you and Uncle Jerry go to Vancouver?"

"Right after he retired. He wanted to get away from the turmoil. We spent a weekend there."

"Did you take any boxes with you?"

"No, but we left a suitcase. The suitcase was not one of our new set. He told me later, after we returned, that it was important and was safely hidden away."

"Dad, I guess we're headed north."

They bid adieu to Lydia and left the house. As they entered the car Tiberius looked at Marcus and said. "We need to delay any trip to Vancouver."

"I agree. You noticed them, too." He nodded.

As they drove away, a black car followed.

At the approach to Interstate 5 south, the black car turned before entering the onramp. Marcus and Tiberius increased speed to match highway driving. Smiling at his father Marc broke the silence. "I guess Uncle Jerry had a few secrets." Tiberius returned the smile and pushed the pedal.

As they approached Alderwood Mall and south Snohomish County, a set of blue lights flashed behind them. Several cars moved right but the lights kept coming. Tiberius moved over to let the state patrol pass but the car pulled in behind them.

When they came to a stop both men displayed badges to the Stater. "May we be of help to you?" Tiberius asked. Marcus readied an exit from his side, not expecting a confrontation but preparing for it.

"No sir, but I may be of help to you. Would you step out of the car? I want to show you something." They vacated their vehicle unsure of what was occurring.

On the passenger side away from highway traffic the WSP patrolman reached in his car and retrieved a paper. "I was asked to give this to you by my sergeant. He said you had come to Marysville about Jeremais Jefferson. You are his brother and nephew, right?"

Marcus took the paper from the patrolman. "Yes, I'm Detective Marcus Jefferson of Kitsap County and this is Sergeant Tiberius Jefferson of Seattle PD. What's this about?"

"I'm not sure, but I know the WSP was not content with the final verdict regarding your uncle. They had nothing more to go on, so the case was closed and sited as a suicide."

"Thank you, officer? I didn't get your name."

"Patrolman Bennie Goodman, and no I don't play a clarinet." They chuckled. "Find out the truth, but be careful. This county is not as clean as it should be. And the mess Jefferson was investigating still exists."

"How is State Patrol entwined?" Tiberius asked.

"An open file exists but is not being pressed until more evidence shows up or somebody makes a mistake. That's all I know. Here's my card. Call if you need anything." Goodman returned to his car and left.

Marcus took the card and placed it in his pocket. "This is more elaborate than I expected. Let's head back to Seattle. I'll arrange for a couple of days off so I can head to Vancouver. Do you want to come?"

"Seattle PD is not going to interfere with a seasoned cop requesting a couple days to unwind. I have plenty of leave time. Your mother will just have to understand."

"Thanks, Dad. I hope Joan will." Returning to the car, they headed south to Seattle. After being dropped off at the ferry terminal, Marc bought a ticket for Wendlesburg and returned to an afternoon of sorting out the information gathered from the trip north.

Reading the paper the WSP patrolman gave him, he understood the need for quiet investigation. Some of the names on the list were a surprise. Some he didn't know. At the office a check of records for the state could open possible reasons for the failed operation.

His cell buzzed. The name on the screen was T. Jefferson. "Hi, Pop. What's up?"

"I ran the license of the black car which followed us. It belongs to an Import/Export business in Everett owned by one Andrew Pepper who also lives in Everett. He runs his business out of a series of warehouses on the waterfront."

"He'd have access to inspectors and other county people." Marcus read the list of names to his father. "Maybe some of these people are mixed up in a dirty industry."

"I sure hope a couple of those names aren't. I'd be disappointed. Check the others though and we'll see what pops."

"Your brain is on track with mine." They clicked off. Aunt Lydia had opened Pandora's Box when she contacted Marcus. Joan was sure to be more than unsympathetic, decrying Marcus's insensitivity to immediate family and her. He had to get this solved and solve it fast.

In the office Fellington called him in. "What did you uncover? Conspiracies galore?"

"Glen, you're obtuse sometimes. And yes, it seems some sort of breach of protocol has been in play in Snohomish. I can't discuss it yet as I don't have enough information but it warrants an investigation."

"This has to be on your time."

"If I uncover ties to Kitsap, I'll let you know. Then we can place it in the hopper with our work. Who's in charge of vice these days?"

"McClelland, but let me deal with him. You do what you need but outside of solving Kitsap crimes. He can come in if you find anything."

Marc thought about the warning. Fellington had been a good leader and retirement was next. This investigation of Jerry had to be concluded before any change of sheriff. Elections weren't for another year. If he cleaned up the county, the electorate would back his being the next head man. Joan's father had approached him already. As a county commissioner, Kendall Jackson had pull and political savviness.

The position would be free of investigation time which kept him away from family, pleasing Joan. It would mean more money, something not really needed, but appreciated.

The downside was his losing friends and colleagues who would become underlings to evaluate and lead. As sheriff, political correctness and public functions became the norm.

For now he needed the support of family and fellow officers. Uncle Jerry's death was not what it seemed. Someone made the scene a suicide. This person did a much better job than Roger Waite, who attempted a scene setting in his last case, but for entirely different reasons. What was being covered up? What did Jerry know which cost him his life? What was Marc getting himself into?

CHAPTER 4

Jerry met with a vice cop known by very few people. Captain Kopinski picked Wiley Fingers because he had a reputation in the area as a bad ass, sleazy sort who would sell his own mother to make a profit. Few of the vice cops in Snohomish knew him, but his arrest rate was good. He took no credit.

Getting him into an organization such as Andrew Pepper ran, might be easier than Jerry first imagined. Once he was in, he could appear to turn a good cop bad and the ruse would be complete. After a few months of evidence gathering the case would be rock solid and the cartel ground to dust.

All the planning seemed to indicate a positive outcome barring unforeseen situations. The contingency plans called for immediate take down of any perpetrators who fell in the net. If fate prevailed, the entire network, including the ring leader or leaders could be swept up and sent to Monroe State Prison for a long time.

Kopinski called Jerry into his office ostensibly to inform him of a promotion. "Are you set to begin?" Jerry assured his captain all was ready.

"Wiley has contacted a key person and is working to set up a deal for narcotics to distribute throughout the eastern part of the county. I have a couple of officers who will assist me with the investigation. We'll make a show of it and then when Wiley is locked in, he'll get me to turn against the department and feed info to the organization. Of course, we'll be controlling what we give and every so often make an arrest to add legitimacy to what we're doing.

"Jefferson, this better work."

"As long as the drug people think they have me in their control, we'll gather evidence and I'll work my way up the ladder, as will Wiley, and when we have the goods we'll pounce with the entire power of Snohomish County and Washington State Patrol."

"I can't be your salvation if things go badly. I'll claim no knowledge of your involvement and will bury you as a crooked cop if this does not work."

"Yes sir, but I'll make it work." Jerry left the office and returned to his desk to implement the first steps in the destruction of the vile and vicious organization of drug dealers ruining young lives and profiting from the illegal activity they committed.

At home he informed Lydia he was knotted in a major case and at times words may be spoken, printed, broadcast, or otherwise transmitted about him which were not true. "Please believe me. I love you and our children with every fiber of my being. What I'm doing will make Snohomish County and the cities a better place to live. I am not straying away from you as much as playing a role in a stage play."

"Will this include other women in your life?" Her question cut to the heart of his soul. He had no reasonable answer for he had no idea the corruption to which he would be subjected, so as to turn an honest, upstanding, respected officer of the law into a depraved antihero.

"I don't think so, but I love you. Remember, whatever happens I am first and foremost your man."

The next few days, he lived his life without change, returning each night to his house and his family. Although his children were adults, they lived at home while attending college. One, a student at Western Washington University's Everett branch, studied environmental science; the other attended the police academy having recently graduated from Washington State University with a criminal law degree.

He began the interrogation of low level drug dealers asking the pertinent questions before releasing them from prison to go about the business of casting a cloud of doubt over their suppliers. Another attempt by the Sheriff's office to restrict drug dealing in the county.

Harassment of these lowlifes allowed Wiley to string them along and build his street cred. He then could make his play for the bigger fish.

"I know we can set that sergeant up," he said one day to a middle level supplier who had been run in for a test of how much Wiley had dug in.

"You sure are a mouthy punk. What can you do? You're a scumbag dealer who doesn't have enough brains left to think through anything except your next fix."

"Interesting you think I'm a user. I may supply, but I leave the shit alone. I don't need my brain fried."

"You sound like a cop."

"That's because if you don't think like them, they catch you in a stupid mistake. When you're sent to Monroe for being stupid, I'll stay here and run your operation for you. Only I'll be making the cash and nothing will go to you. Capisce?"

"Fuck you."

"No, but while you're incarcerated I'll have fun fucking your old lady."

The fight ended when Wiley erased one of the competition. A few days in the hospital for the dealer would allow a crack in the door to move up in the organization. He used the time well.

Jerry had little contact with Wiley. As dealers came in he heard about the fractures in the structure as someone was working their way higher into the gang.

All was going as planned. What could go wrong? Another few weeks and the cartel would collapse as a house of cards.

CHAPTER 5

"I've arranged for some time away. We can go to Vancouver whenever you're ready."

"Dad, sounds good to me. I've arranged for leave, too. Joan's not happy but as long as you're with me, she thinks I'll stay out of trouble." Tiberius laughed.

"She is a smart one. I've liked her from the first day you brought her home. Your mother knew right away she would be a match for you. So while we investigate this mess my brother got into, we'll make sure she remains happy about you."

"Very funny. I can handle my own family." They arranged to meet in Edmonds with another deputy dropping Marc off at the Kingston terminal. He would carry a small bag and the essential documents and badge for easy border crossing in Blaine. A hotel room had been reserved for two nights. No need for anyone to suspect anything other than father and son time away from police business. A show at a local theater completed the ruse.

If the black car occupants suspected anything, they planned to misdirect and obfuscate. Nothing remained except to empower the plan.

"Joan, I'll be gone for two nights. Dad and I are retrieving something for Aunt Lydia. We'll be able to conclude our investigation more quickly."

"You better not be lying to me or I'll make your life a living hell. I'll have your name smeared in mud and dragged through dirt. You'll be useless to the county."

"Where's this coming from? I haven't kept anything from you. Uncle Jerry had something on the county and it cost him his position and his life. It isn't going to be solved unless someone outside of Snohomish starts digging."

"What if the bad guys aren't happy with you excavating their activities? What if they decide to eliminate their antagonists? What if you get killed?" She pounded her fists on his chest as tears rained down her face.

"He held her hands to stop the assault. "I won't let it get that far. I don't want to die. I have you and our children. Living is the better option." They held each other tight as if this moment would end and no other would find a place in their timeline of life.

Sleep came in fits and starts for both Joan and Marcus. As morning broke in the bedroom window, he rose to prepare for his duty call north. Joan lay quiet, at last. He slipped out before anyone woke. Sarah, Marcus, and James knew he was leaving for a couple of days. They suspected the tension of another serious case meaning their attitudes had to be tolerant. Dad was reasonable, while Mom ranted about importance of family. They sailed the stormy seas of the house with care.

At the Edmonds dock Marc said goodbye to Tom Knudson who volunteered to escort his colleague and friend to the terminal.

"I hope you find what you need. Your uncle was a good man who got railroaded. Find the bastards who did this and waste them."

"Tom, sometimes you sound like Rambo or Dirty Harry. Shoot first, apologize later." They laughed while waiting for the Walla Walla to dock and disgorge vehicles and passengers.

"Your father meeting you in Edmonds?"

"Yeah, we set 8:30 as the time since the 7:55 will get in about then. I'll call you when I'm returning if you want to pick me up. I'm not sure Joan wants to be inconvenienced."

"But it's okay to disrupt my life."

"You're not married. Any woman you're lucky enough to convince to stay with you will have to work around my return."

They shook hands and Marc walked the ramp to the entry gangway. The key and letter were secured in his jacket pocket, free from wallet or other items in pants pockets. The ride across Puget Sound gleamed with the morning sun shining on the water. He took it as a portent of good fortune, admirable and gainful.

He found his father engaged in conversation with an Edmonds police officer charged with traffic control at the Edmonds ferry line. "Marc, meet Jim Parsons. He and I went to the state academy together." Introductions made, the conversation ended and they began the journey to find a suitcase which contained evidence of crimes and corruption. At least, that was the consensus of two intrepid peace officers.

"Is there anyone you don't know?" Marc asked. "Where's your car?"

"I figured a little subterfuge was called for. If the people in the black car are dangerous, then we need to be prepared for answering any attack with commensurate force. Being in an unknown car keeps us safer."

"Great thinking. I'm glad I got my brains from Mom, though."

"Funny. But you're right, she is smarter than me and between us you have both sets of genes for intelligence." An hour and thirty minute drive lay ahead. Conversation about family, work, and grandkids filled the time.

In Blaine Canadian Border officers matched badges and passports allowing fellow law enforcement people to continue without hang up. The drive to Vancouver constituted another forty-five minutes.

At the hotel, a moderate downtown Ramada Inn on Grandville Avenue, they checked to see if their room was accessible. Since the tourist season ended and it was midweek, a double occupancy was ready.

Knowing the address of the storage building to be nearby, they walked five blocks to reconnoiter whether anyone followed them to Canada. Returning toward the hotel the destination was two blocks back and one over. They entered the office area and asked the pretty desk clerk for directions to compartment 384, the number on the key.

"How was this locker paid for and for how long?" Tiberius scrutinized the woman for any hint of missing information. He surmised she was an employee two years ago despite her youth.

Looking on the computer screen she found the history and said, "It was paid in cash in advance for five years."

"Is that a common practice?" he asked.

"Sometimes. People come in here and rent space to keep heirlooms, overflow from the house, and downsizing left overs."

"Alright, take us to the locker."

She closed the screen and guided them down a series of halls to a bank of large school-like lockers. Many had padlocks on them. Others awaited servicing clients for a myriad of reasons.

They found the correct one and watched as the girl swayed her hips back to her reception counter. She turned to glance at them as she went around a corner.

"If I were only younger and single."

"Dad, I don't care to hear about your fantasies."

"Tell me she wasn't flirting a little."

"Could be, but maybe she wants the attention of a younger, more attractive male." They laughed.

Pulling the key from his jacket pocket, Marc pushed it in the lock slot and turned it. The padlock dropped open. He removed it and his father opened the door. Inside sat a beat up suitcase which had seen better days of travel. The brown green coloring of the sides did nothing to enhance the value of the contents.

Tiberius spoke first. "Let's take this to the room and examine the contents."

"Is the suitcase locked?" Marc tried the handle locks which snapped open. Placing the case on the floor, he exposed the materials inside. Several folders held pictures, papers, lists, and maps. He closed the case, latching the locks shut.

"Let's go," he said to his father. They carried their prize to the reception area encountering the young clerk.

"Is there a copy company around here," Tiberius asked. Marcus smiled and nodded his head. Copy everything and put the originals back. Safety first.

She flicked her hair behind her ear with a hand and opened the computer screen. A few clicks of the keys and strokes of the mouse and she printed out the nearest office store with copying capabilities.

"Thank you. You have been very helpful."

"Do you need anything else? I can show you around town, if you need." Both men smiled.

"Thank you, but no." She handed them the paper and Marcus wondered if she meant to be friendly or expensive.

Carrying the suitcase to the hotel, they unloaded the contents in their room. Surveillance photos of officers, people, and groups of people, showed scenarios with drug deals happening, exchanges of cash, and a person beaten. Uncle Jerry had, in deed, uncovered hell in Snohomish.

———∞———

"Dad, after we copy all of these documents, what's next?" Marc shuffled through several papers.

"We return the suitcase to the locker and create a similar safety valve for someone of our choice to find and continue the investigation, if something goes wrong.

"I suggest WSP. They already have an open case."

"Good. You figure out what is needed. I'll take these to the copy store." Tiberius left as soon as the suitcase had been refilled.

Marc removed his tablet computer from his bag and created instructions to an unknown person. How to achieve the task would be developed later.

The lock of the door clicked and Tiberius entered without the suitcase. He carried several large envelopes, the copies. "That wasn't too painful," he said. "Did you get something together for WSP?"

"Yes, we can decide how to implement it later."

"Let's go have some fun." After securing the envelopes in the room safe, they cleaned up and left for an early dinner and show at one of the local theaters.

"Dad, thanks for setting this up. I know you want to figure out what happened to Uncle Jerry as much as I do." The ride down the elevator relaxed both men, the increased stress from the afternoon activities released for the moment.

In the lobby a familiar face sat in an overstuffed wing chair near the concierge's desk. Marcus's face fixed a confusion as he stared at his father. "Did you invite her?"

Tiberius grinned and wagged a finger at the young clerk from the storage building. Marc's forehead wrinkled. The girl rose from the chair and approached. "Introduce yourself, please."

"Good afternoon, Mr. Jefferson."

"Excuse me. Who are you and how do you know who I am?" His eyebrows scrunched together.

Tiberius intercepted the conversation. "Marc, I'd like to introduce you to Officer Regina McDonald of the Royal Canadian Mounted Police." Marc's jaw dropped.

Her hand extended for the obligatory shake. He accepted. "You are an enigma. How is it you came to be at the desk when we arrived?"

"Your aunt contacted me yesterday informing me of your appearance. We had an agreement." Marc's arms spayed out with palms open.

"This case gets weirder by the moment. Dad, what is this?" Tiberius laughed.

Regina continued, "When your aunt and uncle came north two years ago, he contacted our office, explained what he was doing and asked for one of our team to be available if either of them ever called us. We didn't expect to hear from them again."

"So when my aunt called, your agency must have been rather surprised." She nodded. "What did she say?"

"She asked that we keep an eye out for you to be sure no one had followed you. What is this about?"

Tiberius spoke, "My brother died two years ago from a self-inflicted gunshot. It now appears there was more to his death than the official report indicated."

"What was in the suitcase?"

"All of the files he accumulated during the investigation of a drug distribution ring in Snohomish County."

McDonald clarified her position. "What he explained to RCMP was that he had infiltrated an organization and needed to keep some evidence up here away from his department. Asked us not to question it, just keep an eye on the locker. At first we checked every week or so. After a couple of months of nothing, we let it go."

"He never informed you about his retirement?" Marcus moved to his father's side.

"No." She looked older than her receptionist persona. Her clothing reflected more the look of a young Canadian business professional.

"Thank you for your help." Marcus said. "Now I'm in need of another favor. I need to know what my uncle said to your department two years ago which convinced you to help him."

"He said he feared something bad was about to happen and he needed assurances his family would be safe. Our challenge was to provide protection of the suitcase since it contained evidence. He described the situation at home and we agreed."

Marcus continued, "So did Uncle Jerry pay in advance for five years?"

"Yes, and as a result we have monitored it off and on, as I described."

Tiberius listened as his detective son questioned Miss McDonald. He then interjected. "How long have you been with RC?"

"This is my third year."

"You looked very young at the locker facility. If may be so bold to ask, how old are you?"

"I'm not offended," she responded, "I have a youthful countenance. I'm actually twenty-seven."

"My nephew, JJ, Jerry's son, is the same age. He is now with the Snohomish County Sheriff's Office. Is there any reason to believe he's in danger if he stays?"

"I wouldn't know. Since you have returned the suitcase to the locker, we will continue to monitor any activity regarding it and inform you as soon as possible." The men handed her business cards and she left.

"Dad, I think Uncle Jerry got in too deep and when he wanted out or had enough to convict, they killed him. How are we going to connect the dots? If all of the information he collected was not enough to convict, we'll have to dig into it and it won't sit well with Snohomish."

"I agree, but now is not the time. Let's go out and celebrate our discovery."

"How did you find out Miss McDonald was with RCMP? She appeared and acted so different at the storage lockers."

"When I returned the suitcase, she approached me and asked if I was Tiberius Jefferson. She also asked if you were Marcus."

"Let's hope all goes well and we find out who is behind all of this and prove Uncle Jerry was murdered."

"We will. Let's leave." As they drove from the hotel another black car seemed to shadow them. Or was it over-imaginative brains?

CHAPTER 6

Jerry sat in the superintendent's office of the RCMP division in North Vancouver, British Columbia. The trip north from Everett had been ordinary, but the conversation about Snohomish County seemed bizarre to the Mountie in charge.

"Sir, I ask only to have evidence, which I plan to secrete at a local storage facility, be guarded."

"And the nature of the materials include what?"

"I've been working for the sheriff's office of Snohomish County as a lead investigator with corrupted morals. It was part of an undercover operation. We were attempting to remove an insidious organization dealing drugs to our citizens. They allegedly are involved in prostitution, money laundering, and burglary, as well." Jerry presented a list of the evidence as a salve for cooperation.

"I see. So we are to investigate this group." The superintendent looked incredulous. "I don't see how we can help you."

"I am not asking for you to participate other than caring for one locker. A liaison will suffice."

"Such an unusual request may require authorization from Victoria. After all, provincial parliament provides our funding and guidance. The provincial super may need to confirm."

"Very well, if you would please see to it. Remember, the fewer who know about this material, the better."

Superintendent Peter Buell picked up his phone, punched in numbers and said, "Come in here, please." Hanging up he studied Jerry. "I'm not sure what you hope to accomplish with this charade, but I have a new officer who will be assigned to carry out your appeal, as bizarre as it is."

A knock on the door alerted them to another person. When commanded, the door opened and an attractive young female in red coat and tan skirt entered, snapping to attention.

"Sir, you asked for me?"

"At ease, McDonald. I'd like to introduce you to Sergeant Jefferson of Snohomish Sheriff's Office in Washington State. He has an unusual request for help." Turning attention to Jerry, he continued. "Maybe you should explain."

"It's a pleasure to meet you. I am investigating a criminal organization in my county which is disrupting lives and creating problems. I have with me a suitcase full of evidence I intend to hide here in Vancouver. I have come to you instead of the Vancouver police because I trust RCMP more than other law enforcement."

"McDonald, take a seat. I'll get us some refreshments while you work out the scheme for this awkward assignment." The superintendent left Jerry and the police woman alone.

"Please, explain what it is you want me to do?" The young lady sat in the chair next to Jerry, leaning toward him.

"I placed a suitcase in a locker in Vancouver near the ferry terminal. It contains evidence which I have gathered but did not turn in at my precinct." McDonald leaned in furrowing her brow. "I do not trust anyone in my district."

"Then why come to us?"

"I have to trust someone and RCMP is the best I know other than my family."

"Is your family not willing or are they unavailable?"

"Miss McDonald, I do not want them involved."

"Please call me Regina or Ginny. What is it they do?"

"My brother is a Seattle cop and his son is a detective in Kitsap County. They do not know about the case yet. If something happens to me, they'll be all over this as soon as they get the word." Jerry finished explaining the details of his plan and elicited a promise to help when called upon. He left the office, returning to Lydia at the hotel. His fear, not abated, but assuaged, for now.

CHAPTER 7

"Dad, the play was a good idea. I'm glad to relax after all that has happened today. Thanks."

"My pleasure. Let's get some sleep and head home tomorrow." The evening air reflected the upbeat mood of the lawmen. The stroll along the waterfront enlivened their steps as they headed to the hotel for a restful slumber.

As they approached the front entry another black car drove away from the parking lot. Coincidence? "Marc, there are too many black cars in this world."

"Yeah, they can't all be after us, can they?" They laughed and pushed the elevator button for the third floor. As it closed, a man slid his hand between the closing doors.

"Excuse me, gentlemen." Entering after the doors slid apart, he continued, "I'm on the second floor." Marc pushed the button.

Tiberius asked, "Are you from around here?"

"No, I came in for a visit with my in-laws. Are you visiting, as well?"

"Yes, we came to see a play." The Elevator stopped and the doors opened. They nodded a good-bye, continuing to the next floor. "Do you think he was telling the truth?"

"Gees, Dad, getting a little paranoid aren't you." The elevator stopped. "I get it though. Something is not right." They stepped out and walked to the room at the end of the hall.

Marcus pushed the key through the slot and watched the green light flash approval. Opening the door, he stood aside to allow his father to enter. Neither of them were carrying weapons, but Tiberius reached for his anyway.

"What's wrong?"

"Hush." The whisper of his voice caused a similar action by Marcus. "Someone's been in here and not to turn down the beds"

They moved deeper into the room allowing the door to close and latch. Touching nothing, they studied subtle differences in the way their items lay around the room. "Someone came in here today." Marcus moved to the safe. "Nothing seems to be missing." He operated the combination releasing the latch.

Tiberius came closer. As the door opened, an envelope slipped out. Marcus removed the others handing them to his father. "They all seem to be here and intact," Tiberius said.

"Think we should contact McDonald so she keeps the locker safe?"

"Maybe. She could bring a print kit just in case our visitor left us a gift. It's late though."

"Call her and I think we need to post these to my office and not carry them with us." He collected the envelopes from his father. "I'll ask down at the desk for postage and discreetly interrogate them as to who came in here. Probably will lead to nothing."

"Alright." His father punched in the number on McDonald's business card, turning away from Marcus, who locked the material back into the safe. "She'll be here in twenty minutes. By the way, to-night I'm checking the locker to be sure the contents are safe. And I'll procure a second locker and move the suitcase to it. Just to be safe."

"Good. I'll be right back." Marcus opened the door, checking for unwanted guests before exiting the room.

On the elevator he prepared a plan of attack for the front desk personnel and the night manager. Whoever came searching for the evidence had not opted for a safe cracking; preferring to open draw-ers, check closets, and move bed sheets. The person, or persons, were amateurs. The tablet had been off when they left and was on when they returned. A closet door stood ajar, not closed. One bed ruffle was folded into the bedding.

As the door of the elevator slid apart he saw McDonald, who must have broken several speed limits to arrive within ten minutes. "What is this about? A break-in of your room? Is anything missing?"

"No, the copies are still in the safe. The intruder either didn't know about them or decided cracking the safe was too much. My father awaits your arrival. Did you bring it with you?"

She held up a small fishing style box and smiled. "Haven't practiced this since training school. What are you doing?"

"I am going to interrogate these fine people until they explode with information. Or I'll ask them a few pertinent questions and see what happens."

"Okay, then. I'll see you upstairs." She strode to the elevator and disappeared. Marc smiled, thinking about the exuberance of youth, a memory for him as he approached a milestone birthday in the next couple of years.

At the desk he encountered another young female, attractive, dressed smartly in the uniform of the Ramada Inn chain. Another older gentleman sat at a desk off to one side. "May I help you?" Her voice strained to be pleasant but waivered with the boredom of late night shifts and little entertainment. Marcus was about to change her evening.

"I am in need of postage for several large envelopes I want to post to my home address. Is there a nearby agency or business still open which can accommodate me?"

The man, dressed in a cheap suit, stood. "How much postage are you needing?" The girl stepped aside and returned to paper work she was sorting when Marc walked up.

"I have four large business sized bubble wrap envelopes." He pulled out his badge and displayed it. "This a police matter."

The manager's eyes widened. "We may be able to help you and can be sure to post them in the morning."

"Thanks, all I need is postage."

"We have a stamp machine here, so we can weigh the envelopes and affix the proper payment." The manager fidgeted.

"We had visitors to our room while we were out. Who is on duty and has access keys? I don't think you want us to call the police." The young desk clerk looked up from her sorting, wide eyed, as if she knew something.

The manager apologized. "Is anything missing?" Marc shook his head. "I appreciate not involving the police."

"You have a staff member letting people in or they are going in on their own. May I see a list? Now?" The manager fumbled with his computer keyboard. The printer whirred as the paper rolled through. He checked the list, crossing off two names with his pen.

"These two are no longer employees here."

"How long ago? Did they quit or were they fired?"

"One is pregnant and now on maternity leave for six weeks, as of two days ago. The other called in today with a lame excuse again and I had to let her go. She was not reliable."

"Did she turn in all of her equipment, yet? If she carried a master key out of here, I need to speak with her."

The manager squirmed and checked his computer again. "She was not issued a key."

"If she was part of the maid service, how did she access rooms?" Marc glared at the manager.

"She was in the laundry. I didn't assign her to housekeeping."

"Could she have procured a key?" Marc leaned over the counter encouraging a better response.

"Not possible, unless she took one from a staff member. No one has reported a missing key."

The desk clerk entered the conversation. "Ramon, she has a boyfriend whose sister works here."

Marc smiled. "Let me speak with her." The clerk picked up a phone, but the manager stopped her.

"Is all of this necessary? I mean I don't want any problems. My staff is very reliable and to be trusted."

"Except for the one you fired today. I want to see this sister or I call the police and report the entry. Ramon, am I speaking clearly enough for you?"

"Yes, sir, I'll go and get her." He left the office alone to the clerk and Marcus.

"Your manager seems a bit uptight. Have rooms been invaded before?"

"Not that I know, but he wants to be the day manager and this won't help."

"You seem like a nice, competent young lady. Are you aware of any activity which might be inappropriate?" Marc's face brightened as he attempted to assuage any fear building in her. Looking at her nametag he continued, "Valerie, I'm not after you, but if your manager knows something it would help us greatly." She nodded as the door opened and a woman about his own age returned with the manager. Trepidation burned in her eyes.

Displaying his badge he said, "Miss, I'm a guest here in the hotel and I want to know if you saw anyone enter our room, 324, without authorization from you or anyone with access keys."

"No sir, I saw no one." Her body shook as she answered. "We cleaned the room, that's all we did."

"Thank you, do you have a brother who has a girl friend who works here?" She looked at the manager and back at Marc. Her silence condemned her answer. "Well?'

"He's a good boy, but his girlfriend is not." Sweat rolled down her forehead.

"What do you mean?" Marcus asked. "Why is she not a good person?"

"She's gotten him into trouble with her family and he has been acting strangely. I don't want any problems."

"I understand, where is your brother right now? I want to help get him out of this trouble." He soothed his comment as best he could. "Has your manager explained who I am? I can help you and your brother."

Ramon interrupted, "I told her to cooperate or she could join her brother's girlfriend on the unemployment line. She knows who you are."

Marc glowered at the manager. Someone was monitoring the locker and watching his family because of Jerry. Was he involved in this and masking his part? An uneasiness wriggled its way into his mind. Into what had his uncle gotten entangled?

Tiberius opened the door when he heard the knock. Had Marc forgotten something? The beautiful face startled him. "McDonald, you got here quickly"

"I live about three minutes from here. Found an apartment near the locker after your uncle's visit. I figured it would be easier to check on it. And please call me Ginny."

Tiberius looked at the box. "I see you have a kit with you. Know how to use it?"

"It has been a while, but we'll get results." She placed the box on the desk and opened it. "Where shall we start, Mr. Jefferson?"

"Call me, Ti, and let's begin at the entry." She unpacked her print kit handing a bottle of black dust to him and a brush. She removed a second bottle and brush.

"I suppose you can use this." He smiled and nodded. They systematically powered the room picking up prints on several surfaces. After using the lifting tape to secure the prints, she took his prints to compare and eliminate.

"My son should be up soon. We'll get his and if we need, we'll print the staff here at the hotel. I don't want to involve Vancouver PD in this, and I know you're out of your jurisdiction, but maybe we can get cooperation in exchange for keeping any illicit activity from being broadcast."

"I haven't heard of anything bad happening here. We have some hotels which are known contact spots for prostitution and drugs, but they're not the best places in town. I would think the chain headquarters would maintain an upstanding reputation."

A portable print reader compared Tiberius's prints which were separated from the remainder of the prints. As they waited, he thought, *she could have worked at many different jobs as a model, actress, or entertainer. She had become a cop. Interesting.*

She broke the silence. "Do you and your son believe someone here in Vancouver is involved?" He relaxed, returning to investigator mode.

"I don't know. We did not expect our room to be searched, but if somebody knows about the locker, then trouble is headed our way. I don't think my brother thought he would be putting you in harm's way."

"It's okay. I can handle it. I'll let the Superintendent of North Vancouver know what's happened. We'll keep you apprised of any changes or developments."

"Let's go down to the lobby and help Marc." She packed the kits with the new pieces of evidence and they left to uncover who left prints in the room.

As the elevator door opened, they saw Marc and staff members of the hotel at the reservation desk. The manager sounded gruff. They caught the last words of his tirade.

"She knows who you are."

Hearing the bell, Marcus turned toward the elevator. "Dad, we have a development. This lady has a brother whose girlfriend worked here until today. He may be in trouble with the girl's family. I don't know any more than that, so far."

"Do you think he may be the one who entered our room?"

"Either he did or she did." Marcus turned his attention to the manager. "Could a person enter the building without you seeing them?"

"No, unless they came in the back door which is locked at night."

"Locked, but operational with a hotel room key. Isn't that correct?" The manager bowed. "So someone has access to the hotel and its rooms, knew which one was ours and violated hotel ethics."

Tiberius interjected with a request. "My friend here is with RCMP. We have lifted prints from the room but need to compare them with your staff so we can eliminate them as suspects. Since this happened tonight, I figure the current staff are the ones to help us with this investigation. If you would gather them, we can print and compare without problems for you and the hotel."

"Is this really necessary? I mean, not everybody has access to the rooms. Val and I haven't left this front desk, except when I went to get my head maid, this woman."

"Good, it won't take long, and we aren't keeping any of the prints after we remove a person from the suspect list." Tiberius decided easing the tense atmosphere had merit. "Ginny, please set up at that table." He pointed to a long narrow table which had brochures and flowers on it. She removed the objects and placed her print reader on the table.

"Marc, you start, since we know your prints are in the room." He cooperated and when the machine had finished four sets of unknown fingers remained.

Tiberius studied the manager with intensity. "Are you coming?" Valerie walked out of the reservation area. Her prints did not match. The head maid comparison resulted in no match. "Sir, I'll only ask one more time. You're next." When his prints cleared, Tiberius ordered him to get the staff together.

Valerie picked up the receiver and punched in a few numbers and asked for all of the maids and laundry personnel to assemble in the lobby. Ramon did not look pleased.

As each person was printed, two of the maids matched. Marcus met each one separately.

"Your prints were found in our room. Why were you there?" The older woman spoke broken English with a Korean accent. She explained working a double shift because of the missing laundress. She had been the day shift maid and worked the night in the laundry room.

He decided she was not a threat. The second girl was a high school dropout who worked both shifts because she had no home to return to and slept in the hotel on a cot in the break room. The day manager allowed her to stay for certain benefits, as she put it.

"Please, don't say anything to the other manager. He wants the day job and I'll lose my job and have nowhere to live. I like the day manager and we're okay with what's going on. Ramon is not exactly my type. I know he's hit on Valerie and she's refused him. She has some sort of pull with the owner and so he leaves her alone. I don't have any of that."

"Your secret is safe with me. I'm not too concerned with the problems here except as they relate to what I'm investigating. What can you tell me about the lady fired tonight?"

"I don't trust her. She'd come to work and skip out when her boyfriend showed up. They'd go to an empty room to…you know. His mom works here. That's her behind the desk. He seemed nice."

"Thank you. I'll keep your secret and if you hear of anything which might be helpful to me or my father, call me." He handed her a card.

"You're a cop?" He smiled.

"Yes, I hope that's not upsetting to you."

"I don't know too many, but you're nicer than the ones I've dealt with." She returned to work as did the remaining nightshift.

Two prints remained, unaccounted for and not likely to be easy to uncover.

"Ramon, do you have the address of your fired laundress?" He rummaged through a card box pulling out a 4 by 6 index and handed it to Marc.

"She's probably with her boyfriend at his mother's house. That's where he lives. With his mother."

Ginny offered, "I can take you there. My car is right outside." Marc checked his watch. It was after midnight and his mind was tiring.

"Thanks." He turned to his dad. "Stay and keep an eye on things. I'll be back as soon as we find our two missing prints." He and Regina departed.

CHAPTER 8

Lydia wondered about Jeremais. She had not entwined herself in his work until now, but something was different. His edginess the last few weeks before he retired raised her antenna of concern. The years with two children at home and his interaction with other cases had not been as complicated as this last year when he acted nervous and irritable most of the time.

"Who are you?" She asked a couple of months before he retired. "What are you involved in which has taken my husband away and replaced him with a manic person your own kids don't like to be around."

"Be patient. I'm almost through with my current assignment. I'll make it up to you and Cammie and JJ."

Now he was morose. His retirement occurred without fanfare. He sat around depressed and aloof. He related to Lydia the problems with the undercover assignment and why it bothered him.

The trip to Vancouver lifted spirits for a moment which collapsed as fast as a house of cards. Jerry stayed home, not leaving for anything. Not for family events, not for shopping, not for entertainment. Church attendance dropped to zero and his children became a lost cause.

"Jerry, what's wrong? You don't have any energy. No one can make you happy. Nothing seems to matter to you." He remained quiet. "Talk to me, damn it."

"Why, nothing makes any sense anymore. You and the kids would be better off without me."

"Don't say that. We need you with us."

Jerry walked out of the room, leaving his wife gawking at his insolence. On the back deck he leaned on the railing. "Damn, stupid life."

She followed him outside. "Ever since that investigation failed and you retired, you've moped around here like a spoiled child who lost his best friend."

"It didn't end right. They got away with it."

"Who? What did they get away with?"

"It doesn't matter anymore. Lydia, I need you to do something for me. It's not going to be easy." He faced her placing hands on her shoulders. "I left all my evidence in our red suitcase when we went to Vancouver. If anything happens to me, contact my nephew, Marcus. He'll know what to do."

"Now you're scaring me more."

"These people are bad and I don't trust the precinct. I want you to wait two years before you send him this letter." He gave her a standard security envelope, sealed and addressed to Marcus at Kitsap County Sheriff. "Keep it hidden away from everyone."

"What if he asks questions? What do I say?"

"When the two years has passed and you have contacted Marc, retrieve another envelope locked in our safety deposit box at the bank and send it. It's already addressed."

Lydia reached for him, to comfort him, and assure him all was right with his world. He turned his shoulder, ducking her movement. "Jerry, it's not good for you to feel this way. Maybe we should seek counseling."

"Maybe you should leave me alone. If I'm still around in the next two years, I'll help Marc with the investigation. If not, then you must promise me you will do as I ask and contact him."

"I will." Her eyes were bleary from the tears sweeping down her cheeks. Jerry turned and plodded into the house, into his den, where he closed the door and locked it, barricading himself from life and living.

CHAPTER 9

"What got you into police work?" Marc and Ginny sped along the parkway to the address on the card. She was talented and proved a capable individual, smart and young. Did her life include a steady man friend?

"My family. I wanted to do something to change the world. My father thought I'd become a wife and mother." Marc guessed her attitude caused a collapse of familial relationships.

"Are you from around here?" His question raised a shaking of her head as they swerved around a corner. No traffic made the streets an easy race course.

"No, I came west from my home in Timmins, Ontario after passing out of the academy in Regina. And yes, I find it ironic my name is the same." Marc chuckled.

He studied the card. "Here's the place." She parked the car away from the address although her vehicle was unmarked, a simple Prius hybrid, issued by the division. On the street they studied the lower middle class neighborhood, a place of contrast, as some homes were well maintained, while others needed reparations.

Their destination exhibited the former as flowers grew in pots on a painted porch, a small yard had few weeds in the grass and bushes were trimmed. The mauve coloring of siding showed little peeling or discolor.

Marc unlatched his revolver. "Take the back, in case someone is reluctant to talk with us." Regina followed instruction releasing her weapon as she went.

At the front door he listened to any sounds which indicated people present and awake. He heard nothing. Peering in the window next to the porch he saw a neat maintained living area. A shadow passed by a door and a light flashed on. Time for contact. He wrapped on the door not declaring his identity.

Lights flared in the room just observed. The door opened a crack. "Who are you?" A young Hispanic man clad in a sleeveless shirt and boxers opened the door when Marc displayed his badge.

"I would like to speak with you about your girlfriend. May I come in?"

"What about her?" He remained a barrier to entry. Marc replaced his badge in his waist band.

"She may be a person of interest in a case I'm working. Is she here?" Marc had a hand on his weapon away from the sight of the young man.

"No, she ain't here." A noise from behind alerted both of them to others entering the scene. Marc pushed his way into the house, drawing his revolver as he moved.

"Look who I found trying to leave by the back door." Regina had a pretty, young Hispanic woman in cuffs, her service weapon trained on the woman. Dressed in bra and panties, little was left to the imagination about her shape.

Marc aimed at the man and said, "I think you need to explain your actions." He removed his cuffs and handed them to his suspect. "Put this on your right wrist." The young man did as requested. Marc snapped the other ring on the girls left wrist.

Regina smiled as she sat the pair on a brown sofa. "I do declare. These two seem to be in need of some convincing that illegal activity is not good for them." Holstering her gun, she stood next to Marc, who did the same.

"Miss, ah, what is your name?" He checked the employee file card. "Yes, Marguerite, where were you this evening between six and ten?"

"You don't have to answer him," The young man interjected. She glared at her boyfriend and then at the two officers.

"I was right here."

"And I suppose you'll support her in this allegation." Marc crossed his arms, awaiting the next lie.

"Yes, we watched television and went to bed." Marc turned to his partner.

"Go get the kit. At least we can eliminate their prints." Regina left the house. "Miss, your boss, Ramon, told us he fired you when you didn't report for work tonight. Did you possess a pass key which needed to be returned?"

"Is this what it's about? That pig makes a move on any female who works there. I told him to fuck off and so he fired me. Now he sends the police for a stupid card. What an ass. He's one who should be fired."

"That may be true, but do you have such a key?" Her eyes burned with rage. She nodded. "And where may I find that key?"

"I don't have it anymore." Her eyes softened as her head lowered. "I gave it to a man who wanted to get in one of the rooms."

"Who is this man?" The boyfriend bumped against his girlfriend.

"Don't say anything. They'll kill us." Marc understood separating suspects so one story could contaminate another. He did not have the luxury.

"If you two are in trouble, we can help." Regina returned with her print kit and scanner. "Tell me about the man." He waited as Regina set up for taking prints.

The girl looked at her boyfriend who shook his head. She whispered to him and turned her attention to Marc. "He's part of a gang." The boyfriend tugged at the manacles trying to stop her talking.

"This gang, what do they do which scares your friend so much?" She sat silent before he pressed her to answer. "You're going to prison for a very long time for conspiracy and impeding an investigation, if you don't cooperate. I guess you think you're man enough to become some big fella's bitch while you're in the tank."

"Look, you don't know who you're dealing with." The young man squirmed, his eyes widened, sweat formed on his brow.

"Then explain to us who they are. After all we're the police. We have resources to help you and your girlfriend stay safe and get free of this man."

The girl spoke first. "He wanted to get into room 324. He claimed to be a cop, but I know cops can get the management to open doors with a warrant. He didn't look like he wanted to debate so I gave him the key."

"How did he know you had a key?" Marc changed his focus to the young man. "How would he know to ask your girlfriend?"

"Can you really help us?" The pleading face broke his stolid composure.

"That depends on what you know and are willing to tell. My partner is with RCMP. I'm sure something can be worked out. Now tell me what I want to know."

"He and I work together." Marc's brow lifted encouraging continuation of the confession. "He's part of a smuggling gang. I help get things together. He's my girlfriend's cousin." Her countenance turned to anger, but she said nothing.

"So she got you into the gang and supplied him with a key to break into a room at the hotel where she used to work. This doesn't look good for either of you."

"You promised to help us."

"I promised nothing, but I'm sure if you cooperate something can be worked out with the prosecutor's office."

Regina stepped into the conversation. "Shall we print?" Marc bowed and she proceeded with her testing for matches. Neither of them matched. "I'll run the unknowns through our data base. Something is sure to pop."

"Well, let's get you kids dressed and off to custody so no one can harm you." He removed the cuffs from the man as Regina removed her cuffs from the girl. They led them to a bedroom in the back watching as the two perps put on clothing.

"Regina, will your precinct hold these two for a while?"

"I think so. We are investigating a smuggling ring and if these two are implicated then we have reason."

The four of them returned to the front room where Regina packed her kit. Cuffs were reattached to the hands of the lovebirds as a precaution. In the Prius comfort for the two prisoners was lacking. But neither complained.

Marc scanned the neighborhood for unwanted advances by other vehicles or pedestrians. Assured they were not followed, he sat in the passenger seat.

They headed to her office in North Vancouver. Explaining Marcus to her sergeant was going to be interesting if not comical. More questions about a cousin and a gang shaped an investigation more complicated than he had envisioned. He called Tiberius to fill him in on the current situation.

Marc checked his watch. Time approached two thirty am. The streets were empty except for the dark truck keeping pace two blocks behind them.

Regina flipped on her imbedded blue lights as she raced to the precinct. "Always wanted to do this. Think that truck can keep up with a Prius?"

CHAPTER 10

Tiberius closed his notebook with new information and returned to room 324. He clicked his holster to his belt and with keys in hand left to check the safety of the suitcase. Uncertain the room would not be entered again, he placed a small piece of paper between the jamb and door mostly hidden from sight.

The early morning air invigorated his walk to the storage facility. The evening had produced surprises he did not anticipate. The play was forgotten like a windy day is soon replaced with sunshine. He arrived at the building within ten minutes, reconnoitered the area for undesirables, and then entered the lobby. The night clerk greeted him asking for the required identification, the keys. He flashed his badge to aid the young man's acceptance.

With the security gate unlocked, he strolled down the hall to the second locker, observing the first as he walked by. The lock on Jerry's door remained undisturbed. The second locker was undisturbed, as well. Opening the combination lock he bought from another clerk at the desk, he checked the contents. Satisfied nothing had been monkeyed with, he closed the door and latched the lock.

At the first locker, he opened it to see the red suitcase still in place, now empty of the files and folders. At the reception desk, he asked about the switch of shifts and who was the next one to come on duty. Assured the place remained a haven of some security, he checked the clock on the wall. It read 1:38. He felt tired.

"Marc and Regina must be at the house by now," he thought. His son would call when convenient so he retraced his steps to the hotel. No one seemed to know about the locker which pleased him. He did not want to fight anyone seeking information about evidence. Nor did he want to deal with the scum which spent the early mornings terrorizing anybody crazy enough to be alone on a street.

Keen eyes scoured the neighborhood for people who did not sleep and searched for victims on which to feed. All was quiet. Arriving at the hotel he asked Valerie if his son had returned.

"I haven't seen him, sir." She smiled and her eyes sparkled. He figured she knew more about the manager than her boss wanted known, hence her ability to work with him without coercion.

"Has Ramon readied the postal machine?"

"Yes sir. Shall I inform him you are needing it?"

"I'll be right back with the envelopes. We can prepare them so I can mail them when the post office opens.

In his room, he opened the safe and removed the envelopes. Returning to the front desk, he found Ramon, night manager, wannabe day manager. "I have my postal machine for you."

"Thank you. Here are the envelopes, but I insist on being present as you place the fee on each envelope."

"Yes sir, Mr. Jefferson." He placed the packages one at a time on the weight scale and printed the proper price sticker and affixed them. He returned all four to Tiberius.

"Now that we've finished, please explain how you allowed an invasion of our room. I don't think the young lady you fired today worked alone. Did you give her the card?"

"No, I would not do that."

"Did she promise to sleep with you if you did?"

"Why would I want to?"

"It seems you have a reputation of sexual harassment of staff members. If they don't cooperate, you fire them. Even in Canada that's against the law. Shall I go on? Or will you be honest with me." Tiberius moved close to intimidate him.

"I didn't fire her because she refused me. She wanted it but for a price, the master key."

"And you complied. I hope the sex was good." The manager said nothing. "I think you need to reinstate her to her job before she files a discrimination suit against you and the hotel." Tiberius realized any chance of that happening was slim, but he cared not at all. "Oh, and the hotel or you can pay for the postage."

Valerie came into the office. "Ramon, I heard what you said. I want a promotion to assistant manager or I'm going to inform the day manager of your nighttime activities, and I still will not sleep with you."

Tiberius stifled a chuckle. He left with his possessions and relocated across to lobby to the elevator. Before he pushed the up arrow, his cell phone chimed.

"Hello, Marc, did you find the young lady?" He walked out to the parking lot for privacy.

"Yes, and her boyfriend. It seems he's enmeshed with the gang which may be supplying Pepper's organization. I'm not sure how they tie together but the girl supplied the key to a man who happens to be her cousin."

"Very interesting. Marc, she got the key by sleeping with the night manager, a condition she employed. He got what he wanted, she got what she wanted, and I don't think she was fired. Where are you?"

"Regina and I brought them to her precinct in North Vancouver. She's very resourceful. I'm not sure, but a truck may have been following us when we left the boy's house. If they were tailing us, it could mean trouble. If they were staking out the house because of the boy's collusion, we picked them up as a result. Anyway, they left us as we pulled into the precinct."

"Can you get back here soon? I think we need to return home."

"Can do. Our two candidates for prison are secured for the moment. Ginny will drive me back." They ended the call.

As he reentered the lobby, Valerie came out from behind the desk. "Mr. Jefferson, what's going on? This has been a most bizarre evening and morning. I haven't had this much excitement in my life."

"I can't discuss it with you, but be assured you have aided an investigation. I think you should be the night manager and get Ramon canned. If you need a recommendation before I leave, let me know." She reached up to his face and kissed his cheek.

"Thank you. You have made my night." She turned and strutted to the door leading to the reception desk. Tiberius pushed the button and thought of younger years.

In the room he locked the envelopes in the safe. The time on the room clock read four twenty-two. Exhaustion smacked him hard as he collapsed on the bed.

He heard the door open and prepared to defend the room. Marc entered with Regina close behind. Reading the clock, it was now five fifteen. He closed his eyes and finally relaxed. What nest of wasps had they stirred?

CHAPTER 11

Jerry knocked on Daniel Kopinski's office, entering when told. "How's the investigation going?"

"I'm meeting with Wiley. He has some stuff for me." Jerry sat in the chair indicated by his captain. "I'm not sure we have enough yet, so we're going to put the corruption into play."

"Be careful. These people are not what we would call nice." Dan stood and walked around his desk. "I can't cover for you if anything happens, as I told you before this began."

"I'm keeping good records of what happens and will be securing evidence for convictions of any and all included."

"Alright, go and do what's needed. I trust you." Jerry stood, shook hands, and left for his rendezvous.

Driving an unmarked car to avoid tails, Jerry arrived at the prearranged site in a remote part of the county near Lake Stevens. Looking around for unwanted intruders, he decided all was well.

"You afraid of visitors?" Wiley appeared from nowhere or so it seemed. Jerry grinned.

"You been here long?"

"Got here to watch you arrive. You were not followed, as best I saw." They shook hands.

"What do have for me?" Jerry left his notepad in his pocket. Time enough to write later.

"One of Pepper's underlings came to me yesterday and asked about finding something to hold against you. He wants someone inside."

"I guess I'm the best one for the job. Does he suspect you of anything?"

"I've been nothing but helpful to him. He's dug deep to find any dirt on me, and he's found it. Of course I planted it for him."

"Good. Do you need anything from me?" Jerry scanned the area wary of any anomaly.

"Do you have any reason to be afraid of being in the back pocket of Pepper?"

"If he goes after my family, I'll hunt him like the dog he is. I don't think he will unless it goes wrong for him. If he feels any threat to his organization he's going to apply pressure to assure results."

Wiley nodded. "He has everything the way he wants, but his confidence can be used for his downfall."

A noise interrupted their conversation. Jerry reached for his service weapon. Wiley placed a hand on his partner "Hush," he whispered. Alert to a movement in bushes about ten yards away, the men crouched into defensive postures.

As they waited, hearts beat with greater energy. Adrenalin surged, pupils widened.

Breathing eased as a black tail doe and her two yearlings emerged. Three pairs of eyes focused on the men who remained still, not wanting to spook them. The family of three guardedly retreated to a small copse of trees, leaping away from perceived danger.

"Kind of jumpy, aren't we." Wiley swiped a drop of perspiration from his brow.

"Better we be cautious than dead."

They confirmed plans to make Jerry's life change from honest cop to susceptible human. Greed seemed the best way to get him, a need for large amounts of money and no source to cover. Wiley would present the problem to one of Pepper's lieutenants and make the set up.

Jerry would accept the money with conditions no bank was allowed to present. He had a place for the money to stay intact, not used but appearing to satisfy the needs. Jerry committed to a path he hoped would create a crushing blow to an organization destroying young lives. He wondered how this could affect a family he loved, and he now made vulnerable.

CHAPTER 12

Marcus awoke to find his father dressed and packed for a return trip to Seattle. Regina had left shortly after they returned to the room from detaining the two suspects. For safety of the evidence, she took the envelopes to mail as soon as the post office opened.

He arose and after a trip to the bathroom, he explained about the change of plans regarding the evidence.

"She seems to be a bright young lady. Are you sure we can trust her?" Tiberius's question was one Marc debated with himself in the car as she drove him back to the hotel.

"She's okay. I know she'll mail them"

"Let's get home then." Meeting with the day manager, they learned of the release of the night manager because of the early morning escapades. He thanked them for their discretion.

As they packed the car, Marcus asked, "Do you think he's giving up his candy girl?"

"Probably not. She didn't seem to mind being his side dish." The parking lot was mostly empty of vehicles so they relaxed as they entered the street heading for the highway south to Blaine. "Think anyone will escort us out of B.C.?" Tiberius giggled as he spoke and checked mirrors for other vehicles, finding none.

"If they are interested in what we have then maybe. But I'm betting we have no followers as much as they'll contact their pals in Snohomish."

At the border they parked the car and entered the office of the United States Border Patrol. With badges displayed they asked to speak to the Deputy Chief of the Blaine Sector. Escorted into the outer office, they waited for several minutes.

"Sorry for the delay, gentlemen. I was on the phone with Washington D.C. What can I do for you?" Deputy Chief Arlen Landrensen pointed to chairs and sat in his desk seat.

"I'm Tiberius Jefferson of the Seattle Police Department. We are investigating the death of my brother, Jeremais Jefferson, a former officer for Snohomish County Sheriff. My son, Marcus, is a detective with Kitsap County Sheriff. Jerry was investigating a drug ring in his county which ended badly. After retiring he died from a self-inflicted gunshot. However, there may be some question as to the final verdict. We think he was murdered."

"You're returning from Canada. Where did you go?"

"We went to Vancouver searching for evidence my brother left there. He was sure his own precinct wasn't safe for what he had gathered. He left directions for his nephew to go get it and continue probing."

"Did you find what you were after?"

"Yes."

"So how can we be of help to you?"

"At the site where Jerry stashed the evidence, we met a young lady, who it turns out, is an RCMP officer. My brother had arranged for surveillance and coverage of the locker where he left his suitcase full of photos and files. RCMP is currently looking into a group exporting drugs to the U.S which may be connected to Snohomish."

Deputy Chief Landrensen opened a file on his desk. "There is a group we're keeping a close eye on."

"You can be of help by keeping us in the loop as things develop here. We'll be in touch with you when we find something useful."

Landrensen removed a piece of paper from the file. "This is a list of the people we suspect of crossing the border with contraband. So far nothing has been found."

"May we keep this?" Landrensen nodded. "Could they be distractors so others might get through easier? Is every car checked for drugs?"

"No, we look for the ones we suspect and have the dogs work them. Homeland Security changed our policy last week. Starting next month all cars get a checkout."

Marcus and Ti stood up. Taking the paper with them they thanked the chief and left. Passing through the check point they headed to Seattle and a ferry ride for Marcus.

As Ti drove, Marcus said, "Let's stop at the WSP in Everett. We can enlighten them about what we have. Maybe the officer who stopped us will be on duty."

"We might want to wait until our envelopes arrive. We don't have any strong leads or ideas about who is involved."

"That is why I listen to you, Pop." Marc sat back and closed his eyes. The trip whizzed by as he slept. He dreamed of times he spent with his uncle, aunt and cousins. Memories corrupted by an unbelievable act. The truth was out there. Where was the question to be answered? And how could it clear Jerry's name without further damage to anyone in the family?

As agreed, Tiberius dropped his son at the ferry in Edmonds. Marc said good-bye to his father and boarded the boat to Kingston. He pulled out the card Regina gave him when she left the hotel room. He punched in the number wanting an update on the two left with her.

"Hello, Detective. I wasn't expecting to hear from you so soon." He wondered how she knew who called, but figured she programed his number into her phone, something he hadn't done to his.

"I'm calling to see if we have any more on those two we ran in this morning. Oh and did you send the packages?"

"Delivery will be tomorrow by express mail. I put the extra postage on for you, so now you owe me. As for our guests, they gave up their friends in exchange for some very intimate relocation. We have enough to move against the cartel here and bust it up a bit."

"Good. Any connection to Snohomish or Kitsap or King Counties down here?"

"Nothing yet, but we'll keep digging. Oh, and I checked on the locker again. Someone entered the area and the surveillance tape showed them at the first one. Nothing more but the outside camera spotted a red truck similar to the one following us last night."

"It seems our two song birds need a new tune. Find out what they know, since no one should have intel on the locker."

"Sure thing." They ended the call. He smiled thinking of his morning resistance to an invitation for breakfast at her place.

He called Joan as time neared seven. "I'm arriving on the 6:45 Kingston. I should be home by eight."

"Did you find what you needed?" Her voice sounded warm, inviting. He didn't rue his morning decision.

"We did. It will be at the office by tomorrow. We sent it as a protection to losing it on the way home."

Her voice chilled. "Did you run into to trouble?"

"Nothing we couldn't handle. The RCMP is helping us. They have an investigation ongoing regarding a drug ring which may be supplying Snohomish County."

"I'll see you when you get here." He clicked off and punched in Tom Knudson's number.

"I'm on the 6:45. I'll wait for you to arrive at the Drifter's Bar and Grill."

"How was the hunt?"

"Productive. I'll tell you about it when you get here." He clicked off and walked to the Kingston end of the ferry. Standing on the outside deck with the breeze blowing across his face, he leaned on the railing. Looking down at the cars and trucks, one looked familiar. He walked back inside and down the stairs to the auto deck. A quick survey of the middle lane, he uncovered the truck which appeared to be similar to the one which followed Regina and him in Vancouver.

The plates were from Washington. He noted them in his booklet. No one was in the truck for the moment. He decided to wait for the announcement for passengers and drivers to return to their vehicles. Pulling out his phone he clicked in the office number for records. After a short period of time, he possessed what he needed.

With the name of the registered owner, he returned to the upper deck. No need to confront anyone at this time. The boat docked and the crew placed the gangway on the upper deck. He walked off with other passengers, down the ramp, to Drifter's.

Marc ordered a coffee and sat at a table. The last two days had been a whirlwind. Now an investigation about Uncle Jerry. Tom arrived within fifteen minutes.

"Hi, Marc. Glad you're back in our area."

"Glad to be here. Let's go. I have a family to assuage."

They left, heading to the lower parking area where Tom's cruiser sat. "So RCMP is part of this analysis. Does the group they're checking have connections here?"

Marc held most of his suspicions inside. The tentacles on this octopus stretched far and wide. He had to uncover where they sucked the life out of innocent people, who was controlled and what they knew. Tom was a friend. Yet, people followed and interfered. How did they know? Why wasn't a trip north uncomplicated, a simple gathering of material without fanfare or difficulty? Something was rotten and the smell permeated aspects of his life and family, an odor of mendacity much as Big Daddy quoted in 'Cat on a Hot Tin Roof' seeped into places which he believed secure.

"Not that I'm aware. Let me get home and rest. We can talk in the morning when I'm fresh." *When I can think clearly and provide only what I want you to know.*

As Tom departed the driveway of his home, Marcus thought about his friend and partner. Nothing he did sparked a debate regarding loyalty to honest police work or living an ethical life. Tom was above reproach. Still.

The front door opened and Joan stood on the porch, her smile building happy thoughts in his head. "Hi, dear. Nice to see you."

"Thank you, I do hope you have what you need to fix this obsession about Jerry." She folded an arm in his as they headed into the house. "The kids are at friends for the evening." Her destination made sense as they ascended the stairs. Unpacking and bed for sleep.

As he placed laundry in the hamper and stored his bag in the closet, Joan sat on the bed unbuttoning her shirt. He chuckled. "I assume the kids are not returning soon."

"You can say that. Sarah is staying the night, Marc Junior is dating a new girl, and James is going to be back about 10. So are you interested?"

He removed his clothing and joined her on the bed. His journey north, forgotten for the moment, could be explained later.

A noise disturbed the restful time after their romp. "James is home." Joan rose from the bed, robed and left. Marc robed his body and followed.

Downstairs they met James as he closed the door and locked it. He peeked out the side window frame, then saw his parents. "Dad, you're home." James hugged his father. Marc reciprocated.

"What have you been doing tonight?" James removed his coat and tossed it on the floor. Looking at his mother, he picked it up and placed it on a hook in the hall.

"I was over at Bobby's playing video games." James reached into his pocket and pulled out an envelope. "Some guy outside asked me to give this to you?" Marc turned but did not look out the window.

Staring at the envelope, he asked, "What did he look like? Had you ever seen him before?"

"No. He was tall and…I don't know. It was dark and I ran in as fast as I could. He scared me."

"You did fine, son. You did fine. Go upstairs and get ready for bed. I'll be up soon to say good night." James departed ascending two steps at a time.

Marc studied the envelope before opening it. Joan moved closer. "What is it? Who would leave it with a kid?"

"I don't know. I just hope this isn't tied to what Dad and I did in Vancouver." He held the paper gently keeping much of it untouched. Heading to the kitchen, he retrieved a pair of latex gloves and put them on. With care he opened the unsealed item and removed a letter.

He read as Joan watched. His eyes closed and he dropped his hand. "What does it say?" She reached for it, but Marc shook his head and moved it away from her grasp. He read it again, aloud.

"Detective Jefferson, do not pursue looking into your uncle's death. He was dishonored and uncovering what he did and who he became will not bring you any peace. He died without honor. Nothing but pain and suffering will result."

Joan sat in the nearest chair. "Is someone threatening you? Us?" He sat with her.

"I don't know. It's difficult to say whether continuing will mean literal pain and suffering, or finding out the truth, finding out Uncle Jerry was crooked in the end, finding out he did commit suicide, will hurt me emotionally, hurt Mom and Dad, hurt Aunt Lydia." Marcus stood, opened a drawer, and withdrew a plastic gallon storage bag from the box. He placed the letter and envelope inside and sealed the zipper lock.

"Maybe you shouldn't chase this shadow." Joan wanted closure but figured she was losing her husband to the hunt until the fox was found and destroyed.

"I'll get this checked for prints, tomorrow." His brain cultivated a scenario of Regina running her machine only to discover a matching set of fingers which searched the hotel room. He wobbled his head. How complex was this hunt for the real reason Uncle Jerry was dead?

CHAPTER 13

Jerry walked into the restaurant looking for an open table without an outside view or interfering customers. As he sat another man strolled in the front door of Buck's American Café on Hewitt, scanning the scene. When he discovered Jerry, he made a beeline for his table.

"You are one challenging cop." The man sat in a seat next to the wall across from Jerry. "Have you decided what to eat? I hear the food is fabulous."

"No, I just arrived. You're sitting at my table without introduction. Either be kind enough to identify who you are or be gracious enough to leave as quiet as the mouse you are."

"Please, Mr. Jefferson, I am here at the behest of a mutual acquaintance. He relayed your challenge regarding financial banking and offered to have us meet your challenge."

"Who are you?" Jerry squeezed the knife handle held in his lap.

"I do apologize. My name is of little consequence, but for the sake of completing our transaction, please call me Mr. Smithers."

"Is that because of the arrangement we are about conduct or the state of anyone failing to meet the financial obligation of mutual agreement?" He squirmed from the waist down, maintaining a calm demeanor despite the adrenalin coursing his arteries and veins.

"I do understand the reticence of making such a large transaction here in public, but rest assured we are as secure as any couple entering a lending institution and asking a manager to hold the baby." He smiled and Jerry noticed a distinct gap in his teeth which Jerry assumed was the result of some unfortunate run-in with a misguided beneficiary of the loaning business conducted without government regulation or legal support.

"All right, I do have a need for the services your organization provides since a more regular request may result in awkward questions being asked and my reticence to answer said questions. Are we to complete our arrangement here or elsewhere?" The knife cut into his hand, a trick learned in a back alley deal to have a reason to leave a bad scene and retreat to the nearest bathroom for medical assistance.

"We can complete our deal nearby. I first must relate our terms and the collateral by which such a loan will be secured. In that way, we are much like a bank or mortgage institution."

Jerry remained silent as the next words sealed his doom if any of this failed to hit the main bull's-eye of the city's most notorious resident, Andrew Pepper. The loan for $50,000 was to be repaid in one year at 10% interest per month. Payments were to begin after the first month and be at least the interest. Any early repayment included a 15% added fee.

"Do I sign any promissory note or are we on a verbal agreement?"

Mr. Smithers pulled a piece of paper from his coat pocket. "Funny you should ask? I have such a document with me." He handed the paper across the table. Jerry's bloodied hand rose from under the table.

Blood dripped on the table cloth as he laid the knife on it. "I do seem to be a bit nervous. Please excuse me while I wash."

Smithers gathered the document before any of it suffered a bloody transfer. "I will be right here when you return." Jerry stood and walked to the men's room around the corner and to the back of the building.

As he passed the first door his mind betrayed his sense of accomplishment for being able to infiltrate his target. The men's room décor reminded him of a bawdy saloon hall in the old B grade oater movies he watched to distract his mind of scum.

The first stall door opened and a grubby looking man stepped out. "Did Smithers offer you the loan?"

"Wiley, you look like a vagrant. Yes, I made an excuse to get in here, so make it quick." Wiley Fingers installed the microphone under the lapel of Jerry's jacket and flipped a switch on a small box he carried in a pocket of his coat.

"This is good for about a quarter mile. If you leave, I'll follow close behind. I'm going outside before you return to the table. Wait about thirty seconds." Wiley departed to plant himself across the street. Jerry came out and sat with Smithers. The paper towel wrapped around his hand staunched the flow of blood.

"Smithers, I'm ready."

"Then let us leave here for my banking facility." The two men walked out after paying for their beverages. Jerry glanced across the intersection finding a beggar sitting on the walkway. As they headed for a parking lot, the man on the sidewalk stood and wandered parallel to them fifty yards back.

In the lot Smithers stopped at a Ford LTD and opened the trunk. Removing a suitcase, he clicked the locks and opened the lid. Fresh fifty dollar bills bundled together in groups of 50. "This is your requested amount. Count it, if you want." He pulled out the document he showed in the restaurant. "Sign here."

"Do I get a copy of the document?"

"No need for a copy which could end up in the wrong hands. Trust me. I'll keep it safe." Jerry signed and left with the suitcase. He was committed.

CHAPTER 14

Tiberius picked up the receiver and dialed his son's house. Joan answered on the third ring. Morning had not started well and fighting with his wife, Gabrielle, the night before set the stage for the next day to be a downer. His return home after dropping off Marcus had onerous consequences for which he enjoyed no solutions.

"Hello, Joan. Is Marc available?"

"Yes, just a minute." Waiting gave the impression of an interminably long pause which ended within ten seconds.

"Dad, what's up?"

"I wanted to see how things were when you got home last night." Hoping his son had a better reception.

"Fine, except for the love note I got from some fool wanting a fight. It said I should not investigate Uncle Jerry's death or there could be pain and suffering. I take that to mean exactly what it says. Joan's upset, of course."

"How does anyone know we're looking into my brother's death? First, Vancouver and now you in Wendlesburg. We have a leak, a mole, a spy, somewhere we did not expect."

"I agree, but thinking about who we've spoken to regarding Jerry narrows the list to a few, not many."

"Meet me in Seattle after the packages arrive. I'm beginning to believe my brother was silenced. Something in those envelopes should shed light on what happened. We have to put two and two together."

"Do you think we can go after this gang of thieves and do it legally?" Marcus was not willing to risk a career he had yet to fulfill. Joan would not forgive his losing his position or worse, his life.

"At this point I'll finish what needs to be done. You keep your family safe."

"Okay, as soon as mail arrives I'll head to you. Where shall we meet?"

"Remember your childhood favorite spot for fishing, but don't say anything. Ears are close and lips slip."

Having arranged a rendezvous, Tiberius hung up the phone. Finding his wife, he said to her, "Gabs, I apologize for last night. I was out of line. You have every right to be upset with me but not with Marcus."

"What are you two doing opening old wounds? Your brother's death hit you hard and now you want it uncovered again? Why?"

"Lydia wants it. As I said last night, Marcus received her request because Jerry set it up. So I offered to help. Please, be understanding and support our son. He is one of the best detectives I know and if anyone can unravel what happened in Snohomish County, he can."

"No matter what ruthless activities ensue because of the hornet's nest which is stirred up?"

"Nothing bad will happen. This is a routine examination of evidence. Jerry left it for Marcus."

The conversation ended, love intact, questions unresolved.

Ti gathered the emblems of his profession and went to work. The envelopes were to arrive in Wendlesburg sometime in the afternoon. A call from Marcus would start the game to be played until finished with Jerry's death fully explained.

At the precinct Ti directed the patrol officers to their destinations and explorations of nightly activities. He sat at his desk studying files of new recruits and old complaints before taking a young female under his wing to learn the ropes.

Three stops to unravel 911 calls about domestic disturbances and a missing child taught the rookie about patience and listening. The child returned home from a friend's apartment. Forgot to tell Mom.

One disturbance for loud noise turned into a counseling session how one should treat neighbors. The last call required a backup car to come take a husband into custody for hitting his abused spouse.

Leaving the scene they drove onto I-5 heading south toward the convention center returning to the precinct. At the James Street exit a large pick-up cut across two lanes nicking the front of the cruiser, sending it into a spin stopped by the wall under the Convention Park above them. The truck slowed checking the car for damage and injuries. Tiberius memorized the license, and then spied the semi-automatic pistol pointed at them.

"Gun. Get down." His rookie stared at him as he opened his door and leaned to the left out the opening. The rain of bullets smashed the windshield and shattered the electronics in the car. Clicking off his belt, Tiberius rolled out to the asphalt, gun in hand. He rose up and emptied the clip into the truck's cab as it sped away.

"Officer involved shooting," he yelled into his shoulder mike. "James Street exit off Interstate 5." He relayed the license number for other cars and police to spot. Turning back to the cruiser, the young female slumped forward in her seat. Tiberius ran around the back of the car, opened the door and checked for a pulse. Finding one he pulled her back up looking for blood.

"Officer down. Send a bus to this location." Sirens indicated help arriving. "Marla, where are you hit? Talk to me."

"What happened?" Her voice was strong and steady. She reached for her chest and felt the sting of a flak jacket working its miracle. Tiberius unbuckled her belt, but ordered her to stay put.

Two Seattle police cars arrived and blocked the I-5 traffic pattern to the exit and one south-bound lane. It didn't take long for the jamming of the main arterial through Seattle.

A command lieutenant arrived and called Tiberius aside. EMT's arrived at the same time and began checking Marla.

"What happened here?" The commander pulled out his notepad to record the testimony.

"We were returning to base and a black Ford 150 cut across the highway and clipped my front end. I spun into the wall as you see.

When I looked at the truck, it had stopped and the driver pointed a pistol at us. I yelled 'Gun' and the next thing I knew bullets flew. I got out and returned fire. I don't know if I hit anyone, but I know I hit the truck."

"And what happened to your rookie?"

"She was hit but it looks like her vest took the brunt. I should check on her." The lieutenant nodded. They would finish the report later.

Tiberius marched to the ambulance and gained attention of one EMT. "Is she alright?"

"She'll feel this for the next week, but no major damage. How are you doing?"

"I'm fine. Save the bullets and vest for us to check." He approached his charge. "Marla, how are you?"

"I feel like shit. It happened so fast. Is this another one of your lessons?" She tried laughing and groaned.

Ti grinned. Her humor remained. "Not the way I set it up, but let's make it one. When I say down, I mean down." He held her hand.

"Yes sir. Down means down. Teach me that trick of getting out of the car so fast."

"Later. Get checked out and come back to work."

The ambulance left with its latest subject. A buzz in his pocket distracted Tiberius. He answered.

"Dad, I have the envelopes and will be on the next ferry to Seattle."

"Hold up for now. I've been in an accident."

"What are you talking about?" Tiberius stalled his response. "Tell me."

"Someone cut me off and took shots at me and my partner."

The shout through the ear piece forced a move away from the ear. "Is this related to our friends?"

"I don't know, but if it is, we need to get moving on this. Meet me tomorrow instead. You study the material. I'll work on some things over here."

After getting a ride to the precinct from another officer, Tiberius learned the truck was abandoned three blocks from the accident-shooting site. The plate was an automobile license, not for a truck. Blood was found in the cab meaning his bullets struck true. No hospital would treat a gunshot wound without reporting. Plenty of places to find help, though.

While sitting at his desk completing the required incident report, his commander called him into the office. "Explain how an accident turned into a shooting."

"Well, I don't really know. Road rage?"

"Don't get cute with me. Is this related to the Vancouver trip?" Ti sat in a chair next to the desk.

"The time off was not for anything dealing with Seattle P.D. That said, someone may be after me for what I am doing in my off time."

"Do you want some unofficial advice? Or do you need some unofficial assistance." Tiberius smiled. His boss was one of the best leaders in Seattle and kept a low profile while dealing with high profile politicians.

"I could use some help. This is about my brother."

"Which one? Never mind. I assume it's about Jeremais. So is this a question about the suicide being bogus?"

Tiberius leaned forward, folding his hands in his lap. "Jerry made a pact with Lydia to contact my son, Marcus. He left evidence behind which was not turned into Snohomish."

The commander stood and came around the desk. "And you think someone is snitching about your activities. What happened in Vancouver?"

Tiberius sat back. His boss sat next to him. "It started in Everett when we met with Lydia. A black vehicle followed us until we got on the highway where a WSP patrolman pulled us over to aid support in our investigation into the drug alliance operating in the county. In Vancouver we located a locker containing the evidence Jerry gathered. We also had an unauthorized entry to our room at the hotel because of a maid whose cousin is part of a group in B.C. They import drugs and pass them into the U.S. and are probably linked to what Jerry was working. Now I get into an accident which included shooting at me. My son received a note with an implied threat if he continued."

"What happened to the maid?"

"She's visiting RCMP North Vancouver as a guest of the government, along with her boy toy who worked with the group. Still someone informed them we were present, looking for the evidence."

"I can't offer you official support. The case is closed and no reason exists to open it. It's out of our jurisdiction and has no bearing on anything here, as of now." Tiberius understood. Get something which connects. Did Marcus have the connection?

———⚭———

At his desk Marcus opened the first of the envelopes which contained photos of meetings and monetary exchanges. He studied the faces of unfamiliar people and read notes on the back of each picture. Cross referencing names, a pattern appeared. Jorge Gonzales seemed to be the most often written name. Using the sheriff's DataWorks Plus Digital Crimescene software, he searched for any records which cross matched the man named Gonzales. As the software combed files of various law enforcement agencies, he turned attention to the other envelopes.

Other names elicited few if any leads but each list produced new questions. He placed the photos aside and opened an envelope which contained e-mails and letters, summaries of police actions against various perpetrators, and several files of men and women associated with Andrew Pepper.

A third envelope contained the actions of the Snohomish Sheriff's office for a three year period of time. In the chronology Marcus noticed a pattern of two officers which matched several actions Jerry followed. The notes about them implied a connective deception of ethical values. "Damn. Uncle Jerry, you found the problem but they stopped you before you could fix it."

Marcus connected to the data base of the interactive law enforcement center in Olympia and checked to see if the two officers still worked in Snohomish. One retired 6 months after Jerry's death. The other died in an automobile accident which included his wife and son. The driver of the other car escaped any serious injury, but was convicted of three counts of vehicular manslaughter and was sentenced to serve three concurrent terms of eight years.

"Clean up." Marcus understood the two year wait. Cleaning up the mess Jerry stumbled onto. He needed to find the retiree. Wiley Fingers. Uncover narcotics cop. Who had to disappear or die?

The fourth envelope contained maps of various areas of the county, marked with drop points and kill spots. Uncle Jerry had it all and he was unable to finish the job. Dad had to see this for himself. In the right hands many people were heading for long prison terms. In the wrong hands many people were going to be dead.

He repacked all of the information into the envelopes. Checking the DataWorks sweep, Gonzales' name linked to several crimes in California, Oregon, and Washington. The biggest hit came out of Vancouver, B.C., with a connection to a group called Shin Chou. "Sheriff Fellington, I need a trip to Seattle. I will be back before the evening shift."

"Marcus, somehow I've lost you to another county's case, haven't I?" Marc raised his eyebrows and set his jaw. "Go solve this and get to me when you need help."

"Yes sir." Marc turned out of the office and left the precinct office. He went to the motor pool and requisitioned an unmarked impound vehicle. Better safe than sorry.

He pulled out his phone and left it in his own car. GPS left on might distract any tail. He headed south down Highway 3 until he arrived at the intersection with State Highway 16. He stopped at the convenience store and asked if he could make a call. A payphone on the outside wall still functioned. He dialed the Seattle P. D. number for his father's office and asked for Tiberius.

"I thought we were meeting tomorrow."

"We need to meet today. I found out what Uncle Jerry had. I think they silenced him. And another officer as well. A third is retired and missing. I'm on my way. Don't contact me as I left my phone in my car at the office. I have an unmarked vehicle." He hung up the receiver, returned to the gray Hyundai Sonata and headed out to share his findings.

He hoped his father would be at the fishing site when he arrived. Traffic east on 16 was tolerable until Interstate 5 north which clogged around the ongoing highway construction and the Tacoma Dome. He kept his frustration in check, no blue lights to clear a path. Had anyone followed him? It didn't matter now. They were just as jammed as he was.

As he approached the sign to downtown Tacoma, he decided to detour around the traffic and take the Puyallup exit, passing the Emerald Queen Casino. Joining up with the old Puyallup road, he continued toward Fife and Milton. The fishing site was off Highway 18 near the Auburn, Black Diamond Road. He drove without other cars impeding his progress. No one followed.

As he approached the Green River, he exited just before crossing the bridge and found his father standing beside a blue Buick LeSabre. He accepted Marc's nonverbal suggestion for caution and commandeered his own unmarked transport.

"Paranoid?" Marc said as he stepped out of the car. "I see you have new transportation."

"Caution seemed to be a virtue, considering our history." They shook hands and hugged. "What got you so fired up?"

Marc opened the back door and withdrew the envelopes of evidence.

"I looked through the materials and found patterns for a couple of the Snohomish deputies which matched the problems Jerry uncovered. One of them is dead, a result of an auto accident. Killed his wife and son, as well. The other was a narcotics cop who had worked undercover. He retired about the same time as Jerry and disappeared. He was working undercover. I'm guessing he went into hiding so he wasn't killed, like Jerry and the other one. Somebody was cleaning up."

"Nice hypothesis. Is there enough here to prove a case and get a prosecution?"

"I think so, but Uncle Jerry didn't trust anyone in the legal system in Snohomish. He indicated in notes the level of incursion made by this cartel and some high ranking individuals are among the corrupted."

Tiberius read through the material. His head rocked side to side as he read and learned what his brother uncovered. "This is going to be difficult to accomplish. We'll need some sophisticated and covert help to purge the county of its corruption, and we'll need to move quickly."

"I think we should find Fingers. Of course, if we find him so will the cartel." Marc sorted through the stacks of notes until he found an encrypted paper.

"Read this." He handed it to Tiberius.

"This makes no sense. Why would he encrypt something, unless he needed to keep certain information from prying hands and eyes?"

"I thought so, too. I haven't found a decoder for it." Marcus sifted papers in one of the envelopes. He passed more papers to his father. "Look through these while I scan this bunch. We have to find meaning to his secret."

After several minutes Tiberius slammed the hood of his car. "This is frustrating." As soon as he ended his tirade, his eyes expanded and his mouth dropped. "I'm an idiot. When we were kids we played spy all the time. We even made a language for us. It included a secret set of words which we used to build the foundation for the language." He pulled out his notepad and began writing.

Marcus watched over his father's shoulder. The strange configuration of letters caused a smile. "You never told me you and Uncle Jerry played games as kids."

"Hey, we had to entertain each other. Living on a farm away from civilization could get lonely."

"I thought you grew up in Seattle." Secrets in the family. A revelation unexpected and surprising. Marcus had lived his youth in a close-knit household with his sister and two brothers, his mother, Gabrielle, and Tiberius. His father's parents lived within ten miles of the Laurelhurst house. Their Italian heritage showed in the names given to children, in the food eaten, in the clothing, and education.

"We all have secrets." He finished scribbling and closed his pad. "Let's go. We'll take my car. I'll have yours picked up by King County and brought to my precinct."

"Where to?" Marcus sat in the passenger seat with four secrets which contributed to the end of a simple life as a county cop. What secrets lay within the papers Jerry encrypted? Had his father remembered a past linked to this moment?

They drove away from the fishing site baited to fish for men and women who destroyed lives for personal gain.

CHAPTER 15

Jerry sat at his home desk writing notes, creating and transcribing into an unknown script. Wiley sat opposite him watching the scribble accumulate. The silence assembled an intriguing moment of calm in an otherwise precarious endeavor.

"When you finish, teach me. I have to know how to crack your messages and nothing you're writing makes any sense." Wiley stood as he spoke. He opened the refrigerator door and rescued a cool beverage from the six-pack of beer.

"I will, but this needs to be fool proof. No one can know what it means or more than you and I will suffer." The writing continued. Wiley twisted the lid from the bottle and swigged a long draught. He sat again in his appointed spot. Jerry propelled a paper toward him.

"What does this say to you?" Wiley picked it up and studied it.

"It seems to be directions for a building a kite."

"Correct. So anyone reading this will think of it as a set of instructions. Now read this." Another paper slid across the table.

Wiley perused the note and smiled. "I need to learn a list of words and substitute them when necessary."

"Again, correct. My brother and I played spy as kids and created this code system. It's simple but leaves anyone trying to decipher it with little if any clue as to how. We can communicate what seems to be legitimate messages, but they can have other meaning."

Wiley nodded. It could be broken if enough time was dedicated, but it didn't seem worth the effort. "Is the list always the same or can it be changed for subsequent messages?"

"The key is in the third word. I'll give you several lists with words which indicate particular places in the sentences you use to complete the message."

The two conspirators set plans for meeting again in another week. Wiley stepped to the front door. Before opening it, he turned back to Jerry. "Are you doing okay?"

"Yeah. I guess. I don't like being beholden to someone like Pepper, but if this works, we'll end the hold they have on the county." They checked out the windows looking for any tail on Fingers. Whether a person following was from the Pepper organization or the County sheriff office didn't matter. Jerry was now part of the corruption pervasive in the county.

Wiley opened the door and stepped out into the darkness of late evening. Jerry closed it, fastening the deadbolt lock. He climbed the stairs to his bedroom searching for his wife, Lydia. He didn't like meeting at home but changing the venue of rendezvous seemed safer than keeping a schedule in a single place.

"Did you get what you needed?" Lydia spoke as he entered the room. She lay in their bed reading a Robert Dugoni novel, *The Conviction.*

"Lydia, if anything happens to me, contact my nephew, Marcus. He needs to finish what I've started."

"You scare me when you talk like this. I don't need a dead husband and Cammie and JJ don't need to lose their father."

"I'm sorry. I don't mean to but what I'm doing is important." He removed his clothing and went to the bathroom to prepare for a night of rest. He wanted nothing more than to have the investigation end. Nothing more than to keep bad people from ruining a wonderful place to live. Nothing more than keeping his family safe from harm.

As he came back to the bedroom his cellphone chimed. "Hello."

"What are you and Wiley planning?" Had someone followed Fingers to his house?

"Who is this?" He took the cordless phone out into the hall, protecting Lydia from the vagaries of his profession.

"You and he are getting rather tight."

"Identify who you are or this call is over." Jerry continued downstairs to his office. He had equipment to record calls and trace what he needed.

"You're getting into an abyss which will consume you and your family. Now what are you planning?"

In the office he clicked the recording machine and started searching the caller's source. "I still don't know who you are."

"I'm a friend who wants you to succeed but fear you're in deep and can find no success."

"I will succeed at what I want. Who are you?"

"I will introduce myself to you at some point in this investigation, but for now, I need to be anonymous. I'm watching you and will provide help as needed, but stay safe and keep out of trouble."

"I'm beyond safe. So who are you working for?" The trace clicked indicating a locale. Jerry checked the site and frowned. It was impossible. How could this person be in another state and know what he was doing in Washington State? The call had to be bouncing from tower to tower and was masked by some sort of computer program.

"Don't be cynical. You're working a wonder and I am sure you can be successful." Jerry listened, attempting to understand the voice on the other end. Did he recognize it? "Have you located this call yet?"

"You don't seem to be anywhere near where the search says you are. You know too much about me. So I assume you're here in the county and masked the call for your safety. Or is it my safety which concerns you."

"Very good. I can stay in touch and we can help each other." The call ended without warning. Jerry played back the recording, wondering about the voice. Modified by some piece of equipment, the voice still had a familiar timbre.

CHAPTER 16

M arc walked into his house from the garage after sitting a moment, a standard action. He noted the emptiness. Joan was at the elder-care facility and their three children were in school. He headed to his office and dropped his briefcase by his desk.

Sitting in the large leather chair, thoughts of how Joan would respond to the progress he and his dad made in solving Uncle Jerry's death flooded his mind. She had a right to suspect his motives for not believing suicide was an option. But nothing in his career changed his observation of a self-motivated death providing any other pattern. Each person ruled a suicide by the M.E. carried a history of abuse and neglect, telling actions of misanthropic and sardonic mental aberrations, or lack of attentive care from family and friends generating a misinformed, unenlightened, and miserable soul.

Jerry was different. He carried a content demeanor with family, friends, and co-workers. One botched case was not enough to throw away a lifetime of good, a career of success. The envelopes contained damning evidence, but he was unable to complete his task.

Placing pictures on an evidence board, Marc sorted them by date and time. They retreated back four years constructing the history of a county in turmoil. Other pictures connected people to events, events which showed his uncle involved in the underside of the beast of drug dealing.

An undercover operation included more than one person. Jerry had to have another accomplice besides Wiley Fingers. Dad would decipher the note and a search would commence. But who still worked in the department? Who carried the burden of knowing the truth and held it tightly to the chest? Who was praying for a miracle?

Noises alerted Marcus to the impending invasion of the house by family. The front door slammed shut as someone entered. "Boys, get in here." He turned the evidence board over to conceal the data.

Upon their entering the office, Marcus glared his best angry eyes but instilled little fear. "Why are we condemning the front door to an early death?"

Marcus Junior answered, "We're in a hurry. Mom told us to be here half an hour ago and we had to make sure to beat her. Is she home, yet?" James smiled as angelic as possible for a guilty person.

The front door endured another forced closing. "Sarah, come here." This father usually had little to do with the discipline of children. The brothers parted to allow Sarah entry to the room. "Where have you been?"

"Mom said I could go." A wrinkle of the brow and puppy posture made no impression on Marc.

"Go where?"

"To Jaiden's. We have a big test in a couple of days and we were studying." Another sound indicated a fourth member of the Jefferson household arrived. The garage door hummed as a well-oiled machine.

"Now that your mother is home, I suggest each of you attend to your various duties and prepare your defenses." Marc watched his three sullen progeny slink into the hall. He followed to find Joan, his own defense needing shoring.

In the kitchen Joan reached into the refrigerator for a chilled water. "Hello, beautiful." He pulled her close as she approached. "Did you miss me?"

"What are you up to?" Her smile belied her question. Her lips connected with his, passionate and inviting. "What have you been doing?"

He released her as he spoke. "Dad and I met in Seattle. We have a lead Uncle Jerry left us but it's encrypted. An answer may be available, though."

Her face screwed into an angry witch about to cast a spell turning her prince into a toad. "Uncle Jerry. You promised. No more crazy cases and now you become obsessed with proving everyone wrong. You have to be the one who's always right." She stormed out of the room.

Marc froze. Another day another time, he might want to explain. Tonight, information and planning held priority. Tomorrow, mending relationships might rise to a higher plane. He reentered his office to find Joan studying the pictures. He froze a second time.

"Jerry had something on Snohomish County, didn't he?" She spoke without turning. Marc thawed and approached. Standing beside her they looked like detectives solving a crime, as partners, not lovers.

"He did, but someone knows about this and followed us to Vancouver. We interacted with a couple there who are involved in the drug trade in B. C. They're spending time with our RCMP friends. The Mountie we met was helping Jerry and the border patrol has been alerted to the trafficking which has to be happening. I get the note, and Dad was involved in an accident which included bullets. He's okay, but his partner, a rookie, took a couple of rounds in her vest. I fear for you and the kids. I'm so sorry." Joan remained tense but locked an arm in his.

"You clear this from your head and come back to me. I'll wait, unless we need to leave." He realized she understood the danger inferred from the board. Tension made for clearer thinking in Marc, but did it aid an angry nurse?

She whirled around, unhooking her arm from his and moved toward the doorway. Stopping, she turned. "Are we in any danger from these people in Everett?"

"I don't think so."

"But you can't promise we're not." Marcus set his mouth in a braced line and shook his head. She turned and exited, children needed attending and dinner was still a mystery. He flipped the board again and followed.

Finding Joan with Sarah, he suggested a solution to the mystery of dinner. "Let's go out tonight. I know it's a school night and we both have work tomorrow, but dinner isn't yet prepared and we can have some time together we don't always get."

Sarah broke in. "Good idea. I'll get the boys." She left before a rebuttal occurred.

"Marc, you're undermining our family with this investigation and bribing the kids with a dinner out is not going to traverse the developing chasm. Finish this quickly and keep us safe."

"I get it. Enough evidence exists to finish it, but I don't have the processes in place to bring down the drug traffickers or the corrupt Snohomish officers." The children broke in on the conversation.

"We're ready." They said in unison. An evening together warmed Marc's heart. Joan was correct. He had to protect his family and prove his case against the adversaries who as yet did not know the depth of his knowledge. Marc's mind wandered as they entered the car. What secrets existed still to be uncovered? Who knew about the investigation and tipped off the opposition? How was he going to trip them up in their defenses?

CHAPTER 17

Tiberius called his captain. "I need some of those vacation days you keep hassling me to take."

"Does this have something to do with cruiser being sideswiped and someone shooting at you on I-5?"

"Could be. I haven't hooked it with my brother's death, but something is rotten. My son is receiving notes to stop investigating and all of the evidence we've found points to corruption in Snohomish County. I need the time to coordinate with Marc and a couple of others who are part of the original investigation."

The silence reminded Tiberius of his captain's thought processing. He waited. "Alright, you have the time you need, but check with me regularly." The call ended and Tiberius returned to decoding Jerry's mysterious messages.

No word lists existed with the evidence, leaving a hole in deciphering six notes. He reread the shortest note. 'Take time to try twelve twisters.'

The code was more complicated than any he and Jerry had created as kids. Using memories of their childhood game, he tried constructing a probable list of words. Nothing made any sense. Third word..., two letters meaning every second word. All letter 't'. He needed the original list, probably memorized and destroyed.

He perused the longest note. 'Call me when the last of the quarters are found in the store.' Third word. Four letters—every fourth word. The, quarters, the. Another enigma. What message could be made with T Q and T?

He put the encoded notes away to let percolation in an idle mind do its job. A call to a friend in Snohomish seemed appropriate.

"I have the notes, but they make no sense to me," the voice on the other end said. Tiberius listened

"Does Marcus know you've been digging into this case as a favor to Sheriff Collins?"

"No, and he can't know until all the pieces are in place. Do you have the lists Jerry made to decipher the notes?"

"They were destroyed but a memory is a wonderful thing. I'll send them to you. Email or USPS?" Fear of interception and deception called for a face to face.

"Neither. Let's meet at the usual place. Bring a reasonable facsimile of the lists. I have six of them unless you know of any others."

"If Jerry kept six they are the keys. Others were not important. Bring them and we'll unlock the messages. I've been waiting a long time to finish this. When did Marc get the evidence Jerry hid away?" Tiberius decided a diversion was best.

"He was sent a message and we retrieved what there was from a locker in Vancouver. It wasn't as much as I would have liked."

"Did the maps come with it?" How did his friend know about the maps? He trusted this person for over twenty years but had to be cryptic for now.

"We got two of the eastern part of the county. Nothing was marked on them except for two drug drops and a safe house." Tiberius thought about one of the other three maps of Everett and the surrounding areas which highlighted several gang hideouts and the bordellos run by Pepper. The other two highlighted meetings and courier routes for the protection rackets and storage locations.

"Marc may be in trouble from some of the people associated with the county crew. Let him in on the secret before it's too late."

"He'll be read in as soon as I understand the messages." The call ended with doubt about his friend's intention to solve a two year old death. Jerry had to know the person who pulled the trigger. He had to know he was to die and be smeared in the eyes of the people with whom he served. But who was still not clear. Several suspects remained on the two year old list he kept in his wallet.

Before he packed up the papers, he copied each note by hand, putting the copies in the envelope he planned to take with him. The originals remained locked in a safe in his home office. Tiberius installed the small security box in the floor next to the desk which he covered with an area rug on the oak panel boards. Without a careful inspection no one would discover the seams of the entryway.

Gabby had left him a lunch before leaving to visit friends and play canasta for the rest of the day. She planned to return before dinner. Tiberius offered to take her to Anthony's Pier 66, a rare date night. He had his leave time and concluded a night out was warranted.

The trip into Snohomish County took less than twenty minutes from his house. He stopped at the small diner in Mountlake Terrace, Time Out Greek and American Restaurant. Few people he associated with stopped in although the reviews were better than average.

He took his prepared lunch but wanted to order a burger and fries. He arrived at 11:05AM, made his order and took a seat near a window. Anxiety was Tiberius's main battle with waiting, but the set up needed to be cryptic. Checking his watch, twelve minutes had elapsed from the time of his arrival. His friend should be showing before lunch was served. He ordered a beer to settle his mind. Nothing surprised Ti any more since his brother's untimely death. This secret, keeping the real story from his son and sister-in-law, tore at his heart. The rest of the family needed to be kept in the dark so the investigation could continue.

Marcus's call about Lydia's request opened the door for the conclusion he had waited two years to find. He didn't know who had killed his brother. He just knew it was a fellow law enforcement officer in Snohomish County. Everett P.D.? WSP? Snohomish Sheriff?

Maybe someone at Monroe State Penitentiary. His quiet trail led to several conclusions, all of which baffled his common sense.

The door opened and a young couple entered. As he checked out the couple, his lunch and beer arrived. Looking out the window a familiar face exited a small Prius.

"Do you always have to eat when we meet?" His friend sat across from him and signaled the wait staff. One of the owner's sons dealt him the courtesy and brought a menu. He ordered a gyro and iced tea. Tiberius slid the envelope across the table.

"Here's what I have. Match the lists with the proper notes."

"What's the hurry? I thought we might eat like regular folks and talk about the weather and politics."

"Very funny. I've wanted this solved since they killed him." The young man glanced at them as if scoping for secrets. Tiberius stared back and the man turned.

"You're rather paranoid today. I don't think the couple is out to get you." His friend pulled out a piece of paper from his jacket pocket, laying it on the table next to the envelope. "Let's see what your brother was up to." He opened the envelope and retrieved the six hand written copies.

Studying them with care he jotted down words which seemed to fit the code. The waiter arrived with the gyro and iced tea as he wrote. He covered the evidence, his own paranoia kicking in.

"Take time to try twelve twisters seems to be instructions for contacting someone." He wrote the three words which had worked with the pattern. He pushed the paper to Tiberius.

'Track Thornton Tuesday.' Ti frowned. "I don't know anybody named Thornton, and I don't remember seeing the name in any of the other evidence."

"Could be an alias." He read a second message and decoded. After writing several words Tiberius took it and laughed.

"My brother did have a sense of humor most of the world didn't get." The note read: 'Three pigs are guilty.' Jerry hadn't named anybody, but it was clear some in the sheriff's office committed a breach of their oath.

"Look, I have to get back to work. I'll contact you when I have the other four finished." The friend stood, took his billing slip to the counter, paid and left.

Tiberius packed his papers into his pocket and followed. Telling Marcus was not in his plans for now. Finding the mole in the grass occupied his focus. Who was following their activity, watching for a moment to pounce and end any further probe?

His cell buzzed. Checking the caller, an unknown source gave no number. "He punched the receive button. "Yes?"

"I am sorry to interrupt you, but I have information from our two intrepid criminal wannabes." Regina called from an untraceable phone. "Can we meet in Seattle today?"

"Where are you? I'm guessing not Vancouver."

"I have taken some vacation time. I'm nearing Seattle. We found the connection to Snohomish County. A woman named Laila Jearene Paulukaitis has a daughter in the Everett area who is involved with Pepper. We think she may be the liaison for trafficking materials from Vancouver to the United States. We're keeping a close eye on her."

"I'm in Mountlake Terrace just north of Seattle. Let's meet at Seattle HQ downtown."

"Copy that." The call ended. Surprised by the call he decided Marcus should know. Another idea diverted his plan. He called JJ.

"Hey, Uncle T, what's up?"

"Are you on duty or available to meet?"

"It's my day off, but I have plans."

"Can they be modified?"

"I guess. Let me make a call and rearrange. I'll get back to you."

Tiberius entered his car, checked the surroundings, and satisfied he was alone, drove to the office on 5th Avenue. As he maneuvered through south bound traffic, he thought about the deciphered messages.

Thornton? Three pigs? And now a person named Laila Jearene Paulukaitis. Did Marcus have any ideas? Had Jerry's investigation contained complications which collapsed the search and led to his death? Time would tell.

CHAPTER 18

The evening cooled, another low marine weather front assaulting the coast, pushing the warmth to eastern Washington. Jerry transcribed a message into the code he and Wiley used, preparing it for transmission to the dummy e-mail address. 'Three grown men want to find a new club to attend.' Wiley had the list associated with the key word, so Jerry trusted the action to be taken appropriately.

He had reported to Kopinski in early afternoon with new evidence which he figured would be in the hands of the enemy, regardless of how careful his captain was. One member of the department was identified as a possible connection to Pepper. Wiley had photographed the person at a meeting with known associates.

"Jerry, you can't accuse one of our own without evidence. This picture is not enough. We need a conversation or another witness to corroborate what this picture seems to indicate."

"I understand. We need to keep eyes on him and I don't think anyone here is trustworthy enough."

"Do you trust me?" Kopinski stood and walked around his desk. Jerry squirmed.

"I have to trust you or you'll make sure I go away for a long time. Prison is not my best residence."

The captain smiled. "See, a sense of humor. I'll keep an eye on him and let you know if anything pops."

"Thanks." His thoughts returned to what issues complicated keeping his wife and children safe from misfortune. Any problems and he was willing to shoot first and ask forgiveness later.

Tamara Delgato connected with him about a late payment on his loan. He promised to make it right. She warned him about consequences to his family if he did not comply. Tamara, a known prostitute, was the money collector for the association. She had propositioned him before establishing the payments schedule. Jerry declined. She flipped her head and grinned. "Your loss. We could have made a great couple and I don't care to interfere with your marriage." She was a beautiful, sexy brunette who exuded a magnetism she exploited for pleasure and financial gain. Her closeness to Pepper represented a connection he did not otherwise have. He associated with her because Pepper had not contacted him.

He spent too much time away from home meeting with small fry dealers, confidential informants, and Wiley and worried Lydia might suspect infidelity problems were imminent. A breach in the plans could upset motives for a successful conclusion.

He punched the send button delivering his message. Keeping the suspected deputy under watch prompted his first message, Track Thornton Tuesday. This second message came as a result of the man's schedule. No one could be seen near him until after noon. If Wiley decoded correctly, *Wait through noon tomorrow*, the tracking device would be attached to his automobile appropriately at the Jackson Park Golf Course near Thornton Creek. The man played there on Tuesdays.

A knock on his den door provoked his closing folders and securing them in a locked drawer. "Come in."

Lydia opened the barrier to his regular life and entered the room. "Are you coming out for dinner soon? Or shall I save it for later?" He checked his watch. It read 6:33.

"Let's eat." He rose and approached her, hugging and kissing his wife. "Something smells great."

He followed her to the kitchenette area to find a meatloaf and potatoes, one of his favorite meals. His angst about her safety increased as they sat. Their children had plans for the evening and missed the camaraderie. A bit of romance might complete the night. They ate in silence not wanting to dredge up the scum polluting their relationship.

He helped with cleanup and they ascended the stairs to the bedroom. As he removed his uniform, Lydia spoke, "I miss our life before we had this convoluted investigation. Do you still love me?" He stopped.

Regarding her with love, he responded, "More than ever. Be patient and let this conclude."

She undressed without answering. For a woman in her late forties, she kept in shape and maintained a healthy lifestyle. He hugged her and said, "I love you." The intimacy of the evening obstructed fears for the moment. He enjoyed her companionship.

They showered and prepared for a restful night. Noises downstairs initiated an exploration. Cammie and JJ had returned home. All was well. Worries put aside, he slept as sound as a puppy.

CHAPTER 19

Marcus woke early, dressed, and descended the stairs to his office. The evidence board remained turned away from view. He flipped it over and studied the material. Using a ball of string, he connected lists to maps and pictures. He connected names and addresses, joining each person with anyone referenced in another group of papers. A pattern emerged.

Joan joined him as he taped another string to another lead. "Oh hi. I'm figuring out what events happened to whom and when and where. All I need is the how and why." He smiled at her as she flexed her face into a steady glare at the board.

"You think someone ensured he died, taking his information with him."

"Yes, but whoever wanted him dead appears to know his evidence didn't disappear with him."

"I'm scared. That note last night was clear. Leave it alone or suffer. Should I be scared?"

"We'll stay vigilant to any anomalies around us. Dad is working on the coded messages. He and Jerry developed them as kids. They should help." Marc put a reassuring arm on her shoulder and she tucked in to it.

Other clamors alerted them to children arising. Marc flipped the board over and followed Joan to the kitchen. They ate a simple breakfast of cereal and muffins.

Lunches were prepared and backpacks checked for homework and other school needs before Sarah, Marc Junior, and James left. Joan dressed for work and checked on Marc. "Please be careful. This is an unusual case and I fear someone is not happy with you. Finish it quickly."

He nodded. "I plan on it. I've taken some time from my regular duties to concentrate on this so Dad and I can wrap it up soon." They hugged and Joan departed for the senior care center.

Marc returned to the board making notes of the ties he uncovered. A sergeant, a lieutenant, and two deputies connected to Pepper. Were they taunting him as part of the organization? Or had Jerry recruited them to help collect evidence. Were they the culprits who ended Jerry's life?

The copy of the usury loan of $50,000, signed and marked as delivered, puzzled Marcus. He had to ask Lydia about the money? Had the loan been repaid? Or did Jerry sacrifice his life for defaulting? Were his family members in hock for recovering the money? A calculation revealed a possible balance of $250,000 or more outstanding. A note explained how Wiley finagled the copy from Smithers by way of a Tamara Delgado.

"Tiberius needs to know this." He mumbled. Another motive for suicide reared an ugly head. Still, Marcus believed Jerry had died at the hands of another person. The suspected deputy? Or another of the deputies? One of Pepper's minions?

As he fixed the time sequence on the board into his computer tablet, something was out of place. Two meetings with Wiley crossed paths with a meeting of known Pepper associates. One of them, a young woman named Helene Paulukaitis, coordinated the meetings, according to Jerry's notes. Scanning pictures, he discovered one which included her with Wiley and his uncle. Who had taken the picture?

Writing on the back indicated a date and place, but no other information. Marc checked one of the maps and found a mark on it with a timestamp. They matched. A reference number prompted a check into a notebook meticulously kept by Uncle Jerry. A meeting discussing future dealings of the syndicate with her mother in Vancouver denoted a large movement of marijuana and opiates into Washington. Jerry had tapped into the trade information which should have begun the process of dismantling the syndicate.

Picking up his cell he dialed his dad. The phone went to voice-mail. "Dad, when you get this call me. I've found a link to Vancouver and Jerry may have enlisted other deputies to aid his investigation. I'm at home." He clicked the phone off and returned to his study of the board.

Jerry had been orderly and putting the pieces together was not difficult. However, conclusive findings did not lend themselves to prosecutorial outcomes.

His phone buzzed on the desk. Recognizing the name, he answered. "Hi, Dad. I've got some news for you."

"Good. I have some interesting news for you, too. What do you have?"

"I uncovered a person named Helene Paulukaitis who coordinated meetings about drug deals. She's pictured with Jerry and this Wiley guy, but I don't know who took the picture."

A laugh crossed the earpiece to Marc. "I am with Regina McDonald and JJ here at Seattle HQ and I have the name of a person in Vancouver with connections to Snohomish, Laila Jearene Paulukaitis."

Marc sat down in his desk chair, mouth gaping open. "Are they related? This is too much of a coincidence."

"Helene is Laila's daughter, near as I can tell. Ginny was sent to assist us and brought the information. She cracked the ring in Vancouver with the help of the young couple who decided to turn on their cohorts. Can you come over with the materials so we can check our facts so far?"

Marc checked his watch. Morning was but half finished. "I have much of the material on an evidence board, but I can remove it and come over."

"Stay there. We'll come to you. You're better set up than we are. There's a boat leaving in twenty."

"Good I'll see you when you get to my house. I'm not at work for a few days." The call ended and Marc returned to the board.

A disturbance in the front yard interrupted his thoughts. He peaked through the window curtain to see a man leaning out of a red truck placing an object in the mail box. Grabbing his spare gun from the unlocked drawer of the desk, he moved to the front door. Opening it with care, he watched as the truck squealed tires leaving a smoky trail. He could not read the plate but thought he recognized a British Columbia design. Was it the same truck which followed Regina and him in Vancouver?

Marc called his supervisor to get help with the mail box. No good would come from exploring it without protection. As he waited, a neighbor came out of his house. "Marc, are you alright? I saw the guy in the truck put something in your box and when he raced out of here I suspected trouble."

"I'm fine, but I'd stay away from the street for now. He might return."

"Are we in danger here?"

"I don't think so, but I have some guys coming to check the box. I can't discuss anything with you right now. Please be wary of strangers in the neighborhood." He nodded and reentered his house.

Marc walked out to the street and observed the tire marks. Tread remained but left no distinguishing evidence. Another object caught his eye. A small metal cylinder lay near the post of the box. He shot a picture with his phone's camera.

Returning to the house, he grabbed a CSI kit he kept with him. Unless the man gloved his hands, prints might be available on the metal or on the face of the mail box.

He removed an evidence bag and picked up the cylinder with a gloved hand and placed it in and sealed the bag. With a pen he wrote the information on the label. Sirens blared in the distance alerting him to aid arriving soon. Observing the periphery of the mail box no other items displayed. He shot pictures of the tire marks and gathered a sample of the rubber left behind when the truck sped away. Composition might detail the manufacturer.

A squad car arrived, siren off, lights flashing. Another van approached as the deputy exited. "What's up, Marc?" They shook hands after Marc removed his latex gloves.

"I've had a visitor. I'm not sure what he placed in my mail box, but if it is an explosive device, I thought it prudent to let the bomb boys work it."

Another car arrived and Tom Knudson got out. "Marc, I heard the call for the bomb squad. What's happening?"

"Not sure yet." He turned to watch a man in a heavy bomb suit approach the box. As he opened it, he checked for any wires or strings which could trigger a bomb. Nothing showed. He pulled the cover down and examined the interior.

Tom, Marc, and the deputy remained at a safe distance. Another person in the van watched the screen which displayed the image of the small camera the suited deputy inserted into the mail box.

"Nothing here to trigger the device. I'm going to remove it and open it." With long forceps he reached in and clamped the box, removing it and placing it on the ground. It looked harmless.

Marc started to approach. "Stay back, sir, until I get it open." Using a shield barrier to protect him from a possible explosion, the deputy snipped the tape on the package and unfolded the neatly wrapped paper. The cardboard was taped as well and he cut through to find the box contained nothing more than a smaller jewelry style box. When it was opened the deputy removed a folded notepaper, placed in an envelope.

Using latex gloves, Marc removed the letter and unfolded it. He shook his head as he read, aloud. "Stop investigating your uncle or people you care about are going to be hurt by what you find."

Handing the paper to a CSI investigator, he continued, "I want anything you can get from this as soon as possible. It may match the other letter."

"Yes sir. I'll get right on it." The forensics expert placed each item in an evidence bag and marked the bag. He left with the treasures to uncover any plot points for Marc to use in his pursuit.

When people had left and all was calm, Marc phoned his father, leaving a message detailing the invasion and the cryptic note in the box. He returned to the board looking for a connection to the Vancouver incursion. Nothing seemed to fit. Nothing pointed to anyone who could be feeding information to the enemy.

Only a close associate to himself or his father or a family member might have enough familiarity to interfere, to attempt a halt to the investigation. But who?

CHAPTER 20

Tiberius checked the caller I.D. on his phone. The message claimed another letter. He expected no prints or other leads from the materials collected at his son's place, but a second warning meant someone was alarmed.

Finished with the decoding of the four messages, he now had a clearer understanding of the severity of his brother's investigation. Thornton was not a person but a place.

What importance was the creek which ran through Seattle from Jackson Park Golf Course to Lake Washington spilling into the lake near Matthews Beach? A piece of information was missing. Did Marcus have it in the envelopes at his house?

Another possibility was Thornton Place, a housing complex near NE 103rd. A meeting place, away from the investigative probing by Snohomish law enforcement? He clicked open his phone and punched in the speed dial number for Marcus.

When Marcus answered, Tiberius asked, "Is there anything in your materials which points to a Thornton Creek or Thornton Place?" A noise like papers and folders being searched flooded the earpiece.

"One of the maps has King County on it and a mark is near Jackson Park Golf Course. Why?" Tiberius reflected a moment about his secret. "Dad, is something wrong?"

"No, I have something to tell you when we meet at your house. Is Joan at work?"

"Yeah, and the kids are at school."

"Good. See you in a couple of hours." He clicked off and turned to his fellow officers. "Marc has some information which can aid the investigation. Let's head for Wendlesburg."

"Uncle T, do you believe my father was eliminated?"

"I don't know for sure. If he did kill himself, it was to keep you all safe. If not, then we'll take those bastards apart and put them where they belong." Regina watched, curious about the young man who shared family traits of good looks and an inquisitive nature.

The ride to the ferry terminal was quick despite construction on the water front. They stayed in the car which was parked on the second deck on the outside north lane, silent for the moment. As the boat moved away from the mooring, Regina broke the calm, directing her question at JJ. "How long have you been with Snohomish County?"

"About a year. Always wanted to follow my dad and uncle. Cousin Marcus has the right idea of detective work. Sorry, Uncle T, although you are more of a detective than a street officer." Tiberius nodded his acknowledgement.

Regina continued, "I enjoy uncovering rascals who inculcate the nastiness of life into others who might not be willing or desirous of a criminal life." JJ scrunched his forehead and roared with laughter.

"Anybody ever wonder what you're talking about when you incorporate such insidious linguistic construct?" Regina grinned, a satisfactory retort accepted. Tiberius sat quietly, watching as the younger generation flirted, his memory of such actions rustled to the forefront of his thinking.

"Are you seeing anyone at the moment?" She raised one eyebrow.

"Are you hitting on me? With my uncle present?" Tiberius snickered, thinking how he would be interested if he was JJ's age. And single.

"Just curious if someone had to try and keep up with your sense of humor." But she earmarked that he could be a good catch.

JJ smiled. "I'm testing the waters with a fellow officer named Samantha, Sammie, Jose. We're not really serious or anything."

"She might be thinking something a little different." JJ didn't answer but pondered her comment.

Tiberius interrupted, "If you two love birds are done displaying your plumes, we should talk about what we expect from our investigation."

The ferry approached the Wendlesburg dock and the announcement cautioned passengers and drivers to return to their cars. Three intrepid officers watched people repopulate the auto deck. "Marcus said he had a connection to the Thornton mentioned in one of the coded messages. One of the maps is of north King County and marks a place near Jackson Park Golf Course. It may be that 'Track Thornton Tuesday' was a request for Wiley Fingers to tail someone who was scheduled to meet another person at the marked site."

———— ❧ ————

The ferry docked and cars disembarked for unknown destinations. Tiberius drove off when the second deck turn came. Silence prevailed until they arrived at Marcus's house.

"Good to see you again, Ginny." Marc's comment initiated a smile from her. "JJ, I'm glad you're part of this."

"Thanks, cousin. I never really believed Dad killed himself, and I want these pieces of…"

"Calm down, JJ," Tiberius interrupted. "Marc, I have been looking into Jerry's death for the last two years. I didn't tell anyone because of the threat of reprisals to Lydia, Cammie and JJ. I didn't think you were in any danger. Now, however, I think caution is important."

"Have you found out anything which we can apply to the materials Uncle Jerry left us?"

"I have a friend who can help us with the messages. He contacted me soon after Jerry died. He wishes to remain anonymous because discovery can be dangerous for him."

Marcus pondered his father's comment "I think I know who you mean, but let's leave it as he wishes. Will he connect with us when we need him?"

"He and I have an arrangement. When we get close to bringing down this organization, he'll help us finish off the details. He knows quite a lot about some of the people engaging in illegal and dishonorable activity who should be enforcing the law and are not."

Studying the board all four police officers looked puzzled. "Dad, what if Uncle Jerry found out the main culprit was someone important in the sheriff's office?"

"Marc, I'm afraid he uncovered the snake's head and couldn't cut it off. We have to be prepared," he said turning to JJ, "that Lydia was threatened and pushed Jerry to halt his activities. She may even be the source of the information being fed to those who are following us, so no harm would come to you and Cammie."

"Mom wouldn't do that." JJ set his jaw and folded arms across his chest. "She told me about Dad's investigation and asked for me to keep a sharp ear and a watchful eye. I've heard and seen nothing to indicate who might be corrupted."

Regina pointed to a picture taped under a question mark. "Why is this picture separate from the others?"

Marc answered her. "I didn't have any indication how it fit within the framework of the patterns which are forming."

"If we place it with Jackson Park Golf Course, doesn't it explain the Thornton meeting on the map?"

"Ginny, you are brilliant. I didn't see it." The picture of Jerry and a woman exchanging packages was fuzzy but indicated the accessories of a golf course.

"Who's the woman?" she asked.

"Helene Paulukaitis."

"Her mother is our suspect in Vancouver."

"Question remains, though. Who's taking the picture?" Marcus looked again at the picture. "Very pretty." He pointed at another picture which showed Uncle Jerry and another man with the young lady. Indeed, the clarity of the photo enhanced her features and the beauty of her face. "She and this other man were contacts with Pepper. Jerry wrote in a journal about the interactions he had with her and how he may have compromised his marriage in order to appear more inclined to cooperate."

"Dad had an affair with her?" JJ dropped his arms to his side. "Did Mom know?"

"Nothing he wrote indicated he engaged in a sexual relationship, but she may have offered it and your father may have played along. Lydia knew nothing of this, as far as I can tell."

JJ shook his head back and forth. Regina placed a hand on his shoulder. "Her mother taught her well. She ran a prostitution ring in Vancouver and is quite beautiful for a woman in her forties." JJ reached up and removed her hand but held it for a moment not brushing it away but keeping hold as the hands descended to their sides.

Tiberius interrupted their interplay. "I'm ready to make contact with Snohomish and see what kind of turmoil rises when we indicate our investigation found something they don't have. JJ, I want you and Regina to pick up Helene and bring her to the WSP office in Everett. They're ready to help us find answers and close the case. Be careful. Some of her associates may get violent if they get wind of your actions." Both nodded.

"Marc, you and I are going to visit Mr. Pepper and offer incentive for his surrender to us. He'll want a warrant and a lawyer, but we aren't going in as an official investigation. Although he may protest, I want to know who he'll contact in the sheriff's office. We'll then meet you two and Miss Paulukaitis at the WSP office."

"Dad, are we ready to move on them? Although there's a lot of circumstantial evidence, I don't think it'll hold up in a court. Jerry probably knew he had enough to threaten but not enough to convict. One of his later journals had a note about him telling Captain Kopinski he was not able to complete the investigation. He indicated corruption in the department and Kopinski cut it off. After another meeting with him, Jerry retired. He wrote about the threat of having his pension and other benefits pulled."

Regina commented next. "Was Kopinski corrupt?"

"I don't think so but who knows."

"Where's Kopinski now?" Her question generated a memory in Tiberius. Something Jeremais had said about a month before his death. 'Tell my captain nothing. He's a coward.'

"He left the police force about a year ago and disappeared."

"Could he have been eliminated?" Her queries sparked a return to one of the folders containing correspondence.

Marc pulled out a memo from then Sheriff Virgil Kastner to Kopinski regarding a mix-up in funding for covert investigations. "He may have been misled about financial coverage and discovered what he thought to be an error. Any requests he made to cover expenses were denied before they were submitted to the county. Jerry made a note on the back of this intra-office communique he obtained from a secretary. He worked his case without financial support from the county."

JJ's comment surprised them. "About six months before Dad's death I overheard him talking with Mom. He complained about the lack of support."

Tiberius stroked his chin. "So Jerry figured someone was sabotaging his undercover operation and it triggered his Vancouver caper."

Marcus nodded. "And Kastner pulled the strings. Think he was crooked?"

"No, but he retired at the same time as Jerry and moved to Chicago. Maybe he ran before it all collapsed around him?"

"How do you know he's is in Chicago?" Three faces scrutinized Tiberius

"I guess I should enlighten you more about what I've been up to for the last two years." The scrutinizing morphed into perplexed looks. "After my brother's death I contacted a couple of friends in Snohomish and asked a few questions. They're to be trusted and I will not reveal who they are until we have enough to finish off the scum who killed Jerry."

Marcus interrupted, "You've actually been investigating and you didn't tell anyone?"

"Sorry son, I knew you wanted to clear his name, but I needed to get into this and you were involved with other cases. I didn't know about Jerry's evidence, he was pretty cagey, so making any headway has been difficult. Finding his stash turned the corner for me."

Marcus grimaced. "Then let's get to Everett and shake up their world." Regina and JJ looked at each other and smiled.

CHAPTER 21

"Lieutenant, what's going on?" Jerry entered Kopinski's office and closed the door. "My financial requisitions are rejected and this investigation is disappearing faster than a snow fall in November."

"Relax, Jerry. Have a seat." Closing a folder, he stood and walked around his desk. Jerry remained standing, feet apart, arms folded across his chest.

'I don't need a seat. I need an explanation."

"I wish I had one. I'm being stonewalled as if someone doesn't want you to continue your investigation. I may have to pull the plug on this one."

Jerry's eyes burned and neck muscles bulged. "I need to finish this. I need to bring these people to justice."

"I know, but it's not happening. There's no money for it and none coming."

"Do you understand what's happening? Someone in our office is feeding them intel. We have a mole and I'm going to find out who and tear out their black heart with my bare hands."

"You can't just come in here and threaten fellow officers and others without any evidence." Jerry remained quiet. He had what he needed but wasn't about to reveal his stash. He trusted no one.

"Alright, then what's to become of me? I've played up the role of corrupted cop. If this gets out, what's to prevent a hungry DA from wanting my badge? How do I stay out of prison for an investigation you supported? Are you going to deny any responsibility?"

Kopinski's silence fueled the fire raging in his heart. "You're a coward, Dan. If you can't back me up on this, you're not the man I thought you were." Jerry turned to leave, but a hand reached for his arm.

"Wait. I can't give you the support you want because of circumstances as they are. I can suggest you take an early retirement. You have enough time in and we can push the paperwork through without any questions about what you were doing."

"That's you're idea of support? Kicking me out? Who got to you? Our mole? Kastner suggest this?"

"I'm retiring also. I'll leave soon after you. It's the best for both of us. I know I got you into this, and now I have to get you out."

"I got myself in because I had to do it. I had to destroy them for what they did to my daughter. Cammie didn't deserve what happened to her." Jerry dropped his arms to his side, tears welling on his lower lids. "She's a good girl and they tried to mess her up. Now I'm going to mess them up. If I can't do it as a cop, then all of you stay out of my way. I'll do what needs to be done."

Kopinski sat on his desk. "That's not helpful, Jerry. They'll squash you like a bug and crucify your family. JJ will never get into the department and Cammie will be dragged back into pulling tricks to support a drug habit." Jerry squared to his boss and friend. "If anything happened to you, Lydia would be devastated."

Jerry stepped to the door and turned. "If I do nothing, they win and this can't be a game they win." With his hand on the door knob he finished his statement. "I'll let you know what I plan to do about retiring. But mark my words, I'm going to find out who's crooked and they're going to regret messing with me. I have no friends in this department anymore." He opened the door and proceeded out. Out to the squad room. Out of the office. Out of his life as a cop.

He racked his brains to understand why someone in the department was sabotaging the case. Pepper had dirt on someone or paid a hefty bribe to an underpaid sheriff employee. Evidenced pointed toward corruption but had not identified the culprit. Or culprits.

He drove home to inform Lydia of his failure as a detective, a first for him. He knew in his heart Kopinski was right. He had taken what amounted to a bribe from Pepper's organization. The money sat in a bag in the trunk of his car. Repayment had come due when a deal was struck to have him feed the enemy information about operations inside as a forgiveness of the interest. He figured it was a way to get closer to Pepper and the higher members of the gang. It was starting to work with low level information transferred to Smithers.

Had the mole confirmed his lack of high level cooperation? Had this person enough clout to kill the money? It was finished. His career was at the end and still he could not let go of the damage inflicted on Lydia and Cammie, and JJ. He had failed and now faced the possibility of charges for violation of his oath as a deputy.

In the house they shared for nearly twenty years he sat in the kitchen waiting for her to enter the room. "You're home early. Is anything wrong?" Jerry smiled without teeth showing, eyes downcast.

"Nothing we can't handle. Nothing, as long as we stick together."

She sat in the chair next to his. "Tell me, so we can plan how to handle whatever it is we have to handle." She understood more about what made him tick than his own parents and brother. Jerry had fallen in love with her from the first moment he met her at the college dance his sophomore year at the University of Washington. He placed her hands in his.

"I'm finished with the county. It looks like someone is tampering with my investigation and financials have dried up. Dan encouraged me to retire before I get charged with corruption." She squeezed his hands with a gentle accepting manner, an understanding of the situation.

"What can I do to help?" She understood his desires to be an honest person and to uphold his name and family. Lydia was the backbone he needed at the moment.

"Want to put on a play?" Creases reorganized her forehead. "I have an idea, but it's going to take a lot of patience on your part and hurt some people who are most important to me." Bewilderment shined back from her eyes. "Time has come for one ruse to end and another to begin."

CHAPTER 22

As the four officers of varying departments waited for the Kingston ferry to arrive, the conversation had little to do with their quest and much to do about the one person not related to the others.

"I grew up in a family of educators and business people. I was to inherit my father's wholesale company along with my younger brother and sister. We were to go to college and get degrees in marketing, economics and human resources. Dad's health was suffering and he wanted us to keep the money flowing. I was a big disappointment."

JJ sat in the back seat of the car beside Regina, hardly knowing what to say to her. Her beauty confounded his sense of decorum and interfered with any loyalty to his girlfriend, Samantha. "He has to be proud of you now, doesn't he?" He fumbled the words and she smiled.

"I suppose. My mother was happy to have me pursue what I wanted. She encouraged me to go to the academy, but it caused some issues between my parents."

The horn on the ferry announced its arrival. As they watched the bicycles and motorcycles disembark, Marcus thought about his father's revelation. An investigation of his uncle's death had begun almost as soon as the body was discovered. Why was he left out of the loop? He missed Jerry and wanted to prove a murder had been committed. Jerry could not and would not pull the trigger.

As the last of the cars departed the decks of the MV Spokane, Tiberius started his car. Marc needed time alone to ask his father about what he uncovered without his help. Lydia had been so calm after Jerry's death. Why? Marc attributed it to shock. Two years later and she seemed immune to any depression associated with such a severe loss in one's life. She knew about all of the materials gathered during the eight months of detective work. Why the secrecy?

Tiberius put the car in gear and followed a small Kia hybrid onto the loading ramp. Directed to the left outside first deck parking area, he stopped and applied the brake after putting the car in park. All four intrepid investigators ascended the stairs to the passenger deck and found a seat near the staircase.

JJ and Regina sat on one bench while Tiberius and Marc sat across from them. They looked like they belonged together, but Marc thought the distance and differences created a barrier to any relationship developing.

While he stared out the window at Puget Sound and the northern Cascade Range, his mind flitted from one idea and chain of thought to another as if he distinguished no immediate threat to himself or any member of his family.

"What's on your mind?" Tiberius asked. He swiveled his body and head to face his father.

"You withheld your involvement after Jerry's death. Why?"

Tiberius contemplated how much to tell his son. "Jerry asked me to leave you out of it. After his retirement, he and I met to discuss what to do about the lost investigation. He wanted to keep you out of danger."

"What danger? Who threatened him? Pepper or someone in the department?"

"He wasn't sure, so the fewer people involved the safer. I'm sorry for the past, but we now have the means to destroy these people and their organization. We can help Snohomish clean up the department and affect changes to King and Kitsap Counties at the same time. As we get more done more information will reveal itself to us. Don't worry about it."

"You're withholding from us even now." Tiberius didn't deny the allegation.

"Uncle Ti, Dad acted strangely after he retired. I saw little of him and I lived at home. Cammie moved to Bellingham to go to school and Mom kept to herself most of the time. So I agree with Marc. You know more than you're telling us."

Tiberius regarded JJ's words and said, "Be patient and watch as things unfold. We're engaging these people on their turf and they'll resist any overtures for them to surrender." Smiling at Ginny, he continued, "I am sorry you got mixed up in this. It really is a family fight."

"I may not be family, but I know what's at stake."

Marcus retorted, "You're in on this? Even before we came to Vancouver?" Her eyes widened as she shrug her shoulders. A slight grin coursed her face which burnt a pale red.

"As you know I met your uncle when he and Lydia came to Vancouver to secure the evidence you now have at your house. He asked for our help which we gave. You came and we captured part of the contingent operation which connects to what is happening in Snohomish County. Tiberius and I met once before you and he arrived. I do apologize for the deception, but we had our reasons."

"And now? What reasons do you two have for keeping secrets? If we are to be successful, it might be helpful to know what's going on." Marcus narrowed his eyes and stared at his father. "Well?"

"Well, Jerry's suicide…"

"Alleged suicide," Marc interrupted.

Tiberius corrected. "Alleged suicide. Anyway, Jerry's death changed everything. He prepped Lydia for the danger threatening him and the family. He decided to do something outrageous to protect all of us from the retaliation of Pepper and three unidentified members of the department. Unfortunately for you and others, we lost a good man."

"You are not explaining. What is being kept from us?" Marcus glared his best at his father. "What are you holding back from me?"

"Your uncle had a plan for exacting revenge on the people who corrupted your cousin. Cammie fell in with a bad crowd and when he pulled her out, he vowed to get even."

"Are you saying she did something wrong?" Marcus's eyes widened.

JJ answered first, "She got hooked on oxy and started turning tricks to cover the cost. Dad got her into a rehab program in Bellingham and moved her there to go to school. She's okay but he was pissed. It's one of the reasons I joined the department."

Regina joined the conversation. "Your uncle came to Canada to secure his evidence and find a place to hide, if needed."

Marcus closed his eyes. "He didn't get the chance to escape before they killed him." The Mountie did not respond. "Alright, then we get to complete his business with Pepper."

The announcement for drivers and their passengers to return to vehicles halted further conversation. They descended the stairs to the auto deck and prepared for a journey to hell.

As Tiberius awaited his turn to disembark, he looked at his son and apologized. "I needed to complete what Jerry started, but I had little with which to work. When Granger became sheriff, he suspected a mole or two still remained in the department, but he had no leads. He asked me as Jerry's friend and as the sheriff to dig up anything I could."

When time came to leave silence reigned. The drive from Edmonds to Everett was uneventful. The nearer the group got to their destination, the eerier the car's atmosphere became.

Tension caused different reactions within the car's occupants. JJ checked his phone for messages. Marcus closed his eyes trying to relax. Regina texted a message to her office. Tiberius gripped the steering wheel with white knuckles.

Their journey into the heart of the beast compromised nothing in the pursuit of justice. "I'm going to the State Patrol first. We can share what we have and move on to Pepper and give him the news."

"What about the sheriff's office?" Marcus's eyes remained closed.

"JJ and I can contact people we know who are above reproach. For now, we'll leave them out. Whoever is on Pepper's payroll will find out after we get to Pepper."

"Uncle T, I heard a rumor about Dad that he was on the take with him."

"It was part of the ruse. He was to become bound to the organization and in lieu of interest payments for a usury loan, he was to feed them intelligence from the sheriff's office."

Regina commented, "When he was in Vancouver, Jerry told me the organization paid him $50,000 to cover his indebtedness. It was this ruse, as you called it, which helped him to identify at least one person in the department who was on the payroll of your person of interest. He placed the money in our custody."

Marcus opened his eyes and turned. "You have the money in Vancouver? You haven't been honest from the beginning. Spill the beans."

Regina returned his question with her own. "Do you want the truth about your uncle immediately or can you wait until we strike the fuse which destroys this group?"

JJ spoke next, "I want to get the people responsible for my father's death. I want my office clean of any corruption. I need them dead, figuratively and if necessary, literally. I can wait, but what you have to tell us better be good."

"It is."

Tiberius turned into the parking garage of the Washington State Patrol office and parked. "Let's see if we can find Goodman."

In the office a secretary directed the team to communications where a contact with Officer Goodman was made. A request to return from patrol was made.

"While we wait, what say we plan an assault on Pepper's warehouse?"

"We'll need to commandeer another car." JJ said.

"I'll ask the senior officer for one. JJ, Ginny, go get Paulukaitis. We'll wait for Goodman and then see Pepper and leave him with a few questions." Tiberius and Marcus left to see the officer in charge.

CHAPTER 23

As they drove toward the waterfront in Everett, Tiberius and Marcus prepared for the worst and hoped for the best.

"Do you think Pepper will be happy to see us? I sure hope so, because I want to see his face when we destroy his empire. I want to cut his throat for what he did to Cammie and Jerry." Tiberius kept his eyes forward as he spoke. "The son-of-a-bitch deserves to die."

"We can't just kill him. He needs to stand trial for his crimes." As Marcus responded to Tiberius's tirade, his cell phone buzzed. Checking the caller, his jawed dropped. "Joan, what's up?"

"I came home to get something and found the house unlocked."

"Anything missing?" His thoughts pictured the evidence board being destroyed or contents stolen. "Anything happen to the board?"

"Your concern is about your precious evidence? I could be dead or worse?" Tiberius peered at his son.

"I'm sorry. I didn't mean to downplay the seriousness of this."

"Nothing is missing. However, you need to come home and see what is here. I don't know how to describe it. Everything is intact but you have some new evidence."

"Joan, you're being cryptic. What is it?"

"It's more who it is." The phone clicked silent. Tiberius pulled the car to the side of the street. Marcus paled with fear.

"Someone's at the house with Joan. I don't think she can call for help. I'll get some deputies to her. Dad, we have to go home."

The phone buzzed again as they sat. "Hello." Sweat beaded on his forehead. He pushed the audio button for his father to hear.

"Mr. Jefferson, don't call anyone to come over. Your wife is a lovely person and I would hate for bad things to occur. You have quite a collection of evidence. I guess Jerry was a very thorough and careful investigator."

"What do you want?"

"I want you to stop chasing daydreams before they become nightmares. You can have your fun with this evidence, but remember what Isaac Newton postulated. For every action there is an opposite and equal reaction. Don't push too hard or the rebound might be troubling." The phone went silent.

"Who the hell was that?" Tiberius eyes screwed into narrow slits as anger welled up inside. "We need to let Pepper alone for now. Call JJ and have them abort and return to WSP. I think I know what's up."

Marcus pushed the speed dial for his cousin, but it went to voice mail. "Forget about Paulukaitis. Return to the WSP office as soon as you get this." He clicked off. "Let me try Ginny." He dialed her number and got the same result.

Tiberius returned the car to the street squealing tires as he spun 180 and raced back to where the journey began. "Something's not right." He flipped the cruiser's blue lights on and hit the siren. "Something's not right," he repeated.

The car maneuvered through traffic as fast as possible. "Should I radio ahead about the problem?"

"Marc, no. It's not what you think, but I have to gather all of you together and explain something. Something else which I didn't think was possible." The siren shrieked for traffic to move aside. They arrived within minutes.

At the WSP office they entered the squad room hoping the find JJ and Ginny. "They haven't had time to return with or without Paulukaitis."

"Try them again." Tiberius confronted the sergeant who had outfitted their partners with an unmarked car. "Does the car have a radio in it?"

He checked the log book and shook his head.

"Shit. I hope they aren't entering a trap. We have to find who is feeding information to them." Heading to Goodman's desk, he asked, "Did you get what I asked of you?" He placed both hands on the top surface and glared.

"Yes, but I don't understand why you wanted this particular report. It has nothing to do with our investigation of your brother." Goodman handed him a folder which he opened and read.

"Thanks. You're right. It has nothing to do with Jerry, but everything to do with someone who is helping our foes." He hoped the others would arrive soon.

"Dad, what is it?" Tiberius handed him the folder which he opened and read. "Oh my. This explains a lot." He returned it to his father. "Let me call home again." He walked away for privacy, fearing the worst.

"Hello, Marc." Her voice sounded calm and reassuring. "Are you coming home soon?"

"Are you in any danger?"

"No, but our mystery guest left. He'll contact you when you get back. What's going on? I'm frightened for you. I don't want to lose you." Her calm increased his angst. He sat in a chair.

"Did he hurt you? Did he threaten you in any way?"

"No. He says he's here to help but must remain anonymous. He didn't tell me his name or anything about him. I found him sitting in your office analyzing your board. He called my name when I entered and told me not to be afraid. He knew about us and our family. How does this happen?"

"Alright, we'll finish here and head home." He clicked off the call and returned to his father.

"Is everything alright at home?"

"Yes, but it's crazy. Joan told me the person who was in the house came to help." His eyes wandered away from his father's gaze. "Who wants to help? Who knows about me, my family, and what happened to Uncle Jerry? Who the hell comes to my house, enters it, and confronts Joan?"

"You know who. It's in that report. We'll see more of him as this unfolds and the trap is set." He turned to Goodman who sat nearby. "Officer Goodman, would you be kind and get me your file on my brother? I left my copy in Seattle." Tiberius watched as he left. "Marc, we are not necessarily in the clear being here. I don't think we need to stay any longer than needed."

"Is Goodman on the take?"

"Not sure and not willing to test it." JJ and Regina entered the room with a beautiful young woman who discharged disapprovals about the treatment she received from her captors. As she realized her environment kept prying outside eyes at bay, she calmed her awkward activity. She straightened her frame projecting her chest and lifting her chin. The elegance exhibited belied her profession.

"Uncle T, I would like you to meet Helene Laila Paulukaitis."

"It is my honor to meet you. I understand from JJ, you are working with Officer Jose to break free of Mr. Andrew Pepper and his organization." He remained a gentleman as he began questioning her. "Please have a seat. JJ, remove the restraints. No more need for acting in here."

Goodman returned with the requested file and stared at the siren who entrapped unsuspecting men much as the Greek Sirens lured unsuspecting sailors onto the reefs around their island. "Here you are." He held the folder out without looking where it would land. Tiberius grabbed it as it began a descent to the floor.

"I don't believe you've had the pleasure of meeting Ms. Paulukaitis." Goodman's head rocked back and forth in a slow pattern much as those captured by beasts lost in mythology. "Would you please leave us for the moment so we can interrogate our witness?" His head bobbed as he backed out of the room.

"JJ, I need you to leave, as well. You shouldn't hear what she may tell about our family."

"I know her role in keeping Cammie enslaved, hooking for her. I'd like to stay." He sat across from her, remaining silent.

Marcus and Regina leaned against a wall to watch Tiberius unravel the mystery of Mr. Andrew Pepper as related from Helene.

After an hour of questions and answers, a picture of the life and times of Andrew Pepper spread before them.

"Regina, please go with JJ and take Helene to a safe place." Speaking to their guest, "I do apologize for the rough treatment, but eyes and ears seem prevalent in the county and I want it to appear as if you are not a cooperative person."

"Mr. Jefferson, my life has been faulty from an early age. My mother became pregnant by a john in Los Angeles, so she came to Vancouver to start fresh. As you know it did not work out as she wanted. As I grew up I watched her bring home different men each night. When I became old enough to understand, I believed I had one choice in life. I began turning tricks at the age of thirteen and now that I am twenty four, I want out. There has to be more to living than providing lurid fantasy for men and women's perverted lasciviousness."

Turning to JJ she continued, "I do apologize for what I put your sister through. I had little choice myself. She and I must be about the same age. I'm glad she got the help she needed."

Regina placed cuffs on her and led her to the door. JJ followed. With Pepper's movements more clearly defined Tiberius and Marcus could head back to home in Seattle and Wendlesburg. The only hindrance was the pair of officers escorting a prime snitch to a safe place since each of their transports were in Seattle.

"JJ, Ginny deliver her to our secure location and come to the Sheriff's office in Everett. Marc and I are going there to meet an old friend." They nodded and left.

Marc sat in the passenger side of the patrol car, then said, "Time to shake up their world, isn't it?" Tiberius smiled and drove away from the State Patrol Office. Another domain was about to be breeched.

CHAPTER 24

"I don't understand what you want? " Lydia remained seated at the kitchen table next to Jerry.

"I need to disappear and you have to act normal around other people." She stared at him "What?"

"You need to disappear and I have to act normal. You are making no sense at all. Are these people you investigated coming after you?"

Jerry stood and walked away. Turning to her, his eyes downcast, he answered, "I don't know, but I can't take any chances. You and the kids are important to me and the only way to keep you safe from harm is for me to leave until I can figure out a way to destroy them."

Lydia strolled to her husband. Taking his hands in hers she kissed him. "We can face this together. I don't want you gone."

"I know, but they'll come after me and you could be hurt in the crossfire, literal or not. And if they go after Cammie and get her hung up and turning again, I'd have to kill someone and that wouldn't be good for me or you." She kissed him again.

"What do have in mind?"

"I'm not sure yet. Can you live here without me for a little while, take care to see JJ getting into the department, and planning for Cammie finishing college?"

As they stood together, before she could answer, the kitchen door from the garage opened and Jeremais Junior entered the room.

"Why hello. Did I come home too soon? You look like you two need some privacy." He winked.

"Your mother and I were talking about you finishing school in Pullman and getting an assignment to the patrol academy. You still want to be a cop, don't you? I still have some pull in the county, I think."

"Yeah, I guess."

"By the way, what are you doing here? Why aren't you in school?"

"I finished with finals and left for the weekend to be with you guys. I have no life at WSU."

His mother grinned, "You are such a liar. I happen to know you're seeing the Jose girl who's in your program and plans to join the county force when she graduates." His smile broadened at the mention of her name.

"Guilty, but we're not serious or anything. We just want to capture bad guys and shoot guns."

"Are you two involved?" His mother glowered at him as she spoke.

"Gees, Mom. That's kind of personal. I am a grown man and can take care of my own sex life, ah, if I have one." He blushed.

"Good, get her pregnant so we can have grandchildren." JJ's jaw fell open.

"What happened to the great ethical upbringing and the moral compass implanted in my skull? Has it failed to detect a massive change in your ethos?" He laughed and turned to retrieve a suitcase, left in the garage. Jerry separated from the cluster and went to his bedroom. Lydia joined him after JJ returned and placed the bag in his own bedroom.

Alone with Jerry, Lydia closed the door. "What's going on with you, lately? You act like nothing is okay, like you lost the game single-handedly and now you want to run away. It's not like you to avoid a battle."

"I can't win this battle or the war in which it's being fought. I have to change the rules and strategies of the conflict, so no one comes here. If I'm gone, there's not much to draw their ire or desire for revenge. I have one shot at being successful in getting away and I need your help."

"Alright, what do you have in mind?" He smiled at her and began relating a plot for an adventure movie, a script for an idea outrageous in concept and improbable in construct. He would be the producer, director, and main character in this play to be forged in the confines of a small select group.

"I'll need to speak with some people I trust and get them on board, but if they agree to help, as well, I see no reason for failure of my plans."

They left the room to join their son for a dinner fit for a king or a condemned person's last meal.

CHAPTER 25

Tiberius and Marcus sat awaiting an answer to the question of whom he suspected of malfeasance in the department. An innocent question about a lack of productivity by deputies and secretaries brought a smile to Granger Collin's face. "I know you think I run a tight ship, but you're right, someone in this organization is not dealing properly with their duties."

"Do you have any idea who to suspect?"

"Sadly no, but Pepper is able to thwart our efforts to destroy his organization. Someone has to be feeding him intelligence. Can you help? I really could use it."

"Jerry left a stash of evidence for us to use which he didn't leave with you, or rather Kastner and Kopinski."

"Anything which helps?" Collins leaned in wide-eyed. Tiberius continued, "We may be able to ferret out one of the problems. Tell us about the undercover vice deputy, Wiley Fingers."

"Kopinski enlisted his aid when Jerry set up the sting. He was supposed to be one of the best undercover men in the area. Hardly anyone knew who he was. So he made the best partner for what they wanted to do."

"Do you know how to contact him?"

Granger punched some buttons on his computer retrieving personnel files. "Huh, that's strange." Marcus and Tiberius cocked their heads in tandem.

Marcus spoke first, "Something wrong?"

"I don't usually interface with personnel files, but his name is not on the registry, as either active or retired. There's no record of any Wiley Fingers working for the county."

"Was it an alias?" Marc asked. "Who retired around the same time as Uncle Jerry?"

"Let's see. Besides Kastner and Kopinski, a deputy Timothy Knudson left the force, Bentley Zacharias died in an auto accident which killed his family, and a couple administrative personnel and a secretary. We don't have a lot of turnover here."

Tiberius spoke, "What happened with the accident? Hit and run or standard run-of-the-mill?"

Collins manipulated the computer mouse and punched a few buttons. "He was sideswiped by an SUV which caused his car to go over a ravine into the Snohomish River. They all drowned. Driver of the SUV stopped and tried to help. Claimed he did not see Bentley's car. He pled guilty to 3rd degree vehicular manslaughter. According to this record, he doing a dime in Monroe."

"Isn't that a bit light for four deaths? Who did he work for before the accident?"

"Don't have it listed." A knock interrupted them. "Come in."

"Sheriff, Deputy Jefferson is here with a young woman. Says his cousin and uncle are meeting with you."

"Ti, Marc, I don't know if you have met one of my sergeants. This is Lincoln Orwell. He worked directly with Sheriff Kastner before me. I couldn't run this place without him." They shook hands.

"Nice to meet you. So you are the famous detectives Jerry always spoke about. Your nephew is quite a good officer."

"I don't know how famous, but yes, Jerry was my brother and this is my son Detective Marcus Jefferson of Kitsap County."

"Oh yeah, you took down the ADA who killed that woman and tried to set up the husband. Good work."

Marcus smiled, "Thanks."

"I guess we should get out of your hair, Grange. I'll talk with you later. Marc, let's go find JJ and Ginny." Granger handed Tiberius the page he printed with the names they had discussed.

In the squad room JJ and Ginny sat at a desk where he worked some files. Sergeant Orwell tapped Marc on the shoulder and handed him a card. The card had a message on it. 'Call me later.'

"Our guest safely ensconced?" JJ nodded at his uncle. "Then let's get back to our respective homes. Ginny are you staying in Seattle tonight or heading back north?"

"I planned to stay here and help you with your problem. I've cleared it with Superintendent Buell."

They walked out to their cars but did not drive away. JJ said, "Sam is with Helene to be sure she stays put and to keep her out of harm's way. Ginny is going to stay there, as well. I'll drop off this car and return to my apartment."

"Sounds good. I'll get your cousin home and uncover who came over to their house this afternoon. We'll be in touch." Tiberius and Marcus returned to the squad car and left for Edmonds and a ferry to Kingston.

"Do you think anyone will come after Helene tonight? I hate leaving Ginny and Sam alone with her."

"Marc, those two ladies can more than hold their own. Lydia asked me to check up on Miss Jose when she and JJ started dating. The girl is a black belt in Tai Kwon Do and a master marksperson with a semi-automatic. Ginny probably has similar skills and she is a sure-handed bet to out think any perp who would go against her."

"Do you think Miss Paulukaitis will press charges for kidnapping?"

"Pepper's lawyer probably will want to, but if JJ is correct and she wants out of the business, then we need to trust Sam and Ginny to keep her safe."

Tiberius cell phone buzzed as he drove on Interstate 5. Pushing the button on his steering wheel, he answered. "May I help you?"

"Ti, this is your commander. Coast Guard just fished a body out of Shilshole Bay with a bullet wound and a broken neck. Prints matched the ones found in the black truck which slammed into you. Seems your attacker lost his bid to be hero of the day. His wound was not fatal and we have the bullet. It is one of our issue. We need to test it against your piece."

"Sure thing. His neck was broken?"

"Seems someone with large hands squeezed too hard. He has ties to your mob in Everett. Someone does not want you investigating your uncle."

I get that. We have people poking around us from several sources."

"Be careful. Let me know when you need anything. This just became official Seattle business."

"Yes, sir." He punched the wheel button disconnecting the call. Marcus hand stroked his face, lost in thought about what he heard.

"Care to elaborate on the shooting?" He said.

"I guess the bad guy pissed off his mentor. One less for us worry about." They arrived at the ferry terminal, paid for passage across the Sound and waited in the parking lot with several dozen other cars.

Looking around the collection of vehicles, Marcus noticed a red truck enter behind them. A truck with familiar design and British Columbia plates. "Dad, we may have a tail."

"What? How does anyone know where we are or where we go?" He clicked the steering wheel button and said, "JJ Jefferson." Waiting for the connection, he adjusted his mirror to view the truck. Finding it two rows over and three cars back, he studied the face. Nothing about it was familiar. Marcus opened his door and exited acting as if he was stretching tired and cramped legs.

Walking away from the patrol car he ignored the red truck as he moved toward the end of his row. Tiberius offered assistance distracting the driver, who stared at the officer approaching him. Tiberius stopped by another vehicle and began a conversation with the startled occupants. The driver seemed to relax while Marcus moved around the end and started toward his father's car out of mirror sight of the truck. Clicking his holster free, he relocated to a car beside the truck, staying out of view.

Tiberius finished his conversation with the unsuspecting occupants of the vehicle in front of the truck. Looking at the driver again, he smiled and nodded his head. The man's eyes widened. Marcus changed his station to the side of the truck and tapped the window. With his gun drawn but hidden from view, he said, "Please roll down your window and make no sudden moves."

Tiberius pulled his Beretta from the holster and smiled again. The window descended. Marcus said, "Please step out of your vehicle." He stepped back as the door opened. His gun pointed at the man who exited

"What's this about? Who are you?"

"My name is unimportant. I'm a detective with the Kitsap County Sheriff's Office and the other officer is with Seattle Police. Show me some identification."

The man reached into his hip pocket and removed his wallet. Marc took it from him and opened to find a British Columbia driver's license with the name, Trevor Wilkins, and a Vancouver address. He handed the wallet to Tiberius.

By this time a state patrolman advanced with weapon drawn. An Edmonds city police officer approached from the ticket booth end.

"What's going on here?" the state patrolman asked. The Edmonds officer drew his weapon and pointed at Marcus.

Tiberius responded, "We are investigating a criminal organization operating in the area and this man may be a person of interest. We have been followed by a red truck with BC plates and this one matches.

"Who are you?"

Showing his badge, he said, "My name is Sergeant Tiberius Jefferson and this is my son Detective Marcus Jefferson of Kitsap Sheriff's Office. I am with Seattle Police. Let me run this name and plate to uncover who our driver is." The state patrolman nodded as he holstered his weapon.

The announcement for the loading of the ferry happened and startled drivers left the scene for transport across Puget Sound. Marcus detached his cuffs and placed them on the quiet driver. Removing him from the parking lot to the curb, he asked the Edmonds officer to keep an eye on the suspect. The surprised officer complied. Such extreme criminal investigations seldom occurred in Edmonds.

Marc returned to the truck to search for anything which might tie it to them. Tiberius drew near and said, "Mr. Wilkins is a fisherman from Vancouver and is employed as a boat captain's mate. Seems he also has a history of B and E and assault. No current warrants for him exist here or in Canada."

Marcus turned around with a small folded envelope in his hand. Opening it, he pulled out a paper with his name and family on it. Tiberius and Gabrielle, JJ, Lydia, Camilla were written, also. Addresses and contact information accompanied each name.

"I think we're missing this boat." Tiberius chuckled as he spoke. They retraced steps to the driver who sat on the edge of the parking area. "Mind explaining why you have information about my family in your possession?" He handed the paper to the state patrol officer who read it and returned it to Tiberius.

"It might be a good idea to answer the man," the patrolman said. He stared at the driver who remained quiet. "I'll call for transport and towing. We'll hold him for you so you can sort this out. You need to catch a boat?" Marcus nodded his head.

"Dad, I have to get home. You stay here and help get this guy a comfortable 6 by 9. I can call one of my buddies to get me to the house." The lot was nearly empty of cars as the state patrolman radioed the dock crew to hold for a foot passenger.

Marcus sprinted to the main street and crossed over to the loading dock. He had another question which needed answering and the person who knew was on the other side of the Sound.

CHAPTER 26

Tiberius waited with the state patrol while they hooked the truck for a tow to the Edmonds compound lot. Wilkins invoked his right to a lawyer and a call to someone for help. Another state patrolman arrived to relocate the driver to a holding cell for interrogation. As the suspect left for less accommodating residence, Tiberius spoke with the state patrolman explaining what had occurred.

"I'll run up to your office and have a few words with him. He doesn't have to answer, but I'll get something out of him before an attorney arrives."

In the confinement cell Wilkins sat on the bench, eyes darting about looking for a way to escape. Tiberius approached and asked, "Do you know me? Do you know my brother Jerry?" The driver locked his gaze on him but remained mute. "I guess you don't care if you rot in a jail cell or out in the public where I can spread word of your complicity with law enforcement. How long do you think you'd last before Pepper has you exterminated?" He sat in a chair provided him and continued. "Your buddy who took a shot at me in Seattle ended up in Puget Sound since he failed to kill me. Somebody snapped his neck like a pretzel. Did you know him?" Tiberius grinned and stood. Without another word he left Wilkins sitting, stewing about his future.

"I'm heading to Seattle and would like to have Mr. Wilkins accompany me." The lieutenant in charge acknowledged the request but declined.

"Since he is from B.C. and appears to be operating against you and your family, I want to keep him here and contact Homeland Security about interrogating him without counsel. We may get out of him what you want. I'll contact you when we're finished. If you want him after we're done, we'll transfer him to you."

"Thanks for your help today. I know it was a surprise, but my son recognized the vehicle. We had to act." The officers shook hands and he left for Seattle.

At the downtown precinct a report about the body recovered from Shilshole sat on his desk. He read and his mouth dropped open. The name of the dead man was Max Wilkins. Coincidence? He thought not. Picking up his desk phone he called the number on the business card from the Edmonds state patrol lieutenant.

"We have a body here identified as Max Wilkins. Ask your guest if he has a brother. You may be able to crack him if he doesn't yet know what Pepper had done to this other Wilkins."

"His attorney arrived about a half hour ago and insisted on his release. We didn't have any real reason to hold him, so we cut him loose."

Under his breath an oath of frustration escaped. "Thanks. You have his address, don't you?"

The lieutenant gave him the information and wished him good hunting. Tiberius hung up and checked the folder again for next of kin. Max was survived by a mother and father. No mention of a brother. He was twenty six years old, too young to be dead. The red truck driver, Wilkins, was two years younger.

He called Edmonds again and asked if the truck was still in custody. "Check for any DNA from the truck so I can compare it to our dead body here."

"Can do. Are you sure they are related?"

"No, but the results will confirm or deny. Thanks for your help." Tiberius disconnected. He decided to call the parents. They were to be notified soon enough.

When the phone connected he asked, "Is this the Wilkins residence?"

"Who wants to know?" The gruffness alerted him to be careful.

"My name is Sergeant Jefferson. I am with the Seattle Police. I am calling regarding one Max Wilkins. We have this number as a contact reference. Are you his father, by any chance?"

"What's this about? Has something happened to Maxwell?" A momentary silence spoke many words. "What'd he do this time?"

"Sir, I need you to come down to our office and help identify a man in our custody as being your son, Max…Maxwell." Tiberius held silent for a response, favorable and not confrontational.

"Alright, where to?"

"I'll send an officer to pick you up, if that's okay with you." The agreement for transportation relieved Tiberius of the building stress. Explaining the death of a family member was traumatic and heart-rending. He had no desire to inform the family over the phone.

Next he called Marcus to update him about the two men. The call went directly to voice mail. Leaving a message to call as soon as possible he clicked off and called JJ. "How are the women? Safe and secure, I trust."

"I don't know, Uncle T. I went to see Mom and ascertain how she's holding up. I'll drop by the safe house later tonight."

"How is Samantha doing with you riding alongside Regina?"

"She's fine with it. We don't have a huge commitment to each other and I do not have any feelings for the Canadian. She is pretty, though."

"Make sure Paulukaitis is tight with us and wants to turn state's evidence. Did Ginny explain her mother's position in Vancouver?"

"Not yet, but she will. Helene is done with Pepper and his gang. Our problem will be ferreting out the people in the department. You've known Collins for a long time. Can he stand up to the pressure?"

Tiberius had some doubts but did not want to relay them to his nephew. "Sure, he's a tough bird. Keep those ladies safe but move them if you must." The call ended with a promise to keep their one witness out of harm.

His cell phone chimed. "Hello, Marc. I called to let you know the person in the red truck may have had a brother who took shots at me and my rookie. Coast Guard found him floating in Puget Sound."

"What happened to him?" Marcus asked.

"Somebody broke his neck and threw him in Shilshole Bay. One of my bullets wounded him but not fatally. I'm running DNA to check against any found in the truck. There has to be a connection."

"Dad, Joan was right. Someone came into my house and left a present for us."

"What is it?" Tiberius frowned because of his son's subterfuge.

"Our visitor told her it was a package of cocaine to be tested, but the note which came with it said Pepper would be looking for it. Also, one of the names on the list we got from Sheriff Collins is the same name as my partner. When I find him I'm going to ask him a few questions." Tiberius laughed. They exchanged a few more words and he clicked off. He had had enough surprises for one day and wanted to get home to Gabby to relax. What more could happen before the night ended?

CHAPTER 27

Jerry sat with Wiley in an obscure hole-in-the-wall diner in Oso. "I need something from you to help me get away from here before anyone from Pepper gets me. Everything is crashing around me. Kopinski and Kastner turned on me and forced me to retire."

"What do you need?" He leaned in and locked his hands together, supporting his body on the table.

"I have to disappear. To be dead to everyone. To lose everything I have so those who live after me are safe from this rabble of people I cannot take down."

"Are you thinking…? You cannot do it." He reached out to Jerry. "I won't let you."

"What are you talking about? All I want to do is escape from here and leave the investigation to someone else. You have connections. Find me a safe house."

"Okay. I can do that for you. I need to get out also. I'll disappear with you, but not to the same location since Pepper will send operatives after us. You still have his money?"

"Yeah, but I'm sure he wants it back with interest. He'll come after my family if he thinks he can leverage me. I need a way to assure him it is not recoverable."

"I'll work on it for you. Lydia going with you?"

"We haven't discussed it yet."

"What about your brother? Can he help you?" Jerry shifted in his seat, grimaced and grunted.

"He's busy with his own problems. I can't involve him in this, but his son Marcus is a top notch detective who should be able to finish this job." He tilted his head as his eyes roved upward to the ceiling of the room. "I have an idea."

He explained his plan to Wiley who listened and nodded. "You get Lydia to agree, but you'll need to get a couple of others on board; Jerry, we can make this work."

They parted company and began a subterfuge to confound Pepper and the sheriff's department. Whether they were to be successful depended on the silence of all involved.

At home Jerry discussed his requests with Lydia. He had not described in detail to Wiley what he intended to do but knew his undercover partner would decipher the action. .

"Can you do this for us?" His question held deep responsibilities to keep faithful to a clearly bitter future.

"Why must you do this? It seems so dangerous and fraught with failure. I would be lost without you. How do you expect me to do this and not involve our children?"

Jerry hugged her a lengthy moment and with deep love. His request had a disquieting absurdity to it. "I cannot think of any other way to make Pepper go away than to be lost to him. If I do this, he will stop searching, otherwise he will hound me or you or the kids until he gets what he wants."

Lydia wept. The plan included notes to Marcus and two years of waiting. Waiting without any comfort. Withdrawing from happiness and satisfaction with living. Having nothing to explain to children, brothers, nephews and nieces. Nothing but living a lie. Lydia promised and knew the challenge could break her.

Failure to play out the plot could mean death for her, as well as the children. He hated failure and bad guys escaping justice. He despised the idea of living a lie and losing the respect of those he loved most.

Lydia said, "Can't we leave the area, move down to Seattle and be near your brother and his wife. Gabby is so nice. We can be away from these people and safe."

"Pepper will not leave us alone, even in Seattle. I'm going to finish this even if it takes the rest of my life."

She closed her eyes and sighed. "Alright then, how soon shall we put this into motion?"

"We'll run the suitcase up to Vancouver over the weekend, come home, and set up the plan. If you can stay the course, Pepper is going to receive the justice he deserves."

Jerry stood, as did Lydia. Her tears fell, silent but upsetting. "When? When will it start?"

CHAPTER 28

As the ferry landed in Kingston, Marc pulled out his cell and punched Tom's number. Waiting for his partner to answer, he paced the passenger seating area on the docking end of the boat. Other passengers lined up near the safety net placed by ferry personnel before the gang plank lowered.

The phone went to voice. "Tom, I need a pick-up in Kingston. Something has happened and I need to speak with you. I'll wait at Drifter's." Closing the cell, Marc stood away from the crowd and watched the process for debarking. As the crowd moved off the ferry he clicked the cell open and punched in Joan's number.

"Where are you?" Her first comment, not hello or I miss you. Her voice hinted at anger but held steady.

"I'm on the Kingston ferry. We're docked and I'm about to get off. I wanted you to know I'll be home as soon as Tom comes and gets me." They finished and disconnected. He shook his head knowing his night would be challenged.

At Drifter's he ordered a coffee and a sandwich to sate sudden hunger pangs. Returning a call to Tiberius enlightened his knowledge of the man in the truck. He was surprised to find a brother but not surprised to hear about the death. "Dad, these two have connections with Pepper which means they have been fed Information about our movements. Any idea who the link is?"

"Not yet, but I'll check on Mr. Wilkins whereabouts and get some details." The call ended with Marcus sure his partner could shed light on the retired Knudson. He sat alone and quiet, reflecting on the challenges which lay ahead.

Any threat to family had to be dealt a swift defense. No one else was to die. Losing his uncle had been difficult enough. To have another member of the family harmed would be intolerable.

An hour passed and Marcus decided to call for a deputy to come and rescue him. His cell chimed with Tom's picture. "Hello, can you pick me up?"

"I'm on my way and looking forward to hearing of your progress. I should be there in ten minutes. Sorry for the delay. I was dealing with a domestic case which sent a man to jail and his girlfriend to a shelter."

"Good, I'll see you when you get here." He clicked off and checked the time. Evening began five minutes prior to the call. He hoped another call to Joan might assuage the evening confrontation he dreaded was coming.

"I got hold of Tom. He's picking me up in ten minutes. I'll stop at the office and pick up my car and be home by seven."

"Is everything okay?" Her earlier angry voice dismissed, he tried to keep an upbeat spirit. "Did you get what you needed today to finish this?"

He stayed calm. "Yes, and we are close to wrapping this up. I know this is not what you wanted from me, but if we can clear Jerry's name, so much the better."

"I love you. With you gone so much of the time, I question your commitment to our marriage. I know I shouldn't, but I do." He listened understanding his commitment to work often surpassed commitment to family. He had to be more attentive.

"Tom's here. We'll continue this when I get home."

"I'll see you whenever you get here." They ended the call. Tom came over and sat down.

"What's the skinny on your trek to Everett?"

"We had another meeting with our red truck person. Turns out his name is Trevor Wilkins and he has a BC license and the truck is registered in BC. He had a brother, Max, who took the shots at Tiberius and his rookie."

"Had?"

"Yeah, he was fished out of Shilshole Bay this morning with a bullet wound and a broken neck. Dad's following up on it to find a connection with Pepper." Tom nodded an acceptance of the information.

"You ready to get out of here?"

Marcus stood when Tom did. "Let's go. I have another question for you when we get to your car." He paid his tab and they left.

In the unmarked vehicle, Tom asked, "What's your question?" He had not yet turned on the ignition. Marc decided it best to ask before they started the drive.

"We received a list of retirees and others who left Snohomish County in the last couple of years. One of the names was a Timothy Knudson. Is he related to you in any way?" Marcus locked onto Tom's eyes.

Turning to look out the window, he answered, "He's my older brother. Why? Is it important to your investigation?" He turned back to look at Marc.

"I don't know, yet. What did he do for Snohomish?"

"We didn't speak much. He was working undercover and I lost touch with him until a month ago."

Jerry shifted to face Tom. "What kind of undercover? Did he tell you anything about his work?"

Tom looked away again. "He asked me not to say anything to you, but you need to know." He regarded Marc. "After you began your investigation of Jerry, he contacted me about his job. He's Wiley Fingers, Jerry's silent partner."

"Has he been contacting me without letting me know who he is? Somebody was at my house today and scared Joan half to death."

"I don't know, but he's ready to meet with you and fill you in about what they did. You have to keep it quiet, though. Pepper doesn't know who he is and whoever in the county is on Pepper's payroll doesn't know, either. He retired and disappeared for very good reasons."

Tom started the car and began the drive to deeper involvement with Marcus's investigation. Marc asked, "If he came to my house, today, leaving a package of cocaine and saying Pepper will be looking for it, where did he get the drugs? Unless he's still working with Pepper?"

"You'll have to ask him. As far as I know, he's retired from the force and living a quiet life in Seabeck."

The ride continued without any conversation. Marcus thought about the people surrounding his uncle and again contemplated the chances of a murder versus a suicide. He concluded a suicide was not what happened. Who committed the murder was the real question. Who wanted his uncle out of the way? Cop or criminal? Friend? Foe? Family member? He feared the idea of a relative incurring such a task.

At the department headquarters they stood a moment before Tom spoke. "Tim asked me to give you this. It's his burner to contact him. He has more information for you about your uncle and the investigation. He's awaiting a call from you." Tom handed Marcus a cheap cell phone with no traceability.

"Does he want me to call now?" Tom nodded and Marc clicked open the phone. A preset number displayed on the screen. He pushed the send button and listened as the tone indicated connection was imminent.

"Hello, Marcus. I'll not mention my name but I think you have been informed about who I am."

"Yes, and I have it on good authority you want to meet. When and where?"

"You'll receive a text tonight with instructions." The call ended.

"Rather cryptic. How come you never told me about having a brother?"

"We're not very close. He's eleven years older than me and a private type. He went to work with the Snohomish County Sheriff's office at the age of twenty-four and spent twenty years with them."

"You knew he retired shortly after Jerry and said nothing to me."

"I didn't know about his retirement until last month. As I said, we didn't have much contact with each other." Marcus thanked his partner for the ride and left for his own home and uncertain closeness. What thread next would unravel from the tapestry woven by Uncle Jerry?

CHAPTER 29

Tiberius knocked on his commander's door. "Come in." The bellow surprised him.

"Captain, I'm going to need your help with my investigation."

"I wondered how long it would be before you came to me. What do you want?"

"I have a lead on a person related to the scoundrel who took shots at me last week. One Trevor Wilkins. I need to have him picked up with no undue fanfare and brought here. His brother Max went swimming in Shilshole Bay with a bullet and a broken neck."

"Sounds to me like you want him kidnapped. Didn't his lawyer get him out of State's custody?"

"You do have connections all over, don't you?" Tiberius leaned in to his commander, placing his hands on the desk. "We need information from him about Pepper and he's not likely to offer it without incentives."

"Get off my desk." Tiberius straightened and repeated.

"Incentives which will keep him alive, unlike his brother. Failure to please Mr. Pepper has a way of shortening one's availability. If we can get him away from Everett, then maybe he can be shown the error of his ways." Ti folded his arms, awaiting an answer.

The captain rose from his seat. "What makes you think he'll stay here in Washington? Isn't he from Vancouver?"

"Yes, but he cannot return without being picked up at the border. And if he tries by water, the RCMP has been alerted to that possibility." He uncrossed his arms and let them hang. "I have contacted Superintendent Buell in Vancouver and Deputy Chief Landrensen at the border. Wilkins has nowhere he can go without someone capturing him. I want it to be us, but someone he doesn't know has to be the one to pick him up."

"When his brother was found, a search for next of kin revealed parents here in Seattle."

"Yes, I spoke with the father. He came in and identified his son. I asked about Trevor and he said he was the younger of his two boys. I asked about his Vancouver address. He related a story of Trevor leaving to get away from a girl who wanted to marry him. He didn't see eye to eye with her."

"Did he get to stay without a visa?"

"He's visiting, but has a red truck registered in BC. His name is on a watch list, but he makes regular trips south and has not been flagged as a mule for any of the outfits working here or up in Canada."

"Something is not right with that. Can you trust this Landrensen person?"

"I've only talked with him once, but he cooperated with Marcus and me when we came back from Canada. He gave us a copy of the watch list and Wilkins is on it."

"Do you know where Wilkins is?" The captain sat on the edge of the desk.

"Last we knew, he was visiting a girl in Everett; his marriage proposal girl."

"I don't know how you know that, but give me the address and I'll send Murphy and Sandoval. What about the girl?"

"I know nothing about her."

"Get out and catch me some bad guys before you and your son get killed." Ti nodded and curled his mouth downward. He turned and walked to the door.

Looking back, he said, "Thank you. We're close to wrapping this up." He left and strolled to his car for a trip home. Doubt about wrapping it up remained.

"Gabs, are you home?" He wandered the halls of his house and found his wife in their bedroom. "How was your day?" Upon entering the room he realized something was wrong.

He sat on the bed next to her. "Antonio's in the hospital."

"What happened?" He held her hands as tears dropped in his lap.

"He had an accident after work. He was going to his car and another car hit him. He's in surgery to stop internal bleeding."

"We need to get to him. I'm surprised you didn't leave already? What hospital?"

"Providence in Everett. I just found out before you came home."

He rose pulling Gabrielle with him. "Call Marcus and let him know. This was not an accident."

"What? What? Not an accident? What are you saying? Somebody deliberately hit our son? You get shot at and now Antonio is injured. What have you and Marcus gotten mixed up in?" Her tears flooded again.

Putting an arm around her shoulder he pulled her close allowing her need to cry. Better to remain silent for the moment.

After a few seconds he said, "Let's go." On the drive north Gabby called their eldest son.

"Marc, Antonio's in the hospital in Everett. He was hit by a car in a parking lot at work. Your father thinks it has something to do with your investigation of Jerry. We're heading there now."

"I'm on my way home. I'll get there when I can. Tell Dad I have some news about Wiley Fingers." The called ended with a promise to come to Everett.

At the hospital they inquired as to where to find their son and were directed to a Sheriff's deputy who explained the details as she knew them.

"A witness saw a black Lincoln race into the parking lot and head for your son, who didn't see what hit him."

Tiberius asked, "Does this witness think the car targeted Antonio?" Before she answered another deputy appeared.

"Hello, Ti, Gabs." Sergeant Lincoln Orwell shook hands with them and continued. "It may have been a warning to you and Marc. The witness says the car slowed when it got near him."

"Pepper. Damn it. I'll kill the son-of-a-bitch if we can't nail him. First they hook my niece on Oxy and force her into pro work and now my own son." Lincoln pulled Tiberius arm and directed him away from the other people.

"I think I know who's behind this, but I don't have enough evidence."

"Who? Who are you talking about? I need to know so I can beat the crap out of him."

"Calm down, Ti. We've known each other a long time and this has to be by the book. If you go after this person without the proper evidence, she'll skate. I think my lieutenant's secretary may be working for Pepper. She has a boyfriend who's an enforcer but lives in Canada."

"Wilkins. Trevor Wilkins. My captain is sending a couple of plain clothes to pick him up and bring him to Seattle." His eyes flitted from one side of the room to the other. "Are you sure about the girl? I understand she wanted marriage and he ran."

"True enough, but if you're already onto him, then I need to tell you one more interesting bit. My lieutenant, Allenby, may also be involved with Pepper. I go along with being interested but keep out of any direct contact."

"Allenby? Isn't he the undersheriff?"

"Yes, it's why you need enough intelligence to put him away. I haven't told Granger yet because he will definitely pounce too soon and ruin any chance of breaking this bunch up."

"Thanks, Linc, I'll let Marcus know since he has Jerry's secret stash of evidence. There may be a connection already which he hasn't seen or uncovered."

Returning to Gabriella, they sat in the waiting area for news of the surgical procedure. The day had begun with promise and ended with disaster. He and Marcus needed to fix this before another week passed and more people got hurt.

CHAPTER 30

"Are you out of your mind?" Medical Examiner Thomas Eric Beaumont paced the room hand on head, eyes rolling in their sockets. "This is suicide."

"Precisely. Now can you help me to pull it off?" Jerry sat calm as a duck on a springtime pond. He had proposed to his friend and confederate in solving crimes of a grisly nature an act of selfishness which Thomas found incredulous.

M.E. Beaumont had the ability to crack through the egregious misfortunes of myriad Snohomish County mysteries and enlighten the people who mattered with the causes of said deaths. His pacing increased. "What brain affliction possesses you to this mad and insane endeavor? I cannot, in true medical fashion condone what you have in mind."

"I know it sounds preposterous but…"

"Preposterous? You're talking about ending your life and you act like it's no big deal." The pacing began to unnerve Jerry.

"Will you stop reacting so negatively, please? I really need to do this." Thomas halted his progress around the room. "If I don't die, Lydia is in trouble with Pepper and I'll have to work for him, breaking all the laws I swore to uphold. Now, will you help me?" Jerry placed his hands on his friend's shoulders pleading for acceptance with his eyes.

"Explain to me again what it is you propose to do. I'm not sure it's feasible." Jerry related his idea for a suicide which had dangers incorporated into its construct. It was to be a suicide like none which Beaumont had encountered in his years of medical work.

The idea, as incredulous as it seemed, intrigued the doctor. Thinking of the materials needed to complete the deed, he wrote in a notepad as his mind unearthed surprising concepts for eliminating Jerry and his problems. "Let me research what needs to be done."

Jerry looked over the doctor's shoulder. "Those are some big words. What do they do?"

"Don't think about them for now. I have to contact a mortician friend to arrange for the transportation and burial of your body."

"Let me know when you have what you need, and I'll set everything up to make it happen as planned."

Thomas Beaumont rocked his head as he thought about his tasks and the dangers they entailed. His career was on the line if he was caught aiding his friend in the end days of a person's life. "I understand what it is you seek to accomplish. I wish another way was possible, but this truly may be the best idea, so let's make it work for you." They shook hands and the medical examiner departed to procure ingredients for an improbable suicide which confounded his mind.

Jerry returned to the family room where Lydia sat at the desk writing. "Tom's on board. What are you doing?"

"We need to be sure you're dead when they come to investigate."

"Lydia, I love you more than anyone can love someone. I hope you endure what I am planning. I wouldn't ask this of you except for the need to dismantle these vile and morally empty people and their organization."

She rose from the chair. "I love you, too." She embraced him, eyes closed as tears formed. "I fear losing everything."

He cupped her face in his hands and kissed her lips, gentle as a breeze caresses a tree. "I don't want you to be afraid. My friends are capable of protecting you."

She smiled. "You are the bravest man I know. Please be careful until this is finished." She returned to the desk and continued writing her list. Jerry left for his office and phone calls.

"Granger, I need to see you as soon as possible. Can we meet away from the department?" Jerry paced his office awaiting response.

"Sure, I know a place. What's on your mind?" Granger had been a friend and companion in the department for many years. Now he needed to be a confidante and companion in Jerry's charade. What could go wrong? They arranged a place.

"I'll meet you there in twenty. And don't worry, I won't shoot you or anything. I need a favor and it means being discreet, which I know you can be."

"Alright, I'll see you in twenty minutes." They clicked off and Jerry wrote a list of his needs for the coming event.

"Lydia, I'm heading out to see Granger. I'll be back in a while." She looked up with eyes filling with large drops. She turned her head as the overflow commenced.

Stroking her hair, he said, "I have to make this work. Granger will be sure to keep control. He'll get Zach to help. I trust them with my life." Ironic, he thought.

"I believe you. Go. Get them to understand what you want and need. Go." He stroked her once more and left for his rendezvous.

As he drove another idea entered his mind. If he went straight to his tormentor and eliminated any threat, he could move without any further difficulty. But what of his future with a murder or more on his hands? What would Granger think? How would Sheriff Kastner react? No, he thought, better to deceive and win a war than own a battle and lose any prospect of satisfaction and safety.

When he entered the café in Mountlake Terrace, he spotted Granger at a table by the kitchen. His friend dipped his head and smiled. Jerry sat opposite.

"Thanks for meeting with me on short notice."

"Jerry, you and I have been friends a long time. When you need me, I come. I would expect no less from you or Tiberius. What's up?"

"I've decided I need to be out of the picture. Gone from the clutches of Pepper and his scum. So I'm putting together a party of sorts which will get him away from my family and leave him thinking he has won."

"You're being rather cryptic. Please, explain what you mean." Jerry related his plans to which Granger dropped his jaw, gaping in disbelief. "You want me to assist you to die."

"I don't need a small army of deputies and detectives trampling my death scene. I need you and Deputy Bentley Zacharias to keep control of the area and let Beaumont do his job without any interference. He should be able to get me to autopsy as quickly and quietly as possible. Please do this for me. Tiberius is to know nothing about what transpires here or then. Please." He handed the list to Granger, who opened the folded paper and read.

"I don't understand why you think dying is going to solve your problems. I get what it is you want, but isn't there another way which is less dramatic?"

"I want it to be dramatic. I want Pepper and whoever in the department is feeding him information to know they have nothing more to squeeze out of me. It is over. Done. Finished. I am serious about this, so can I rely on you and your discretion? I have to speak with Zach about it, but with you supporting me, I do not think he will waver from assisting."

"How is Lydia taking this idea of your dying?"

"She understands the outcome is more important than my life."

Granger sat a few moments after Jerry left, disparaging the idea and yet, wondering if the outcome was truly more important than his friend's life.

CHAPTER 31

Marcus paced the floor of the hospital. Surgery always took longer than anyone wanted. Tiberius held Gabrielle, consoling her, assuring her, keeping her calm. A door opened and a nurse emerged from the restricted OR area of Providence Hospital.

"Any word about my brother," Marc asked. "He's the guy who got hit by the car. Is he alright?"

"I'm sorry, sir, I don't know anything regarding the accident victim. I'm sure the doctor will be out in a moment. They are finishing right now." She turned and walked down a long corridor, through another door.

Joan had come with Marcus, explaining to the children what had happened. They promised to stay at home, locked securely inside. "Marc, nurses aren't allowed to tell you anything. Let the doctor come out. It'll be okay. I didn't see any remorse in her eyes as she spoke with you."

He nodded agreement, gazing at the swinging double door one hand on his hip, the other hand covering his mouth. He returned to pacing.

"Dad, this has to stop. They're threatening us and we have done nothing against them. All we have accomplished is to make them mad and they're hurting people who have nothing to do with them."

Lydia arrived as they spoke. "Is he going to be alright?" Gabrielle rose and hugged her sister-in-law. "How are you holding up?"

"It's not fair. These people are animals and don't deserve to live in the same world as my family. I want them dead." Gabrielle stared at Lydia. "How can you be so calm after what they did to Jerry?"

"It'll be alright. Tony will be fine and Tiberius and Marcus will finish this before any more pain can happen."

The swinging doors crashed open as a middle-aged man in scrubs strolled through and straight toward the family. "I'm Doctor Chikere Ndiaye. Who are the parents?"

Tiberius responded, "I'm his father, Tiberius Jefferson. This is his mother, Gabrielle Jefferson and his brother Marcus. How is he?"

"We had to find a bleeding vein in his abdomen which complicated his possible survival. That said, we were successful in closing the tear and stabilizing him so we could work on his other injuries. It is why this took longer than expected. He is in recovery and should be fine. Other than the torn vein in his intestines, he sustained only leg and hip fractures. Part of the hip was what punctured the blood vessel."

"Can we see him?"

Before an answer was given, JJ crashed through the hall door, breathing heavily from ascending stairs, impatient for an elevator. "Where's my cousin?"

Lydia stopped him. "He's in recovery and Doctor…" She turned to him. "Your name, again?"

"Doctor Chikere Ndiaye."

"Yes, Doctor Ndiaye says Antonio will be fine."

JJ settled into a chair. "They're going to pay for this. I'll make it my duty to make them pay."

Marcus approached and sat in a chair next to him. "Relax, cousin, we have some leads which are going to help us. Speaking of which, how is our guest?"

"She's okay. Ginny and Sam are taking good care of her. She said something about a friend of hers in the sheriff's office who is on the Pepper payroll."

"Could that be Lieutenant Allenby's secretary?" Marcus smiled as his father spoke. "And does she have a boyfriend named Wilkins?"

"How do you know all of this? I just found out myself from Paulukaitis. Now I see why you are the best detectives in the state of Washington."

"Yes, we have been busy working while you have enjoyed the company of three lovely ladies, two of whom will kick your butt if you mess with the third one." Marcus smirked as he chastened his cousin.

"What?"

The surgeon interrupted. "I have another patient to see. I'll arrange for parents and brother to see him as soon as he wakes and is coherent enough." He followed the nurse who earlier disappeared through the other set of doors.

Tiberius gathered the two policemen and moved to a secluded area past the nurses' station. "We need to get back on track with approaching Pepper and putting him on guard. We need him to react. We have uncovered the evidence needed to nail him."

Marcus explained to JJ, "We know about Misty Rivers and Trevor Wilkins. One of our contacts in your department is playing Pepper and Lieutenant Allenby. He isn't ready to play his ace card with Collins, though."

"Allenby? He's on the take? I guess I am out of the loop. Can we get Rivers to turn against them?"

Tiberius cut in. "Seattle PD is picking up Wilkins for a little ride south so we can work him without his attorney. If he gets off on a tech, it doesn't matter. He's small potatoes compared with the rest. He's getting across the border without any hassles, so we need to contact Landrensen to find out how."

Marcus continued, "Ginny said the crowd in Vancouver is thinning as they pick off the members of that gang. We should find the connection to Snohomish and cut it. Wilkins may be able to enlighten us as a favor to his future lifestyle."

JJ frowned, "Is anyone else in danger? Marc, is your family safe?"

Marc nodded. "My partner, Tom Knudson, is watching the house for me and we uncovered Wiley Fingers. HIs name is Tim Knudson. He's Tom's older brother."

JJ's frown relaxed. "So Dad's undercover partner is alive and well? Do you know where he is?"

"We've been in contact but I am not at liberty to say anything, yet. He's sending me a text tonight as to a location for a meeting." Marc placed a hand on his cousin's shoulder. "I am now sure your father did not kill himself. Someone wanted him out of the way and made it happen. We just have to find out who."

"Thanks. You never did believe it was suicide and now I think the same. Let's nail these bastards."

A nurse arrived and spoke with Gabrielle. The three returned to the family. "Tony's awake and wants to see all of us." They followed the nurse to the recovery ward and enjoyed a reunion, joyful and calming because of the good news.

As they visited, Marc's burner phone buzzed. He checked it and found a message from Tim Knudson. He wrote a simple 'OK' and sent it.

Tiberius pulled Marcus aside. "Was that from Wiley?"

"Yes, we're to meet at the Camp Union Cookhouse. I think I should meet alone and assess what he has for us."

"Alright, but keep me apprised. He may be the best connection to make our case."

Marc nodded. "Joan and I have to get home. We left the kids alone with Tom. He'll definitely stay single after being with them this long." He said goodbye to his brother and hugged his mother. He and Joan left for Wendlesburg and some rest. Tomorrow's meeting with Wiley had more questions than any person should have. Jerry confided in this person and shared the most information with him. What did he ascertain playing the role assigned to him? And did he understand who was taking pictures of them?

—⁂—

"How were they, Tom?" Joan was hanging a coat in the closet, listening for his answer.

"They were fine, but I don't think I'm cut out to be a parent." Marc grunted. "There was one thing though." Marc grimaced. "You had a phone call but no one spoke when Marc Junior answered. He heard someone on the other end but no words. I had a friend at the phone company trace the number, but it led to a prepaid." Another threat against his family?

"I'm meeting with your brother tomorrow. Maybe he can shed some light on who in Pepper's organization is asked to intimidate people."

"Maybe. I'll see you." He departed from the Jefferson house. Joan came up to Marc.

"I don't like what's happening. I don't need you killed or your brother or any other member of this family." Her arms splayed out as her fists rested on her hips. "Well? How soon can you get this finished?"

"I don't know, but we have some leads which we can use to push them to make mistakes." Her fear was real and he had no answer for which she would be satisfied. It was late and he was tired. He checked the security of the house and followed Joan to their bedroom. Was closing curtains and locking doors enough of a barricade against intruders? He placed his service weapon under a book on his nightstand.

"Thanks for keeping your gun out, just in case." Joan squeezed him reassuring herself that safety of the family was his first priority. His feelings for them had to be greater than his frame of mind regarding police work.

His sleep was shallow and fitful. Noises not normally associated with danger alerted him to false threats. He watched Joan who snored light grunts as she dreamed. He imagined her nightmare scenarios and then slept a moment more to create his own curiosities.

In the early hours of morning his phone chimed on the side table. He knocked the book covering his Beretta onto the floor as he reached for it. "Damn." He answered "Hello, you know what time it is?"

"Sorry to wake you, Marc. It's JJ. I thought you should know. Someone attacked Cammie last night in Bellingham. She's alright, just scared. The man said she needed to tell you to back off and forget what happened to her father or next time he might…He threatened to disfigure her, Marc."

"Where is she?"

"She's at her apartment but doesn't feel safe. I told her to pack some clothes and get down here as fast as possible."

"Hang on. I'll contact Goodman at the State Patrol and get someone to bring her."

"Thanks, Marc. Let me know when she's on the way." They clicked off and Marc got out of bed. Joan stirred as he rose.

"What time is it?" she asked.

"Early. Go back to sleep. I have to make a phone call." He put on a robe and left for his office. After finding Bennie Goodman's business card he dialed hoping to get him. Joan strolled in as he answered. He looked at her and smiled.

"Bennie, sorry to awaken you, if I have. I need a favor." He explained the situation as Joan listened to his side of the conversation. She sat in a chair by the desk. "Thanks, Bennie. I owe you one."

He turned to enlighten his wife about their cousin. "She's okay but JJ thinks she should come home where she can be protected. I agreed and asked for the State Patrol to pick her up and drive her here. Bennie said he would call the office in Bellingham and arrange it."

"They're picking on the weakest of us, aren't they? They know a frontal assault will fail, so they're sending you a message that no one is safe. Thanks a lot, Marc. I asked you if this was dangerous and you assured me you could handle it quickly and without problems." She stood to leave but turned to face him. "I'm packing some things for me and the children and going to my mother's place. When you decide we are more important than your uncle, let me know and I'll figure out if I want to come back."

"You don't have to leave. Besides, you're safer with me than at your parents' house. They can get to you there, as well."

"You really don't get it, do you? I'm tired of being less important than your job. We must come first. I can understand in a situation which is assigned by Fellington or which comes under the jurisdiction of the sheriff's office, but this needed no interference from you. Your uncle killed himself and you won't let it be." She walked out before he responded although no retort could soften her remorse about how circumstances had deteriorated.

He needed a miracle breakthrough where none existed. He trailed her hoping to change her mind.

CHAPTER 32

During the evening Murphy and Sandoval returned with Wilkins and placed him in holding. As a bonus for Tiberius, young Misty Rivers joined the trip confused about why. No calls were allowed for either, regardless of their protests.

In the morning Tiberius arrived to interview each in separate rooms without contact between them. His commander approached him and said, "We're breaking several laws holding these two."

"I know, sir, but they have information which will aid us in the investigation. We are not charging them with any crime so they are free to leave. However, I want them to appreciate what will happen to them if Pepper gets word of their cooperation with us."

"Do you expect them to cooperate?"

"Hell, no, but with Antonio in the hospital they better point me in the right direction as to who ran him over yesterday. Or the word will get out there and they need to be ready for the consequences."

"You may be leaving us open to a lawsuit." Tiberius shook his head.

"I don't think so. They'll be happy to help us rather than find an early end to living. Wilkins lost a brother to this group, so he should be more than willing to help."

"I hope so for your sake."

"What's that supposed to mean?"

"I warned you. We cannot have your back on this. I picked up Wilkins as a favor, but if he is not cooperating, cut him loose. And his girlfriend."

"Yes sir." Tiberius left to uncover answers for which he did not have questions. He comprehended the need to play hardball with the two lovebirds. Any invocation for the right to a lawyer would be ignored this day, but his commander was correct. It could lead to a law suit and could end his career. An early retirement. How ironic.

He decided the girl was first. If she was a Pepper employee, she had to answer for her part in giving information to the cartel. A soft touch with her, he thought. No bad cop for now. Opening the door to the room she now inhabited, he found a hardened person, steely eyes, stiff set lips, and a glare of hatred.

"Good morning, Miss Rivers. May I call you Misty?" Help her to relax, put her at ease, and then pounce.

"Why am I here? I have to get to work. Who are you? And no, you may not call me Misty."

"Alright, Miss Rivers, I have a few questions regarding your association with Mr. Wilkins. I understand you and he were engaged to be married and he skipped out on you to Canada." Her glare remained steady. "I'm sure your question of why you're here is legitimate to you. It's not to me. Last night a young man in Marysville was run down by a black automobile."

"I wasn't anywhere near there. I haven't been to Marysville in ages." She averted her eyes to the floor. Tiberius' mouth curled a slight bit.

"No, I'm sure you were not. Nonetheless, the man ended up in Providence and I am sure the parents are asking questions as to why he was the target for the driver of the car." She squirmed, but refused to make eye contact. "Tell me, Miss Rivers, does your boyfriend know about your cooperation with the police of late?"

"He's not talking with anyone."

Tiberius moved closer. "Can you be sure he's not rolling over on you and everyone else associated with Andrew Pepper?" Her pupils widened, her breathing shallow and quick, before she collapsed on the table.

Since nothing came from the meeting for the moment, Tiberius left to confront his other opponent.

"Mr. Wilkins, I just came from Miss Rivers. She has quite a story to tell. You want to add your portion or shall we just go with her version."

"You're full of shit. She has nothing to tell. Why am I here?" The line of his jaw and the set of his eyes depicted defiance. Tiberius changed tactics.

"I may be full of shit, as you said, but you on the other hand will be meeting your brother as soon as you are released and the word of your cooperation gets out."

"You don't scare me. Max screwed up. He was supposed to kill you."

"Are you admitting culpability to what happened? Did you have anything to do with constricting his neck? You look a little bigger than he did."

"What a funny little man you are. Max was not the brightest star in the sky."

"And you are?" Tiberius sat back in his chair.

"I'm not here to admit anything. I had nothing to do with what happened to Max. I heard he had an accident which broke his neck and he drowned in Puget Sound."

"Your parents must love you very much. Do they know what you do? Are you supplying them with money, drugs, or maybe girls?"

Trevor tensed. A vein bulged in his neck and Tiberius knew he had found the trigger.

"Miss Rivers wanted to marry you and you ran. What was it which scared you so much? Maybe you found out about her and Max? Maybe your father had her as well. And yet when you were escorted here, you and she were found together. I'm confused. Are you a chicken or just stupid?"

Wilkins sat listening to the conversation and turning redder, the neck vein bulging more.

"Max and she never did anything and leave my father out of this. Misty and I are in love and plan to get married as soon as this is over."

"You will love wearing orange which is the new black. She'll look great in a prison jumpsuit. So do you want to be free when this happens, or will you wait to complete your prison terms?" Tiberius stood straight and crossed his arms. "Well?"

Wilkins calmed his demeanor, looked up and asked, "What do you want from us?"

Tiberius sat in a chair and opened the folder on the table. "Tell me about Pepper and his operation, and explain Misty Rivers' role in the cartel."

Trevor twisted and leaned forward. "I know nothing, because if I say anything Misty will be assaulted while I get to watch. Then I'm a dead man and she'll be chopped to pieces."

Tiberius smiled. "And you don't think they will do this if I let you go? Word will be planted on the street about how you snitched. Misty will lose her job with the Sheriff and be arrested for her part in the operations. So tell me about Pepper."

"You've got to get me and Misty to a safe place." He pressed a defiant face into Tiberius's space. "I ain't saying nothing until I get assurances."

"Let me talk with the DA. I'll see what can be done. No guarantees, though. You give me squat and you get turned out to the street." He stood to leave, to return to his other antagonist. He needed answers about the assault on his son and the threat against Camilla. If she knew anything, she had to talk.

As he entered the room, her face screwed up in way to turn her pretty face ugly. "What now? I'm still not talking without a lawyer." She folded arms across her chest.

"Fine with me. I'll send you back to the Snohomish County office and explain how you gave us your boss as compensation."

"Allenby doesn't know anything."

"Not as I understand it. He's the mole in the department and when he finds out you betrayed him to us, what do think he'll do?"

"I have nothing to say. He'd kill me if he thought I was not on his side."

"Trevor has been helpful, so I guess you're right, we don't need you. Have fun at the office, while you can." He turned to leave, then faced her again. "Helene says hi." At the door he hesitated a moment to let the comment work its magic. Opening the door he stepped out holding the knob.

"Wait," she said. "How do you know Helene?"

"Oh, I forgot to tell you. She's in our custody and looking to give evidence against Pepper. Since she says you and she are friends, I thought you should know."

"What's she going to say?"

"Have a nice day." He closed the door before she responded. Letting her stew for a few more minutes seemed reasonable.

CHAPTER 33

Marc answered his cell phone to the desperate voice of his cousin. "They got her." His sound included tears as his voice cracked. "Pepper got her before the State Patrol."

"Slow down, JJ. Tell me what you know." Marc remained in his empty house devoid of family. He sat on his bed where Joan had been just an hour before.

"Goodman made a call to the Bellingham office as promised and they sent a trooper to her address. She was gone. At first the trooper thought she might have left, but the door was open so he entered and found the place destroyed as if a fight had occurred. He found blood."

"Did he call in CSI?"

"Yes, they're working the scene right now. One other thing. He found a note addressed to you."

A pause prompted Marc to ask, "What did the note say?" JJ whimpered again. "JJ, what did the note say?"

"You have to go to Pepper and pay off Dad's loan. You also have to end your investigation or we'll never see her again."

"Where are you?"

"I'm at the safe house." Marc thought about an article he read about tracking cell phone communications and realized their danger.

"Get out of the house now and take the ladies with you. Leave your cell phones. They may be tracking the calls since Allenby's involved."

"Alright, where can we meet?" The panic in the young officer was odd, but this included people about whom he cared. Marc decided to meet with his father.

"Go to Seattle PD and meet with Dad. He needs to know and I'll get over there PDQ." They clicked off and Marc gathered all of the evidence from the board, not trusting anyone to leave it alone. His meeting with Wiley Fingers in Camp Union had priority so he called his father to apprise him of the situation.

"Dad, JJ may be in trouble and need help. Since he's out of communications for now, let me know when he arrives. If he doesn't we need to find them."

"I'll call Granger and get some help for them. It's too soon to pick off Allenby, but I have his secretary and he'll suspect something's wrong since she won't be showing up for work."

"I'll get to your place as soon as possible." Marc left his house for the drive through Seabeck to the Camp Union meeting. Nothing mattered more than getting his cousin freed from the clutches of Pepper's crew. His rendezvous with Wiley had to help.

As he drove a radio dispatch contacted him about a shooting near his destination. He asked for any nearby deputy to respond, but no one was closer than twenty minutes. He was only three minutes from the site. Wiley would have to wait. The burner given to him sat on the seat. He picked it up and punched the preset number.

No answer came and he left a message explaining the delay. As he approached a woman ran toward him screaming something about a crazy man shooting at trees and cars. "Where is he, ma'am?" She pointed toward a wooded area behind a building across from the restaurant where he was to meet Wiley. "Get inside and stay there." She disappeared into the Cookhouse.

Marc drew out his Beretta and proceeded toward the trees. A shot rang out as he entered. "Arrest me now, officer, and take me away in cuffs." A man with wild scruffy hair emerged from behind a tree and laid a starter pistol on the ground.

Confused, Marc barked an order to him. "On your knees, hands behind your head. The man complied.

As he placed restraints on his wrists, the man said, "Tom was right about you. Make it look good. Eyes are everywhere." As he picked up the weapon, Marc realized his meeting had commenced.

Driving away he asked, "Are you always this dramatic? I hope Jerry appreciated your acting ability."

"He did. Let's get out of the area so we can talk as one policeman to another." Marc kept an eye on the rear view mirror for any stragglers who might want to join them. None followed.

At Scenic Beach State Park they sat on the benches of a picnic table. "It's a pleasure to meet you. Your brother is a great partner and I think he misses you."

"We haven't been as close because of my work. Most people don't know we are related. That's mostly to keep him safe."

"So tell me about Uncle Jerry and you working vice to nail Pepper and his crew?"

After Kastner contacted me about Jerry's request, I hooked up with him and discovered his motive for wanting to kill the bastard. I thought it legitimate, but we aren't the types to break the law for revenge."

"No, but I need to know where Pepper might stash someone they kidnap. My cousin is missing and I have instructions to pay Jerry's loan and stop investigating or she dies."

"Is it Cammie? Jerry told me about how she was hooked on OxyContin and forced into prostitution for a while. I thought she was in Bellingham?"

"Someone snatched her this morning before we could get the State Patrol to her place. A note was left behind addressed to me. If you have any ideas as to where they might take her, I would sure appreciate it. And so would her brother, JJ."

"Yeah, he's a fine deputy. I haven't been close to their operations for two years, but one place they have in Snohomish is on the waterfront in Northwest Everett, near the golf course. They use it as a storage facility but it's a house occupied by Jorge Gonzalez, also called Mr. Smithers."

"I've seen his name in Jerry's material. What do you know about him?"

"He's the money man who sets up the loan sharking deals and makes sure people pay their debts. Jerry never paid the interest because he was to become a crooked cop in lieu of payment."

Marc nodded an understanding because some of the information resting in the trunk of his car verified his statement. "Who took the pictures of your meetings with my uncle?"

"Another deputy was working with us. His name was Zacharias. Unfortunately, he died in an auto accident soon after Jerry died. The driver of the other car went to Monroe for killing the family."

"It wasn't an accident, was it?"

"Probably not, but proof doesn't exist." He stood from the table. "We have to get going. If you don't turn me in for disturbing the peace somebody will be suspicious and figure out what happened."

Marc believed Wiley was correct. He trusted no one any more. Could he even trust his own partner, Tim's brother? Joan was right. Obsession had serious consequences for serious problems with serious challenges.

They returned to the car where Tim sat in the back while Marc drove to the precinct to reunite his new found friend with a brother known for being dependable and honest.

He radioed in to have Tom meet them at the office in case he was away. No mention of the name of the prisoner was exchanged. How did a simple investigation to prove a suicide was in reality a murder become as convoluted as this situation?" Antonio in a hospital and Cammie kidnapped for ransom. What was next?

CHAPTER 34

As he studied the plan, Jerry anticipated the risks he was under-taking. Dying was easy. Living had more complications than he wanted. So being dead made sense. He would clear the deck for others to live a life with fewer of the complications he created by living.

"Did you get the materials from your friends in Seattle?" he asked Lydia about a month before his planned exit from living. She had returned from her travels to the big city and pulled the suitcase into the corner of the office.

"Yes, although I still think what you're planning is insane." She opened the case to show him the ingredients for making him dead. He nodded an agreement and smiled.

"This will surprise them more than anything else I could do to them. Remember, two years will pass quickly and Marc can then do his thing without many problems."

"Are you sure two years is needed? Can't he start earlier? I want this over as soon as possible."

"Lydia, after two years these people will be relaxed to a point of thinking they are home free. If Granger becomes the next sheriff, and I think he will, he can aid the investigation because he'll know the background and who to suspect. My only regret is not uncovering the mole in the department."

She sat on the couch in their office and cocked her head to the side. "What about Canada? Is the Mountie ready for this?"

"I called her yesterday and apprised her of the situation. The evidence is secure and they are working on the drug trafficking connection with Snohomish. The safe house will be procured in the next week or so."

"I think this is so strange. I don't know if I can survive what you're doing." He sat with her on the couch and hugged her. Tears formed but did not fall.

"I've got to call Ben and be sure he's on board. He has the last of the film he shot before the investigation collapsed. I'll get it and send it to McDonald so she can add it to the stash in the locker." They rose from their seating, hugged and kissed, and separated for different chores.

As he waited for the phone to connect with Deputy Zacharias, he thought about the ordeal Lydia was being asked to endure. Life without him was not what he planned, but it had to be. Nothing made much sense in his life anymore and modifying the outcome to secure his family became paramount in his thinking.

A voice interrupted his contemplation. "Oh, hi Ben. I called to see if you had any connection with Granger lately."

"Yeah, he told me of some cockamamie plan you have for committing suicide and you want me to help keep the crowd at bay when the deed is done. Are you nuts? Suicide? You don't seem the type."

"I get that a lot lately. Let me explain the whole thing to you, in case Granger left anything out." Jerry asked him to meet at their secret place where picture exchanges and meetings with Wiley occurred. Bentley agreed. The call ended and Jerry looked for his wife to inform her he was leaving to meet with his fellow officer.

"Please be careful. Those people still want payback and if they can, they'll hurt you."

"I know, sweetheart. I'll take my Glock with me. I should be back in an hour or two." The afternoon was passing by and Jerry wanted to be home for dinner, to share as much remaining time with Lydia as possible. He left to rendezvous with Zacharias.

At the meeting place, Bentley arrived in his own car dressed in civilian clothing as was the usual business. No need to attract unwanted visitors. Jerry arrived shortly before him and scoped the area for any people not needed or wanted.

"Alright, you have my full and undivided attention. What the hell are you thinking of doing? It can't be you really want to kill yourself."

"Ben, I have been plotting my death for a month and have all of the pieces in place to carry out my demise correctly." He continued to explain the details of his plan and convinced his fellow deputy to participate. "So what about it. Crazy, insane, idiotic?"

"All of those. And desperate. I hope it does for you what you want it to."

"Thanks Ben. I'll be in touch and Granger will fill you in with his part. I've got to see Beaumont. Thanks again for being part of this."

"I think you're out of your mind, but I guess helping is my only option." As they departed Jerry wondered if his plan was best. Ben was right about his being desperate. He was. Desperate for success in crushing the group of people who corrupted his daughter and threatened the entire county. Desperate to have Snohomish cleaned up. Desperate to be exonerated of any criminal wrongdoing.

At the medical examiner's building Thomas welcomed him into the office. "Is all ready?"

"I need to explain what will happen to you." Jerry opened the folder and read some of the instructions.

"I didn't realize dying was as intricate as this. What if something goes wrong?"

"You may be in for some surprises which you can't anticipate. Being crippled is a real possibility. You might not be able to function mentally if you actually live. Lack of control of your body is a reality for surviving this attempt. A few other negative outcomes are possible, but you have a better idea now."

"Thanks, I guess."

"I'll have a friend of mine, an undertaker in town, who will meet with you about the final disposal and destination of your body.

If you have any doubts about what you are planning, let him know so we can end this insanity infecting your brain."

"Tom, this will work, and then everything will conclude as it should. I trust you and what you have to do for me. Granger Collins and Bentley Zacharias are on board. Who's the undertaker you want to help with this?"

"His name is Pharris Blakemore. He has no love for Pepper or any of the people associated with him. As he put it to me when I approached him, he has seen too many corpses who met their end at the hands of someone in Pepper's organization. Although no one could gather enough evidence to end the county reign of terror, Pharris, for some quirky idea, thinks you have the balls to pull this off. Your death will be a welcome condition for him to work magic."

Jerry thanked Tom and left for home. He had been gone for an hour and a half. Lydia would have the rest of his day and his night. She would have the rest of his life to share as short as the time would be.

At home he wrote the last of the instructions for Lydia to memorize and he sealed the key to the locker for Marcus to get in two years. One last encrypted message to Granger might keep the investigation going until Marcus entered. He had to be sure of what he wanted and leave no stone unturned as to what he was about to do.

Could Marcus solve the mystery? Would Lydia survive his plan? Was he sure about what he was about to do? He sealed another envelope with the coded message and went to bed to sleep assured of his plot to foil Pepper.

CHAPTER 35

JJ arrived with three young ladies in tow. Samantha Jose looked sharp in her uniform and Regina was as beautiful as ever. Tiberius studied the third lady who entered between the other women. "JJ, good to see you. Miss Jose, glad all is well with you." They shook hands. "Miss McDonald, glad you joined us. And I assume you are Miss Paulukaitis?" He led her to a chair by his desk. "Please sit." She complied.

"Have you found Cammie?" JJ's concern meant much to his uncle. Her kidnapping created a complication not expected.

"Nothing yet, but Marcus may have a lead we can follow up on later. Let's get our guest to a comfortable place." He reached out for her hand, smiling, caring, a perfect gentleman.

He escorted her to another room with a table and chairs and invited her to sit in a comfortable seat while he occupied a folding chair. JJ followed and stood in a corner. "Miss Paulukaitis, what can we do to help you in your endeavor to escape Andrew Pepper and his rogues' gallery of characters?"

She stared at him, disbelieving he contained any genuinely honest bones. "I want Sam with me. Samantha. I will speak with her."

"Fair enough." Tiberius rose from his chair. He left the room to request the Snohomish officer join him. JJ stayed with their guest. A precaution against unanticipated actions on her part.

"My uncle is not the enemy," he said in a soft tone. "He wants nothing for you but the best he can offer. Sam and I feel the same way."

"Your sister did some things you disapprove of. You blame me for her drug addiction and her prostitution. I had to comply. Gonzales would have hurt her and me. Your father was in deep and they wanted from him what he couldn't produce. I'm not surprised he killed himself." Adrenaline heated JJ's body because of her words. His face warmed as he fought for control of the rage building in him.

"My father was trying to clean up his home town, something you and Pepper were making dirty. And who is this Gonzales person?"

"You don't know much, do you? Are they keeping you in the dark because they see you turning against the department like your old man?" The door opened before he responded. Samantha Jose entered with Tiberius close behind. JJ retreated to his corner, arms tight around his chest.

"Sam, thank you for staying with me. I don't trust these other policemen."

"My pleasure, Helene." She sat in the other comfortable chair while Tiberius regained his seat.

He said, "Miss Paulukaitis, we want to trade information with you for a future much brighter than presently can be provided. If you help us to unravel the organization, we are willing to skate on thin ice to get you away from here, reunited with your mother and safe from Pepper, Smithers, and any other nefarious individuals with whom you have close contact."

"They'll kill me if they find me."

"That's why it's best for you to cooperate with our investigation and destroy these people's operation. You have the inside track for us to dismantle the cartel and detain all of the suspects from ever conducting this kind of business or being free to come after you."

"I don't know who to trust anymore. Sam, here, is the best person I know. But the Mountie is new to me and JJ may hold grudges because of what I did to his sister. And your brother killed himself trying to get even with Pepper and me for what happened to Cammie. So which one of you is lying to me about keeping me safe?"

JJ started to come in, but Sam shot a look of 'don't you dare.' He settled into his corner arms again folded tight. Sam smiled at Helene.

"It is hard to trust anyone. Everyone in here has worked tirelessly to get you and your mother reunited and safely away from those who mean to harm you."

Tiberius continued, "My niece is missing and we have no clue as to where they may have taken her. When they no longer need her, she'll die and I'll then break all the laws I've sworn to uphold getting even. I much prefer to remain outside of prison, as I imagine you do, as well."

Sam again spoke, "The Mounties have your mother in protective custody awaiting the trial of several of the Vancouver crew which we now know had connections here in Snohomish County. Trevor Wilkins and Misty Rivers are here, ready to turn on their former employers, so if you want to be part of crushing Pepper, please help us. We will get you out of here to safety."

Helene's eyes puddled as silence allowed for contemplating the consequences of actions for and against the cartel. Sam slipped a tissue to her. She held it close in her hand before swiping at the drops about to descend her face.

"What do you want to know?" Red eyes beseeched forgiveness but her mouth remained resolute, straight and taut with a slight downturn. Trust was a difficult partner to obtain considering her past. JJ cleared his corner post.

"Where's my sister?" A sneer cursed at her.

"He has asked a fair question of you. We need to find her before anyone hurts her." Tiberius pushed a pad of paper and a pen toward their guest. "Write down any possible locations and we'll go get her from them." He sat back awaiting her writing to begin.

Sam coaxed her to write, "If you give us the information, we can make all of this better. Your mother would be proud of you." Helene began constructing a litany of places she knew and visited with girls who were forced into selling themselves for sexual activities in lieu of more harmful results.

As the list grew longer, Tiberius's cell chimed. "Hello, Marc." He listened and excused himself from the group. In the hall he continued the conversation. "Is he sure about the place?"

"As sure as any of the others. It seems to him the most plausible one."

Tiberius signaled to Regina who sat in a chair by his desk. "Marc, I'm giving you over to Regina. Our third guest is making a list of places she knows. I want to see if she matches what Fingers gave you." He handed the phone to Ginny and reentered the room.

"I do hope your cousin is not harmed," she said, a shiver coursing her body, doubt in her eyes.

"We'll be heading to you as soon as we finish the processing to make the arrest look good. His brother is my partner and all three of us are coming to get her out."

Tiberius returned and took the phone. "Miss Paulukaitis had the same place on her list. I asked her the probability of Cammie being there but she couldn't be sure."

"Tom, Tim, and I are heading your way right now. We plan on a raid which has drawbacks if she is not at the location. I figure you, JJ and Ginny want to tag along."

"Okay, see you soon." He clicked off but the phone chimed again. "Hello."

"Tiberius, Granger here. I have an angry undersheriff who says his secretary was kidnapped by Seattle PD last night. What's up?"

"Does he think I did it?" Tiberius smiled. "You do understand what we're up to, don't you?"

"Of course, we haven't been working together on crushing this group for the last two years for nothing. Remember, though, Allenby is smart and cagey. He's not going to let this go without a fight."

"Pepper has Cammie and we're trying to uncover a possible location where they may have her. I haven't told Lydia as she would freak and do something which might get her hurt, or worse. Marc has a lead on a place in Everett, but I'm asking your people to stay away and let us investigate. If anything comes up we'll call you in."

Granger understood, "Ti, Allenby is crooked. I've known it for a long time, but with you seeking answers about your brother and now your nephew being involved, I'll wait to finish him off. But he is furious about Rivers being snatched. He probably suspects you're on to him. He left the station about an hour after talking with me. He'll have a lengthy head start on you. He can be dangerous if cornered."

"Thanks for the warning. Care will be taken." The called ended and Tiberius decided it was time to gather all of the Pepper people in one place to sort through the various minutia gathered from them.

He signaled Ginny to follow him into the room. "Miss Paulukaitis, you've met Miss McDonald of the Royal Mounties. She has your mother in a safe house and wants to relate to you a message." He then motioned for Sam and JJ to depart with him so the two women could be alone.

In the hallway he explained, "Marc is on his way here with two more deputies, his partner in Kitsap, and a former Snohomish deputy, who retired right after Jerry. We are heading to Everett for an evening raid on a house where Cammie may be kept. I have spoken with Sheriff Collins and asked that other deputies be kept away from the house unless I contact him. You two are the liaisons for the County to this task force we are creating. Nothing we are doing is sanctioned as yet, but when we find her, we need to be as official as we can be."

"Uncle Ti, what if we don't find her? What if we make things worse for her? If we fail and they decide she's too big a liability and kill her, I don't want to think about what I'd do."

"You're a good cop, so keep a perspective. They can't kill without every other good cop coming down on them with a vengeance. Other than Allenby, I don't think the county has any other cops on the take. Everett may be a different tale. But I'm not concerned with their problems. State Patrol is not on the take or Olympia would be hounding them into non-existence."

Samantha offered her opinion, "JJ, your uncle is right. We have no evidence she's been hurt. All we know is they have her. So let's go get her." She held his hand to assure him. He radiated.

Tiberius entered the room to retrieve Paulukaitis and McDonald. "Let's go meet your friends and see what can be done to get our little girl home safely." They walked out to another floor and holding area.

"Hey, sergeant, how are our two people doing?" His eyes widened and his mouth curled into a circle. "What's wrong?"

"An attorney showed up and demanded their release." An awkward moment ended with his continued talking. "He's in the room with them and I'm filing the release forms, but I'm having trouble finding the correct ones. He's not getting any happier with the delay." Tiberius muffled a guffaw. "Go get him, Ti."

Tiberius, along with JJ and Samantha entered the room. Ginny and Helene stayed in an adjoining room which contained video and audio of the holding room.

"Afternoon, I'm Tiberius Jefferson, and you are who?" The face was familiar, but unrecalled. Two sets of eyes flitted between the Seattle officer and the attorney.

"My name is Stanford. I came to pick up my clients and this delay tactic is not appropriate. I'll be filing a complaint against the department as soon as I return to my office."

"And which law firm is it?" As the conversation continued, Helene recognized the man claiming to be a lawyer.

"I know him." Her breathing increased as her body froze. She reached for Ginny's hand. "He's one of Pepper's enforcers. Trevor and Misty will be dead before they reach Everett."

Ginny watched Tiberius for signs he realized the truth. "Stay calm and watch. This is going to be good."

"I asked you a question. Which law firm are you with?" Sam and JJ unlatched the safety straps of their service weapons. The man licked his lips and glanced at the three armed policemen.

"I'm with Welling, Brewster and Bartok in Everett. I want my clients to be released to me so we can leave." His voice faltered. "Are we going to be able to leave or do I call my office and inform them of this gross miscarriage of justice?"

"You go right ahead and call but no one leaves here until I uncover who you are in reality. You're not an attorney." Tiberius leaned closer, eyes raging with anger. "So who sent you? Pepper?" He placed a hand on the man's shoulder. "Tell us where Camilla Jefferson is and I won't hurt you." He squeezed the muscle under the suit jacket.

"What kind of a cop are you? You can't threaten me. I don't know any Camilla whoever or where she's at." He wriggled to free himself from the hand.

Tiberius squeezed more. "Wrong answer." The man winced. Without looking away he said, "Sam, JJ, take our friends next door. I want them to see how we'll be sure to keep them safe from Pepper's people. And take my service weapon." With his empty hand he un-hitched the holster. JJ took it and motioned to Trevor and Misty who stood and followed without hesitation.

In the next room Helene, eyes widening and mouth dropping, watched as four people exited. "Is he going to hurt him?"

Ginny grinned. "No, once he's finished, the man will feel no pain, unless he lives. Then he'll hurt for the rest of his life." The door opened and four young participants in the drama unfolding in the Seattle precinct entered. Misty and Helene hugged as Trevor moved closer to the window.

"He killed my brother."

"How do you know?" JJ asked. "Who is he?"

"His name is Jorge Gonzalez and he is as nasty as they come. He has ways of attacking a person who thinks they are in no danger. That other cop better be careful."

"Well, then the show should get interesting very soon. Have a seat people." The three transgressors sat as the three police officers stood with guns at the ready.

CHAPTER 36

Marcus and the Knudson brothers stayed in the cruiser on the trip across Puget Sound. No need for any individual recognition. With Tiberius, JJ, Samantha, and Ginny he calculated the outcome of rescuing Cammie as a positive.

"Let's talk about my uncle and your relationship with him." Tim, AKA Wiley Fingers, grinned. "You and he worked against Pepper by working with him, undercover as they say. What went wrong?"

"All started well in the beginning. We mapped meetings and photographed people's gatherings. We plotted for my climb into the upper echelons of the organization and it was moving swimmingly along, except for the one person we did not suspect of treason who swore an oath to the Sheriff's Department."

"And who was this traitorous person?" Marc believed he knew the name but needed confirmation.

"We had a lead on one of the deputies who fed Pepper information about what we were doing. Suddenly funds dried up and Jerry had to leave the department or face criminal charges of corruption. A few months later he was dead. The evidence we had gathered and not given over to the department vanished. I feared discovery, so Wiley Fingers vanished. I retired and moved away with no forwarding address. My pension is deposited in an account and accumulates as we speak. I have nearly a hundred thousand I dare not touch for fear of being found and executed. Fortunate for me, I had stashed the money gathered from the despicable activities of being Fingers and I have lived on it for the last two years."

"What about the deputy?"

"He's now the undersheriff and I can't say whether Collins is aware of the man's disloyalty or not. His secretary was the connection Jerry and I made when we saw her meeting with Paulukaitis and others." Revelations can comprise a strange brew of odd ingredients and Marc now anticipated the secrecy which ultimately ended his uncle's career and life.

"I have the missing evidence. Uncle Jerry stashed it in Vancouver and my Aunt Lydia retained the knowledge for these two years as a favor to her husband. He left instructions for me to retrieve it and reopen the case. I did not anticipate the complexity or the danger. I only wanted to provide evidence of my uncle's murder and clear the suicide from his history."

Tim watched his brother, Tom, from the back seat. "We should save your cousin, then," he said.

The announcement for passenger and drivers to return to the automobiles prompted no reply. Marc drove off the ferry as soon as the cars in front of him debarked the vessel. He directed the automobile to the Seattle Police office and his father.

With credentials verified and the prisoner delivery papers displayed, he parked the car in the parking lot reserved for official business. Inside the building he asked the clerk at the reception desk to inform Sergeant Jefferson of his son's arrival and was directed to the interrogation floor and wing.

In the interrogation observation room Marc and JJ shook hands. "Afternoon, what's Dad doing?"

"He's convincing that guy to reveal Cammie's location. Who'd you bring with you?"

"I brought a couple of deputies to help recover her." He scrutinized the three young people. "And we have three of Pepper's finest, I see."

"Yeah, they're getting a little taste of what happens to those who misuse other people. Trevor Wilkins, there by the window, says the guy in with your Dad is the one who killed his brother, the man who shot at Uncle Ti last week. Our female guests are Misty Rivers, Undersheriff Allenby's secretary, and Helene Paulukaitis who had charge of Cammie when she was working for drugs."

"So are they saving themselves lots of headaches?"

"We'll, see. Nothing yet. Who are the deputies?"

"One is my partner, Tom Knudson. The other wishes to remain anonymous for now, but he has inside knowledge of the organization."

Misty approached them. "Who are those two men who came with you?" She glanced over her shoulder peering at the two deputies accompanying Marc.

"They're deputy friends of mine, here to help find my cousin. Why? Do you want to tell me something about them? Do you know them?"

"No, probably not. One looks familiar, that's all." She slunk back to her position next to Helene.

Marc strolled to Tom and Tim. "Tim, do you recognize the young ladies?"

Without changing expression or looking toward them he whispered, "Misty and Helene. They both knew Wiley Fingers. Did Misty recognize me?"

"She thought so, but you're out of context and probably don't look the same anymore. She dismissed it."

"When she broke up with Trevor, she and I shared some time together. That's when I figured out that Allenby was on the take, but we couldn't make his downfall happen."

Tiberius left the room leaving Gonzalez in cuffs and shaking. Marc and JJ met him in the hall between the rooms. "Marc, glad to see you made it."

"Did he give up anything?"

"No. He's a tough nut to crack, but he's spending time with us until we sort out his role in Pepper's organization."

JJ spoke, "Wilkins says he's an enforcer. He recognized him and accused him of killing his brother, Max. Can we go now that Marc is here?"

"Patience, JJ. We need a plan. Marc you said you were bringing help. Can I meet them?"

"Sure, Tom you know. The other deputy is Tom's older brother, Tim Knudson, better known to us as Wiley Fingers. He wants to keep it secret for now. Misty thought she recognized him but couldn't be sure."

"Wiley Fingers. Well, well, this makes everything more interesting." He fiddled with his holster belt, empty of a service weapon. "I asked for each of our friends to be held in detention until we get Cammie. Although, it might be easier to have Helene go with us to break the ice with whoever has her."

Marc responded, "According to Tim, the house is owned by a Jorge Gonzalez."

"Uncle Ti, according to Wilkins the man you have been interrogating is Jorge Gonzalez," JJ cocked his head toward the room.

Marc glanced at the room where Gonzalez remained. "Maybe he can tell us where Cammie is or suffer for his silence."

"I didn't know who he was until now. Let me convince him of the folly of silence." Tiberius reentered the room to finish his questioning.

Marc entered the viewing room to watch the sounds of silence die an ignoble death. JJ followed.

Tom and Tim stood in the back corner of the room as three offenders waited in their own veil of silence.

Misty stared at Tim who attempted to shield his face from her. Her eyes widened and mouth dropped. "Oh my god, I thought you were dead." Trevor turned to scrutinize her and then peered at Tim. "Wiley Fingers."

"I'm sorry miss. That's not my name."

"Whatever your name is now, doesn't matter. You're Wiley Fingers. Don't you know me?"

Trevor's mouth formed an 'oh' as he spoke, "Wiley, Wiley Fingers. You son of a bitch. He rose from his chair. Before he could attack Knudson, JJ and Marc forcedly replanted him to the seat.

"Stay put or I'll place you in cuffs and arrest you for assaulting an officer of the law." Marc glared at him.

Trevor's anger remained as he said, "He dishonored my girlfriend."

"You and I broke up. Remember? You ran away to Canada because I brought up the subject of marriage. We just kind of hooked up. It didn't mean anything."

Tim watched the interplay of a love going down the proverbial sewer. He had been involved with her and enjoyed the time. The information gained had brought recognition of Allenby's involvement. He decided to work a hunch, but wanted to ask Marc first. He nodded to him in the door's direction and walked out. Marc trailed out, as well.

"What's up? Did she really recognize you as Wiley?"

"Yeah, and I think we can play those two against each other. Misty will turn on Trevor because she doesn't trust him. Trevor is mad at her for sleeping with me. One of them will break this wide open."

"Are you going in to admit to being Wiley? It might be dangerous to expose yourself to them."

"Helene is the one who should know who I am, since I worked with her closely getting to know which of her girls was not happy and might be a source of information."

"She didn't act like she knew you, though."

"She is a crafty one. We never had a relationship like I did with Rivers, but she knows who I am. Is she turning state's evidence?"

"Yes, she wants out of working with Pepper and the Mountie has her mother in protective custody in Vancouver, another incentive for her to be on our side."

"Good. Let's play the game, then." As they spoke, Tiberius came out of the interrogation room.

"He's not budging."

Marc answered, "Tim has an idea to break two of our guests."

They reverted to the room to confront Rivers and Wilkins, Cammie's safe return, the objective.

CHAPTER 37

As they approached the house in Everett, each person examined equipment and attitude. No gun play was acceptable and yet was possible. Resistance could be deadly to Cammie. Surprise was the antidote. Breaking in had no court order backing the raid. An assault on the property might be construed as a personal privacy invasion. Each accepted the responsibility of actions which could be condemned by judicial reactions. Was someone in the court system corrupted? The raid might expose one or more compromised judges or prosecutors.

The unmarked cars were parked away from sight lines and the markings on the officers were concealed from prying eyes in adjacent houses. The armament carried by each person remained concealed from informants who, aware of the captive in the house, could notify the occupants. One owner was in custody in Seattle, confined and secure from ratting them out to the others.

Paulukaitis accompanied them to help retrieve her former charge, pretending to return her to her former trade of sex for life. Misty Rivers and Trevor Wilkins agreed with the concept of living free and protected instead of imprisoned and subject to the tribulations of stronger men and women.

Tom, Marcus and JJ comprised one phalanx of the operation. Tiberius, Tim Knudson, and Samantha Jose composed the other. Helene remained in custody of Samantha Jose who was to knock on the front door to gain entrance for the officers.

Tom, Marcus, and JJ relocated to the rear entry of the house as Helene convinced anyone at the front she was present at the request of Andrew Pepper.

When no one answered the doorbell Tiberius, unlocked the door with a key supplied by Gonzalez as he argued about personal rights infringements. Opening the door with care to not trip any alarms, the two men slipped in and spread out. The living room appeared to be recently occupied with a cigarette glowing in an ashtray. Tiberius pointed to another room which had a table and chairs with papers scattered across it. A man scanned the collection, reading, not aware of the intrusion because of headphones. He bobbed to the music assailing his ears at probable deafening levels.

Guns were released from holsters as Tim and Tiberius moved to neutralize the first of the occupants of the house. A tap on his shoulder alerted the man to his guests. Tiberius placed a finger on his lips as he pointed his Beretta at the man's face.

As hands rose in surrender, Tim removed restraint straps from a pocket and secured them to the tremoring prisoner's wrists. Another man crossed into the living room noticing the officers. He pulled a gun from his waistband. The reverberation of gunfire alerted Marcus to the conflict beginning inside. He kicked the backdoor, shattering the frame and flimsy lock.

The bullet found its mark and the man dropped to the floor before he could harm either Tim or Tiberius. Samantha had startled him and caused a flinch. The alarm brought a flurry of noises from other rooms. Doors opened and eyes peeked out to scan for the source of the gunfire. Officers dropped into hiding as a machine gun raked the living room. Tiberius returned fire hitting the holder of the gun who retreated and closed the door.

In the kitchen area of the house Marcus, Tom, and JJ spread out expecting withdrawing occupants to attempt an escape through the rear. One person opened a swinging door without observing the room. As he turned, three weapons pointed at his body. He raised a pistol to defend himself and fell with a hail of bullets.

Caution now became the method of transiting the various rooms and levels of the house. Caution for keeping Cammie out of harm and caution to not be wounded by other assailants still hiding.

A voice yelled from a basement entry. "Keep back or she dies." Tiberius moved toward the door where the machine gun fired. Crouching low he tried the knob and opened the door a bit. More bullets crashed through the wood above his head.

At the door where the voice emanated Marcus yelled in response. "You cannot escape. Let the girl go and surrender to us or die. Your choice. If any harm comes to her, you will be leaving here in a body bag." Three shots smashed into the basement door framework, answering his statement.

Samantha retraced Helene to the car, keeping her out of harm, and then returned to secure the headset man outside away from the gunfight. "How many are in the house?" He kept his mouth shut. She pointed her weapon at his knee and smiled. "How many?"

He cringed and said, "Four."

"What about the girl? Where is she?"

"In a cellar room in the basement."

"How many are with her."

"I don't know." She strapped him securely to the railing of the porch and reentered to house.

In the kitchen area JJ said, "I think there was a basement entry by the side of the house. I'll check it out." Tom nodded. As he left the room another hail of gunfire erupted somewhere on the same level.

Outside he found the stairs leading to a door which was opening slow and steady as a man holding a woman in front of him backed out and up the stairs. The gun pointed at her head made caution paramount for JJ. He crouched and pointed his revolver.

"Drop the weapon." The man turned with the woman and pointed his weapon at JJ. JJ's bullet found its target before the man pulled the trigger and both people fell down the stairs. JJ stood and advanced to the stairwell assessing the situation with care. An unknown female pushed the wounded man from atop her.

"Don't shoot. Please help me." JJ pointed his weapon at her and the writhing figure laying at the doorway. He waved her toward him careful to keep his distance from her. He signaled her to kneel and place her hands above her head. She did as told.

"Stay where you are and don't move a muscle." He descend the stairs to the wounded gunman kicking the weapon out of reach. His shoulder bled as the bullet had penetrated and fled in an instant. JJ turned him over and strapped his wrists together, ignoring complaints of pain and suffering. Returning to the young woman, he asked, "Anyone else in the basement?"

"There's another girl in the cellar storage room. She's been drugged but I don't know anymore."

JJ took out straps and said, "As a precaution I have to place these on you." She protested but he tied her wrists together.

With silence again ruling the day, the officers collected the living and moved about the house to uncover other prisoners.

CHAPTER 38

Sirens rang out from a distance. Granger had restrained the sheriff's officers, but Everett police responded to 911 calls of shots fired. Badges were displayed to offer identification to complications arising from the raid.

Tiberius started the instructions for actions before city responders arrived and interfered with goals. "Marc and Tom, go investigate the cellar storage. JJ and Sam, gather our perps into the front yard regardless of their wounds. I think we have one dead, three wounded, and one in restraints. Keep the girl with them for now. Watch Paulukaitis for any stray actions on her part. Tim and I will meet our fellow officers and explain."

Descending the stairs to the basement, Marc and Tom were not prepared for the scene about to be uncovered. A lock on the door to the cellar needed forceful removal or a key. Neither implement was available. Tom found a peg board on a wall with several items hanging on it. One was a key.

Removing it from the peg, he placed it in the slot and opened the lock. Inside was a large room with beds, a table, and a portable watering seat. The odor of unbathed bodies, human waste material and rotting food assailed their nostrils. On the four beds lay young women of different ages. Marc guessed one to be a teenager, younger than Cammie. The other three he did not recognized. All three appeared to be drugged.

"Help me remove them to fresh air." Tom nodded and picked up the smallest one who moaned as if in fear. He spoke gentle assuring words to let her know of her rescue. Eyes remained closed but arms secured around his neck. He found a couch on which he placed her limp body.

Marc followed with another heavily sedated brunette who offered not complaint nor assistance. The third person out was the teenager who wakened with Tom's touch and lashed at him with flailing hands and feet.

"Hey, I'm here to help you. I'm a sheriff in Kitsap County and we are destroying this organization to free you from bondage." He reached for her again but she slapped his hands away.

"I'll take care of myself." She sat up and glared at her savior. Her demeanor softened with recognition of Kitsap County. "Do you know Marc Jefferson?" He smiled.

"Yes, he and I work together. Are you Camilla Jefferson?"

"Who wants to know?"

"I'm Detective Tom Knudson. So are you?"

"Am I what?"

"Are you Cammie Jefferson?" Her face lightened as she became more coherent about her situation.

"I can be if you want me to be." Marc entered the room listening to the banter. The last of the women twisted on her bed and groaned. Attention spun to her before Marc saw the young lady conversing with Tom.

He attended to her needs carrying her to the couch where the other two rested. Tom and the fourth girl walked into the room. She needed help as she staggered toward another chair. Tom sat her down.

Marc faced them and smiled. "Well, I see we have our lost lady of the lake." He knelt next to her and held her hands. "I am so sorry for what you've endured." He hugged her. "JJ is here and will go berserk."

"Let's go find him. I want to squeeze him until he cries," she said. Everett police officers entered the basement.

"Good, glad to see you're here. Take care of these women." His hand swept air toward the couch. He started to leave when a policeman put up his hand.

"We need you to stay here and explain what happened."

"I'd be glad to, but these ladies need attention from a doctor and to be questioned regarding what happened to them." He approached the officer who placed a hand on his weapon. "I am not your enemy and neither are you mine, but this young lady awaits seeing her brother and uncle who are outside. So attend to the other three and get them aid."

He walked by him motioning to Tom to bring Cammie along. The officer did not halt their progress. Outside they found JJ and Tiberius speaking with a lieutenant and a captain from the Everett Department. They waited for a suitable time to intervene.

JJ turned to see his sister and separated from the others. "Cammie." He embraced her, then turned back to the commanders from the city. "This person is the reason for our incursion into this house and the gun play began with the prisoners. We are not in the wrong. We need to ally with you and the State Patrol and most of the sheriff's department to ruin the scourge which is allowed to exist here. Are you with us or against us?"

The captain rejoined the young deputy. "Sir, you are out of line, speaking to a superior officer in such a way. I should have you all arrested for this egregious assault within our boundary. You have no jurisdiction here and have violated several state, county, and city laws and ordinances."

JJ stood his ground. "Sir, I mean no disrespect but your city force has allowed this abomination to exist without abatement for several years. My father worked to do your job for you and died as a result. My sister suffered at the hands of this scourge and has now been rescued. Either help us or get out of the way." He walked his sister to his car and sat her in the back seat with Helene. Turning around his eyes pierced the atmosphere as he signaled his fellow deputy to join him. Together they sat in the front seats and JJ started the car and drove away.

"Well," Tiberius said, "I guess we'll leave the cleanup to you and your fine men and women. Oh, there is a body in the kitchen. He attacked three officers who defended themselves at his expense. You can have the other four and, please, see to the needs of the women who were held prisoner." Marcus, Tom, Tim, and Tiberius strolled to the other car and after a gracious but satirical gesture of goodbye, got in and drove away.

"I'm not sure we made any friends with Everett today," Marc commented. "Where is JJ taking his passengers?"

As he drove the car, his father, laughed. "I guess we need to contact them and find out, but I can guess we will meet them where the most good will be done.

As they approached the Sheriff's office nearest the encounter site, Marc said, "We probably should file a report with Everett so they have a record of what happened. They'll be contacting us anyway."

His father agreed. "They were pissed that we didn't stay for afternoon tea. I'm guessing we will endure a serious reprimand and sanctions but we got who we came for and I don't care what they think. Granger will back us, if we need."

"I'm not so sure about Fellington, though." Marc's comment cooled the conversation. After a period of reflection as his father parked the car, he continued. "I'm not going to worry much about what he says to me. I have other concerns which include clearing Uncle Jerry. Tim, do you think he would have ended his life by his own hand?"

Tim furrowed his brow, eyes scanning nowhere in particular, and tilting his head. "I didn't believe he would, but the evidence pointed to suicide and the M.E. sanctioned the action."

They exited the car, spotting JJ's car in another row. The plan had gone well despite the fire fight with Pepper's people. The rescue meant much to the Jefferson clan.

In the station house they met up with the others and strutted to see Sheriff Collins for an accounting of the action which commenced only an hour earlier.

Collins waited in his office, having alerted his staff and deputies to refrain from communication with any other law enforcement group when CenCom calls were dispatched. His action had consequences for his department from the County officials who oversaw it. He was going to take heat for the raid.

Calling them into a conference room, he invited them to relate to him and his undersheriff, Lieutenant Allenby, the significances of their actions.

Allenby listened with intent, knowing his secretary was in Seattle, restrained from contacting him and that Gonzalez had not reported back to Pepper or himself what transpired at the Police headquarters. He eyed each intruder, discreet motions belying anxious thinking.

When the tale was complete, Granger said, "I must say, you Jefferson boys know how to take a fight to the enemy. I'm glad I have one of you on my side and I do miss the other one. I will take your statements as record and forward them to Everett for their report. They may have additional questions which I will intervene for you and allow you time to respond."

Tiberius spoke, "Thank you, Granger. You have been of great service to our family and to law enforcement in your county."

Granger directed his next comments to Allenby. "Robert, be sure to forward any files we have on the operations against Pepper which we have here. And make sure to find out what happened to Misty." He nodded and left the room.

"We should get back to our respective jurisdictions, although JJ and Sam are here already. We'll take Cammie and Helene with us to Seattle."

"Good, before you leave I need a word with you, Ti, and Marc."

Questioning looks coursed each face. "Meet us in the squad room." Tiberius directed his remark to JJ and Sam. Tom and Tim waited with the women.

When they had gone, Granger asked his friends to sit. "I am happy for each of you. You have saved a cousin and niece and broken a hole in the walls of Pepper's organization. I think Allenby will be very cautious with his activities for the next few days and weeks. He's next on my agenda, but I need Misty to turn on him. How is she doing in Seattle?"

"She's fine. When Gonzalez showed up acting as an attorney, they thought they were dead. When we didn't let him leave with them and we reunited Helene and Misty, I think she may have made up her mind. We'll see when we return."

"That's what I wanted to hear." He moved closer to the Jefferson men with a paper in his hand which read; 'office may be bugged.' "I have something to tell you which will be of interest to your case against Pepper. Let me walk you out and we'll discuss it."

In the parking lot Tiberius and Marcus placed Cammie and Helene in the backseat of Tiberius's car and bade JJ and Sam good-bye. Tom and Tim waited by Marcus's car for a ride to Kitsap. Granger continued, "I have a bit of information for you which is going to change your ideas about this case in which you're investing so much time."

He scanned the area for telltale ears. Seeing no one near, he said, "I have some material regarding Jerry which I know you do not have. He planned his investigation carefully so nothing could corrupt the outcome. He took steps to assure his family was safe and that others involved with him would not suffer. Unfortunate for all of us, one such person and his family died in that awful homicidal automobile wreck."

He cast an eye over the parked cars again. "What I am about to tell you cannot leave your lips for any reason. You must keep it quiet and tell no one. Only four people, beside myself, know what I am about to tell you. Do I have your promise?"

Tiberius shook his head. "I can't promise something I don't know. Tell us so we can decide for ourselves. We can make up our minds afterward."

Collins stroked his chin. "Alright, but after I tell you, then you must swear to say nothing until it is clear from me that you can." Both men agreed to his conditions, and he began a story as unbelievable as any told by the most creative of writers.

CHAPTER 39

Tiberius stood passive as his captain paced the office thinking of words to craft a tirade regarding the raid. The Everett police chief had called and berated him for allowing a rogue cop to invade another jurisdiction without professional protocol of informing them of the pending action. With one dead and three wounded and another left for them to take into custody for whatever reason, the chief's justification for pressing for an apology seemed appropriate.

Tiberius folded his arms behind his back, patient, calm, with a slight grin creeping across his mouth.

"Sergeant, I should have your stripes for this."

"Yes, sir."

"I should put you on crowd control at a Seahawks game without the possibility of seeing it."

"Yes, sir."

"I should have you writing parking tickets in the south end and then doing desk duty for a hundred years."

"Yes, sir."

The captain stopped moving and faced his inglorious officer. Staring a moment longer than needed, he continued. "I should make you retire on the spot. But, I realize you only were doing what others have refused or at least ignored doing up there. And after hearing from them about the exploits, I say you and your son had quite a good time. I understand help from the Sheriff's Office accompanied you."

"Yes, sir. My nephew, JJ, and Deputy Samantha Jose, along with Kitsap detective Tom Knudson and his brother, Tim, a retired Snohomish deputy, all participated. We rescued five young ladies from prostitution, one of whom was my niece. We have evidence which links a house owner pretending to be a lawyer. And we have three informants willing to preserve their own skin at the expense of Pepper and his gang." His cracked into a smile. "Yes, sir, a very productive afternoon."

"Does Granger think he can hold off the Everett police while he investigates his own department? I understand they are upset two deputies were involved and that your nephew told off one of the captains. Professional courtesy and all."

"He was quite articulate about the reasons for the raid and confident about his role in it. They threatened to arrest us but didn't, professional courtesy and all."

"Where is your niece?"

"She went to Swedish for an examination last night. They determined she had been assaulted and beaten. She will recover, but the sexual activity was rape and those charges will be filed against the men in Snohomish Superior Court later today. She has an attorney and Gabby and I are covering her expenses."

"Does Lydia know she's safe? That's dumb of me, of course she does. You would have informed her immediately."

"We stopped by the house after we left Granger. She wanted to keep her, but I convinced her it was best to have her out of Pepper's range of contact."

"Get out of here. And remember, I still cannot acknowledge any involvement in your off duty behavior, unless it does become criminal." Tiberius departed the office for his home and an interview with Camilla about how Pepper found her in Bellingham and who directed the kidnapping. Picking up Regina from the squad room where she awaited his return, they headed for the parking garage.

As he drove home his mind wandered back to his conversation with Collins and the tale of two people, one living and one not. A tale as fantastic as any he had ever heard, gave him and Marcus hope for a successful scuttling of criminal activity in Snohomish County. Jerry had begun a multi-act play performed for these last two years with the directorship as cunning and sly as any on Broadway.

North by Northwest, Dial M for Murder, and *Charades* had devilish plotlines as did *The Maltese Falcon.* And nothing in them had the creative inventiveness his brother produced.

Marcus and he, as flabbergasted as they were, appreciated the detail and energy placed in the production and the attention to detail laid out to follow. It was clear. Marcus had learned the truth that his uncle had pulled the trigger, committing the act so egregious. The case was finished and Joan could relax knowing, he was not injured or dead, or fired from Kitsap County.

But the criminal element remained and Granger's story meant a continuation of the investigation and an increase in the dangers of breaking the back of the cartel.

"Ginny, you are one sly fox. Keeping your knowledge of my brother's activities from me must have been difficult. When you met us in Vancouver, you acted so calm and reassured, I never would have guessed you had as much involvement as you have had. Well, played."

"I do want to apologize for the misdirection I gave you and Marcus, but I promised Jerry and Lydia to play it out. When she called to warn me of your impending trip north, I had no choice but to be the best actress I could be."

I swear, you should be working with us in Seattle or in Kitsap. You're one of the best young detectives I've ever met. I know Marc probably thinks the same."

"You two are quite good, yourselves. I am surprised at the speed with which this is moving. Once we connect all of the pieces, all can return to normal and your family will have the closure you have been wanting for two years."

"What about you and my nephew? You seem to have made a connection."

Her radiant smile gave away her feelings. "He is a fine deputy and a wonderful person. I have enjoyed making his acquaintance.

I do think, though, he is more interested in the other deputy than he is in me."

"So you are interested in him." She glanced out the passenger window ignoring or dispelling his comment.

They arrived at the house and entered to find Lydia present, fawning over her daughter, who did not resist. Gabrielle had made a feast for lunch so everyone sat at the dining room table and indulged their appetites.

A phone call broke up the conversations as Tiberius left to answer his cell. "What's up, Marc?"

"Dad, after last night's revelations, I hardly slept. How could Uncle Jerry do what he did and leave us out of the loop? He knows me well enough to leave me out, but I am surprised he left you out."

"I'm not. He always had the brains of the family, until you came along. He knew what needed to be done. What we have to do now will complete his plan and all will be as it should be. We can gather later at your house and finish our plans for collapsing Pepper's organization and finishing Allenby's reign of error."

"Don't you mean terror?"

"No, error, because he should have been loyal to the people who entrusted him with a badge."

"I get it. Alright, I have to meet Joan after lunch and convince her returning home is safe."

"Is she still mad at you?"

"Of course, and she has a right to be, but that doesn't mean we won't work it out again."

"My son, the eternal optimist. See you in about two hours, then." They ended the call. He turned to finish lunch and question his niece and then head out with Regina McDonald for a sail across Puget Sound to Wendlesburg.

As they boarded the ferry with a long line of other intrepid commuters and tourists and visitors, Tiberius thought about the talented, intelligent, beautiful woman next to him who kept secrets and manipulated people and garnered the faith of others so as to accomplish her goals.

A few years difference shouldn't be a barrier, but his love for Gabrielle was a wall stronger than Berlin and higher than in China. He admired her verve, her nerve, her curve.

"What is occupying your brain, Mr. Jefferson?" Her formality, used as a portal through the walls, ended his dream with abruptness.

He matched her eye to eye. "I was thinking about you. You and your subterfuge with my son and me. You are a crafty…and wonderful person, who knows how to build the finest case against anyone wanting to cross you."

"I do believe you are jealous of my knowing and you being left in the dark."

"Not jealousy so much as incredulity that Jerry trusted an un-known entity over his own family. He gave you the keys to the king-dom without as much as a blink of the eye and sacrificed having us master his plan with him. Would he be so unforgiving of us today?"

Regina reached across the space and clasp his hand in hers. "He loved you and his nephew such that his choice was deliberate and fully vetted for any anomalies ruining his plan. He had to protect the family and get out of the way of your investigation."

His heart raced with her touch. Was a telltale hint transmitted to her? "He didn't have to perform his play without us in the audience."

"But you were in the audience. You were even part of the cast of characters who had a part and now are acting as the director and producer he wanted. You are the stars and you have the audience's attention. We'll gather your son and Tim and finish the last act."

"When we complete this, I suppose you will return to duties in Vancouver."

"My assignment will be over, and Superintendent Buell wants me to pick up the last pieces of the shattered cartel in our area."

"Too bad, you would be a welcome addition to the family."

"You mean JJ and me." Her eyes squinted and her mouth curled. "JJ," she repeated.

Tiberius smiled, teeth bared, "Yes, JJ."

"And his involvement with Deputy Jose?"

"They are good together, but she's not the type of family member I would want for my son."

Tiberius knew the cesspool he dug had become deeper than he wanted. Her craftiness intrigued him, though, and when the conversation morphed into matchmaking; he needed to remain quiet, but Regina had qualities admirable for any person. If JJ and Samantha failed, then maybe...

CHAPTER 40

Marc rested his woeful mind. His conversation with Joan about the investigation proceeded poorly and he realized her intent was to stay away from him. He wanted nothing more than to explain the revelation he gained from Collins, but knew she would insist on the exploration coming to a conclusion. Pepper remained the target and nothing he could tell her would assuage the anger brewing in a cauldron of irritation.

Sitting in the café awaiting Tim Knudson's impending arrival was hard. He wanted to share life with the one woman who captured his heart. But what if he failed to win her back? What if this time, marriage continuance eluded him? What if his children sided with her and abandoned him? He rested his woeful mind.

"What're you deep in thought about?" Tim arrived, stirring other considerations into retention parts of his brain.

"Nothing, really. Dad's on his way with McDonald. Today, we should finish this before anyone else gets hurt."

"McDonald is sure a catch. I wonder if she'd be interested in a well-seasoned veteran."

"You're a sick, bastard."

"You haven't known me long enough to make that call. After all I could be a wonderful person."

"If you and Uncle Jerry collaborated on corruption in Snohomish and waded into the seamiest parts of life, I doubt it. But you are correct. She is quite a catch." His other considerations returned and the conversation lagged a moment. The waitress arrived to refill his cup and offered one to Tim, who accepted.

"Where are we meeting the others?"

"At the State Patrol office. Bennie Goodman is orchestrating the assault on Pepper's warehouses, including the Everett police so as to assuage their hurt feelings for yesterday. Allenby is going to be included at the last second to avoid any tipping off of the gang. He is to be on the front line of the attack and will be arrested as soon as the others are."

"Is there enough evidence to tie him to Pepper?"

Marc wrinkled his brow, knowing the last ingredient for the recipe concocted to end the reign of Pepper and his cohorts was to be in place by the time they arrived in Everett. "With what Jerry gathered for us and the testimony of Misty Rivers, Trevor Wilkins, and Helene Paulukaitis, I think so. We have not found any corruption in the judicial branches of Snohomish, but that doesn't mean there isn't any."

"Are you thinking rulings might deny convictions because of the sketchiness of some of our activity?"

"In the county, maybe. But this can be kicked to state courts and federal courts since it involves other jurisdictions and countries."

"B.C., Canada. Are the Mounties cooperating?"

"Ginny assures us they have the right people covered and have dissected the Vancouver organization enough to cause Pepper angst. His supply is drying up and he will be scrambling for sources."

They finished their coffees, paid, and departed for the house where his father and Ginny were to meet them. In the parking lot a familiar man approached. "Collins sent me. You're a hard one to track."

Tim spoke first, "Hello, Michael. It's been a while." They shook hands. Tim introduced his fellow deputy. "Marc, this is Michael Kensington. Mike, Marcus Jefferson."

"Nice to meet you," Michael said. "Your father and I have worked together for the last two years gathering information to end the operations in my county. Your uncle and I were friends."

"Glad to have you on board, unless, of course, you and Allenby have complicity."

"Fair enough. Granger and I have worked for some time now to weed out the corruption in the office. Sergeant Orwell and I are working together and have in place the needed evidence. Now we should act."

The three men retreated to automobiles for the trip to Marc's house and awaiting the arrival of the next two in the party.

Marc's cell phone buzzed when they reached his house. Checking the screen he grinned and punched the answer button. "Good morning, Joan. I'm sure glad to hear your voice."

"Can we meet?" Her voice offered command over request and Marc realized a postponement of the Everett business was a must.

"Where? Here or at the Senior Center?"

"Come over to my parent's house. The children are at school and I have time now before I go to work. I requested some time off." He considered her appeal as paramount and was not going to blow it off.

"Alright, I'll be there in twenty minutes." He ended the call and informed his cohorts of the need to visit his wife and the delay it may cause.

Kensington spoke, "I'll call Granger and let him know we may be delayed."

"If you need to leave before I get back, do so. I can catch up." He left the others at his house and drove to his in-laws fearing the worst and hoping the best.

After entry into the house, Joan directed him to the kitchen where he sat in a chair while she offered him some coffee.

"I'm glad you called," he said. She placed a mug on the table.

"I want to know where you are in the investigation. Are you finished with your fantasy or do you miss our trip?"

"We're heading to Everett to complete our goals. Dad's coming over here and we'll leave with the full force of the legal departments of Snohomish County. The State Patrol, County and Everett will all be involved in the round up of Pepper and his gang of thugs."

"Then I will be at home with the children awaiting your return. And please, no more gunfights."

"I'll see what I can do. However, Andrew Pepper is not one to fall on his sword unless he has planted it in his enemies first."

"No secrets. You will have a war before this is over and Jerry will still be dead and gone." He thought about his uncle and what Granger Collins explained about the day of reckoning. No secrets. He promised not to say anything to anyone. No secrets. Could this one secret assuage her anxiety or derail their marriage? He made a decision which determined his fate and his future. No secrets.

CHAPTER 41

Tiberius gathered the crew of invaders together just as Marcus returned from his side trip to Joan. The information gathered from Wilkins, Rivers, and Paulukaitis offered an edge in the upcoming battle. With victory the war would end, and everyone could resume their lives and plans.

"We are meeting Granger and Allenby at the State Patrol Office where Goodman and a squad of Everett Swat will be waiting. Let's pack up and catch a ferry to destiny."

Marc pulled his Dad aside. "I met with Joan, as I'm sure the others told you."

"You guys doing okay?"

"I think so. She's not happy about our impending fight. She doesn't want us in another gun battle. I understand her point of view. But that's not the important piece. I explained Granger's revelation about Uncle Jerry's suicide. She asked me not to come, but acquiesced to my wishes."

"Alright, let's finish this." They joined the others who clambered into the van appropriated by Marc from the motor pool for the ride to Kingston and the drive north from Edmonds to Everett.

The supply of weaponry in the back included a rocket launcher confiscated from a gun enthusiast who obtained the weapon illegally and had blown up a barn on his property in a fit of drunkenness. No harm occurred, but neighbors called for assistance and the man was convicted of possession.

"Michael," Tiberius said, "has Granger made arrangements for Allenby to be the commander of the county swat team?"

"Yes, loyalties are going to be tried in the court of frontline fighting. If he tries to warn Pepper, he'll be detained and not participate. If he does his job, then maybe some consideration will soften the judgement against him."

Marc drove past Everett to the north office of the State Patrol where they found Bennie Goodman reviewing the assault guidelines with his fellow Staters. Everett had sent a Swat team headed by the lieutenant Marc and Tiberius had met at Gonzalez's house. Granger and the County Swat team arrived shortly after.

With the team assembled, they gathered around a table covered in schematics of the waterfront warehouses where Pepper and his minions were supposedly operating. Two undercover Everett cops had reported the arrival of their target at 10 AM and the arrival of a large truck with Canadian licensing.

The spies remained in place to coordinate the next few hours. Granger stayed close to Allenby to prevent signals. Lincoln Orwell spoke in quiet tones with his boss and nodded. He moved to another room but signaled for JJ to follow.

"Allenby made his move, wants me to contact Pepper." JJ nodded acknowledgement and returned to the taskforce. Orwell made the call but changed the message. Allenby needed to meet and wanted assurance of where it was to occur. When he returned, a slight wriggle of his head to Allenby gave assurance of message delivered. The ruse was set.

Bennie Goodman aligned the method of the advance upon the warehouses and the ensuing round up of the gang. Lookouts were the first targets and a few of the officers remained in plainclothes to accomplish the sortie. The second wave included the assault on the outer buildings with the goal of no gunfire. The third attack would be against the main offices where Pepper was known to be.

Orwell connected with Collins out of sight of Allenby. "He wanted me to warn Pepper. I changed the message to a meeting and guaranteed his staying put for the next hour. I explained that a task force was being put together for a raid in the next couple of days and that Allenby wanted to give him heads up."

"Good work, Linc. Now maybe we can catch the son-of-a-bitch and hopefully a large stash of drugs and other illegal materials. I'll let the Jefferson boys know."

As the various teams outfitted and plotted moves, Tiberius and Granger stood aside to discuss the addition of the last member of the assault team. JJ agreed to stay behind and accompany the person upon arrival. He was not informed of the name but maintained an open mind regarding the importance.

"Okay, people. Our first team has moved into position." Goodman held a tablet with the global positions of each group and the instructions given to them. The second team was on its way, staying out of sight until the arrival of the last team which included Tiberius and Marc, Snohomish Swat, and a Royal Mountie.

Allenby glanced at Collins and then Orwell. Granger and Tiberius engaged in conversation, but Orwell returned the look and smirked. A slight waggle of the head assured the undersheriff; a message delivered.

Near the waterfront the assemblage spread out to various attack points removing unsuspecting citizens and guests of the city. Certain businesses closed relieving the teams of securing the lives of innocent targets. Downtown was as quiet as the eye of a hurricane. The storm commenced with the ripple of watchmen being neutralized.

Reports on secured radio bandwidths spread the word of headway made prior to the influx of the big trucks and swat teams.

As the assault continued gunfire erupted in a waterfront warehouse next to the final target. The mission, now compromised, resorted to plan B, an all-out push into the properties of Andrew Pepper. Tiberius and Marc maneuvered their team of four into Pepper's large building, removing obstacles who fired on them wild and uncontrolled.

"There's a concentration of men on the second floor," Tim said as a hail of bullets ricocheted above his head. Before he could signal, McDonald moved left into a shadow from which her angle of approach created a diversion for the other three to advance. The second floor firing, aimed at her, signaled them to switch to a stairwell to climb.

Carrying a sniper rifle, she aimed at a target and pulled the trigger. A machine gun rattled over a railing as a thump sounded on the floor. She relocated to offset the expected return fire, which came in bursts, bullets skidding off the concrete or crashing into boxes of shipping crates.

Tiberius signaled Marc to cover him as he ascended the stairs to a landing without much protective shelter. As a shooter appeared at the top to halt further progress, a bullet lifted his body off the floor and back toward the wall behind him. McDonald scored a second hit. Marc joined his father while Tim Knudson gave cover fire. They ascended the stairs to find a wounded criminal begging for help. With little regard to the pain being suffered they placed security ties on his wrists and ankles.

The cover of a wall blinded their advancement. Knudson scrambled up and joined them. Regina was alone with whomever remained on the first floor. Radioing for assistance, Goodman signaled a squad of five into the building as backup.

A noise alerted the three men to a change of weapons as a ball-like object rolled down the corridor toward them. Lying on the floor Marc reached for it only to have a shell nick the wall above his arm. He retreated. The grenade fell down the stairs and exploded. The percussion ringing in ears and dismantling the upper stairs.

Another shot from below caused a yowl. A third body thumped on the floor. Tim stood and yelling a rebel charge rounded the corner before anyone stopped him. Tiberius and Marc followed in close order. Firing his pair of semi-automatics, he emptied the clips into the doorway ahead as a body flittered in and slammed it shut.

A shout from below offered additional support as more officers entered and secured the remaining persons of interest on the ground floor. Regina scrambled up the stairs to the damaged area, surveyed the remnant and cast a grappling hook over the railing which remained. Pulling her body up and over, she joined her cohorts.

"You boys having fun yet?"

"Where did you learn to shoot?" Tiberius asked, his admiration for the young woman increasing with each extraordinary fait accompli.

"We have an outstanding range and I learned as a young girl from my father. It wasn't best being female in my family." She placed herself in a position to offset any movement from the room in front of them. Quiet prevailed for the moment.

The radio crackled. Granger's voice cleared the silence with a message from the command area. "Building two is cleared and we have a cache of weapons. Report in about your progress." Other teams called in with positive results and collection of materials, legal and illegal. Tiberius said little.

"Team 4 under fire. Enemy casualties. Team 4 intact." Turning to the others, he said, "We need to finish this." He peered around the corner while Regina aimed at the door. Recognizing another doorway, he signaled his intent to move forward. Ginny placed two rounds into the door crushing any locking mechanism.

Tiberius raced to the room and checked the door which slipped open with a slight touch. Entering he found three people crouching behind a desk. While aiming he ordered arms up and bodies prone. Each complied. Marcus followed as another round of bullets pierced the first door at the end of the hall.

"Cuff them while I look around." Investigating the files and books on the desk, he smiled. Balance ledgers, assets and liability records, and lists of warehouse holdings, nothing illegal.

Marc sat the three women on a couch next to a wall. "What do you do here?" Each looked at the others. He repeated his question. They confessed to being secretaries seeking sanctuary when they heard the first shots. "Stay here for your safety." Tim and Regina joined them.

Four intrepid people moved toward the shattered door. Marcus asked the women, "Where is Andrew Pepper?" Three pairs of eyes glared at them. "Okay, suit yourselves. We'll be back." They left for the other entry now full of bullet holes.

CHAPTER 42

"Do you think we should assault the room he entered?" Marc asked his father as he peered around the corner. Silence reigned for the moment.

"Ginny, keep an eye on the door as we move down the hall on the opposite side from you." The men crouched and skittered across the way and proceeded to converge on the doorway.

As the men surrounded the framework, Tiberius signaled the Mountie to advance. With rifle poised for an offensive movement, she joined the men. The door creaked as Marc pushed on it. No other sound emanated.

Tim tossed a percussion grenade in and backed away. A scattering sound revealed the presence of antagonists escaping the pressure of the concussion. A blast followed and four people scurried into the room to face whatever onslaught awaited them.

The flash and explosion of a pistol sent a bullet wild and undirected toward the intruders. "Damn it," answered the shot.

Three weapons fired at the source to no avail. Another door, hidden by the haze of the percussion grenade, slammed shut. "Everyone alright?" Tiberius asked with unknown results.

Tim answered, "He nicked me but I'll live." He crawled toward the sound of the door slamming. "Let's get him." Others joined in pursuit.

At the door, Marc said, "One of us should return to the hall in case he has an exit from this other room."

"Got it covered." Regina backtracked to the hall and waited from a prone position. "Ready."

"Alright, let's push on and force him out in the open." Tiberius whispered and approached the next door. As he pushed it open a shot rang but from behind them. He sat on the floor. "What happened, Ginny?"

"We have a couple of baddies hanging around the exit with nowhere to go. I have their exit blocked."

Marc pushed the door again and crawled into the room. He located a table with chairs around it which he used for cover. "Give it up. You have no place to go without getting hurt."

"Neither do you," a voice screeched.

"Alright then, die where you sit for the other door is covered with a marksman."

Another shot rang out from beyond the walls. Tiberius moved to the other side of the room finding a file cabinet. Tim remained at the doorway. Blood leaked faster and stained his shoulder more as he moved. "Damn it." He understood his precarious situation.

A gun skittered across the room. "Don't shoot. I'm coming out." A form materialized from near the other doorway. Hands held high the man had another object in one of them.

"Drop what you're holding." Tiberius's order was ignored. Marcus recognized the grenade with a pin missing. Shifting to his right, he saw the second gunman training a semiautomatic at his father. He fired.

The grenade rolled toward the door where Tim sat staunching his wound. Marc yelled, "Grenade." He slid behind a larger shelf of books and boxes as the first man retraced steps in a hurry. Tiberius pulled the file cabinet to the floor and lay behind it. The explosion rocked the room, pushing the cabinet to the wall and shattering the shelving, boxes and books flying from it.

As the air cleared as slow as the weekend haze in Seattle, Marcus lifted debris from his body and watched for any movement. A gaping hole replaced the frame through which they had followed the two men. He feared the worst for his new acquaintance. Checking for his father, the cabinet slid away from the wall.

One man lay near a window which now had no glass and a second man crawled toward the first. Marc rose to full height and trained his pistol at the movement.

"Lie still and we'll get you some help. Make another move and it will be your last."

"I give up." Hands stuck out from a prone body and Marc grabbed one arm and then the other, twisting them with little regard to any pain inflicted.

"You have the right to remain silent, like your dead friend over there. You have the right to an attorney, although the last one sent turned out to be false and was arrested. If you cannot afford one, then one will be assigned to you and will probably advise you to plead stupid. Anything you say can and will be used against you in a court of law because anything you say will only dig a deeper hole into which we'll throw you."

Tiberius approached and checked the other body. He wagged his head. Only one person captured. "I'll check on Tim and Ginny." His radio crackled to life.

"What the hell just happened?" Granger's anxious voice cracked as he spoke.

Marc answered, "One of the men here had a grenade and used it. He's in custody. The other is dead."

"How is the team?"

"Dad's checking on the others. I'll know soon. Out." He left the man cuffed to his dead friend and retreated to check the damage.

"Tim, hold this tight. Help is coming. Ginny, get me another bandage." She opened her kit and tossed one to Tiberius. "Some nick, Tim. I am glad the grenade didn't blow a hole in you."

"I heard Marc and rolled away from the door. Not much left of where I had been." His face, covered in soot and sweat still paled as his wound bled. "I don't feel so good." His breathing slowed and was shallow.

"Stay with me, Tim. Stay alert." Tiberius strained face beheld his son. Doubt permeated the look.

Marc clicked his radio and spoke. "We have an officer in need of immediate assistance. Get medical here ASAP. All others are okay. One prisoner in custody, one dead. Do not know the whereabouts of Pepper. Three women in custody in another room. Need aid now."

"On our way, will be there within a minute or two." He knew Tim had little or no time left without help. How was this going to sit with Tom if a brother lost and now found was lost again?

Medics arrived to relieve Tiberius of caring for his wounded comrade. Marc collected the prize in the other room, leaving the body for the CSI people. Ginny secured her sniper rifle which had served the cause well.

Granger arrived to find three people dirty and scratched but intact. The fourth was cared for and carted for transport to the nearest hospital.

"Alright, explain what happened here. This was supposed to be an easy roundup."

Tiberius entered his interpretation. "We encountered some resistance and neutralized it. This young lady is quite remarkable. She ended any threat to us from this floor and isolated the last two before they attempted to break out of here with the grenade. They had one other which destroyed the staircase. How did you get up here?"

"There's another set of stairs on the other end of the building. Did you get Pepper?"

"I don't know. Only one person was left and taken into custody, except for three women who claimed to be secretaries seeking the safety of an office."

"We have them and two injured men and three bodies. Quite a raid. I am glad we had warrants to pursue this action." Granger turned to the three other people accompanying him.

The Everett captain and lieutenant stood with Allenby who surveyed the area with a slight grin. "Well, I guess this is the end of our cartel."

"How is Tim Knudson?" Marc asked one of the medics as they prepared to leave with him on a stretcher.

"He needs attention. I'll know more at the hospital." They departed with little hope for a positive outcome for him.

"Does anyone know the identity of the body in the next room?" Allenby's question sparked attention to checking for a wallet or other form of ID.

Marc spoke to his prisoner. "Who are you and who is in the other room?"

"I want a lawyer."

"Yeah, I know one in Seattle." Tiberius's snide tone inflicted its intent.

"You can't hold me for anything. I'm innocent. He threw the grenade. Not me. I was here on business and you broke in and started shooting." The man glared at Marc.

"Fine, then I'll check for myself." He removed a wallet from the inside breast pocket and opened it, finding a Washington Driver's license. The city on the card was Longview. The name was Artemis Pepperdine. Marc grinned. Was it to be this easy?

CHAPTER 43

As he thought back to the memorial service and what had just transpired, Marc wondered if all of the last two years had been necessary. The cartel was now a shambles and the leader either dead or incarcerated.

Jerry subjected his family to harsh situations to bring about the end of his investigation. Now people in Snohomish County could honor him instead of vilifying him. His plan, as bizarre as it was, resulted in the end of the corruption and danger for its citizens.

At the Everett City Police office the remnants of Pepper's gang sat in rooms awaiting interrogation. Marc had begun this mess because Aunt Lydia asked him to do it. He sat across from a man claiming to be from out of town. "Mr. Pepperdine, explain what business you had with the people in the warehouse."

"I don't have to explain anything to you. I want my lawyer and you can't keep me here."

"I can because you involved yourself in the firefight at Andrew Pepper's place of business and he is, or was, suspected of trafficking in drugs, prostitution, and guns. So you are under arrest and will be arraigned along with the other conspirators we rounded up today."

He shifted rattling the chains restraining his movement. "I'm Andrew's brother. You shot him dead when he tossed that grenade at you."

"So you're saying his real name was Andrew Pepperdine and you were just visiting."

"I'm not saying anything." The chains rattled again as he searched for comfort.

Marc stood. "Then a DNA sample to corroborate your identity shouldn't be a problem." Before Pepperdine answered he left the room.

In the adjoining hallway he met with Granger and Tiberius who stood with the Everett chief of police. "He does resemble the body in the morgue. Can we compel him to comply with a swab?" Tiberius asked, knowing the answer was 'no'. Another alternative had arrived, as the fugitives collected on the waterfront were processed for the fire fight which cost five people their lives and wounded several others, including Tim Knudson.

Granger smiled. "Let's bring in our surprise and see if any recognition transforms his story." Tiberius nodded and Marcus grinned.

"I can't believe all of this happened as a result of you and my uncle conspiring to lead us and these miscreants down the proverbial primrose path for two years." Granger wriggled his eyebrows and walked out to another room.

He returned with an additional person who knew Andrew Pepper and could solve the mystery of the man in the room. He had aged some from two years ago but looked well enough. He then stared at the alleged ringleader. "He looks a lot different. Wiley would be sure, if he saw him. After all it has been over two years since I last saw the man."

"We'll ask Wiley when we find him." Tiberius remained coy about Tim Knudson's condition. Losing a close ally was not an easy situation to endure.

"Have you seen Lydia, yet?" Marcus asked.

"No. She is expecting me, though."

Granger interrupted. "We need to go to the Sheriff's office and pay a visit to my undersheriff. It's time for him to relinquish reins to his office. He's is going to be so surprised." The four men left after informing the Everett Chief who promised to retain their guest for the night and see to his arraignment in the morning.

At the headquarters of the Snohomish County Sheriff's Department, Tiberius, Marcus, and Granger entered with the fourth man who wore a hat and dark glasses. In his office they sat and awaited the call to Allenby to join them.

Robert Allenby entered after knocking. He looked around the room, unsure of the odd person in the hat. "Well, I guess Pepper won't be a problem anymore." His comment prompted the hatted man to stand and remove the disguise. Allenby stepped back, rocking, trying to catch himself as if he was falling. "You can't be…you're…"

"I do apologize for the ruse. I had to gather enough evidence to ruin you. Now is the time for you to step down and lead us to any others who have followed you in your corruption."

"You can't prove I had anything to do with Pepper."

"I never said you did. However, two witnesses have agreed to testify about your involvement. Isn't that right, Ti?" He nodded and grinned. "You were the one person who had access to what was happening, and you made sure your secretary informed Pepper and his people about the activities. You informed the financial department to kill funding for the investigation, and you conspired to have good cops convicted of corruption for which you will now stand trial."

Two deputies were called in to place cuffs on Allenby and to remove his service weapons and shield. His career at an end, he was escorted to a holding tank away from other inmates, isolated to think about his future. One of the deputies read the Miranda rights to him as they walked.

"JJ should be in soon. I had him called back to see me. And I think our Mountie is with him." Granger sat behind his desk. "Welcome home."

CHAPTER 44

Joan and Marcus drove toward Wendlesburg after picking up Sarah, Marcus Junior, and James from her parents. The silence roared with unspoken questions about their future as a family. Joan warmed to the realization of Jerry's life but not to the fire fight at the warehouse. She accepted the idea of investigations resulting in clear factual evidence but not the frivolous pursuit of cases which threatened unity.

"I need to check on Tim Knudson tomorrow. Tom left to be with him right now." The coolness of the atmosphere didn't build his confidence. Another disruption to family, more severe than before in so short a period of time, wreaked havoc on his future. Could they reinvigorate a marriage tossed on the whims of the seas of discord?

Joan stared ahead as the car led them to house and home. Three pairs of eyes watched the match competing in the front seat. "Call Tom. He'll let you know. I want you home for now; not chasing ghosts."

Marc nodded an agreement to her negotiations. A settlement was preferred to destruction. At the house, he approached her with caution but warmth wanting her response to be as warm. "I'll call Tom and see what's up." Leaving her in the kitchen, a quiet sharing of hands first, he entered his office and dialed on his cell.

"Hi Marc." Tom's voice wavered. "I have some bad news. Tim had a stroke as a result of his wound. Blood transfusion caused an increase in pressure which burst a vessel. The doc says they'll know more in twenty-four hours."

"I'm so sorry, Tom. Did you get to talk with him?" Dead air, except a whimper, answered his question. "He's a good man."

"Thanks. I wish we had had a better history."

"You stay with Tim. I'll let the others know." The call ended. He returned to the kitchen which was empty. He followed her to their bedroom and found her holding her cell phone. "Something wrong?"

"It's not over. You've unleashed the devil."

"I don't understand? Did someone call you?" He stood next to her as she held the phone out so he could read the message.

They shared eyes and his narrowed as the rage surged from deep within. "We wounded the beast and cornered him. Now he's fighting back." He pulled out his cell and dialed his father's number.

"Dad, take Mom and get out of the house. Pepper is still alive and directing an assault against us. Go to our fishing spot."

Joan trembled and yelled for the children. Marc punched numbers on his cell. As it rang he said, "Take the kids and go to the precinct office. Stay there." She left the room, understanding the need for him to confront the snake and kill it.

"Where are you?" He listened. "Mom and Dad are heading to the fishing spot. Joan and the kids are going to the precinct office. I'll be at the spot in an hour. What did you find out?"

"Our crime boss escaped from custody with help from another rogue cop. Can you guess who?"

"We'll deal with that later. Pepper sent a threatening message to Joan and one to Mom. Find JJ and Camilla. Go to Aunt Lydia and get them to safety at the fishing spot."

"Will do." Silence ruled the airwaves again. Punching in the precinct number, the sergeant on duty answered. "This is Jefferson. Is Fellington in or at his home?"

"He's here. I'll connect you." Time crawled again as he waited.

"What's this about, Marc? The sergeant said you sounded frantic."

"Joan and my children are heading for you right now. Pepper escaped. He threatened her and my mother and I'll need the full cooperation of our forces now, if you please. He's massing his army for a frontal assault."

"That doesn't sound very smart on his part. Didn't you destroy his Everett operations?"

"That octopus has many arms and is squeezing out of the trap. Protect my family, and contact Knudson at Providence Hospital in Everett. He's with his brother but I'm not sure anyone is safe. We have another traitor who may be putting my cousin in harm's way. Alert Granger to not trust his youngest deputy and to find JJ."

"Consider it done. What are going to do?"

"I'm meeting my father at our special meeting spot. I'll contact you later." He clicked off. Checking his service weapon he holstered it and descended the stairs two at a time. A noise alerted him to other people in the house. "Joan, haven't you left yet?"

"I'm afraid they got away from me. It's you, though, I've come to see." Andrew Pepper and two others rounded the corner from the garage and stood with weapons drawn. "You and your father have been a pain in my ass. And now it is my turn to be one in yours." One of the men moved toward him and held out a hand.

Marcus unhooked the clasp and with care removed his gun. He handed it to the man by the handle. "I guess you're smarter than I am." He smiled as his other hand hit the send button on the cell phone in his pocket. "Should I put up my hands? Or do you want to just kill me now?" He raised them without a reply.

"Mr. Jefferson, I had a great life in Everett before you stuck your nose in. I had a thriving business, most of which was legitimate, but not as profitable as my other lines of work. I had many people who benefited from employment in my industries, including your cousin for a while. Then your uncle started poking around. I discovered he wasn't as malleable as he made out to be. When I figured out he was using me along with Fingers, I figured he had to go. I'm sorry I didn't do the job myself. So you and your father are going to be punished for interfering. Why don't we head out to your fishing spot so we can complete the business?"

"What are talking about? Fishing spot?" He crinkled his brow. "I was just leaving for the office."

"Is that where you sent your family? I do believe they are not going to make it." Marc contained the rage boiling in him. Three to one was terrible odds, especially unarmed.

"Any harm comes to them and…"

"And what? You'll never know since I will have killed you. Let's head to King County and the Green River."

Awareness of the peril, in which JJ must be, crossed his thoughts. His cousin had worked with Samantha Jose for almost a year and dated her since the academy days. He would not know what hit him until it was too late. McDonald was his only salvation, if she was with him. Marc remained quiet as he was led to his car.

"Get in and drive and stay off the radio. I wouldn't want to spoil our party. One of the men got in beside him while Pepper sat in the back. The other man followed in a black Lincoln.

Marc hoped someone was listening and that Joan and the kids were safe at the precinct.

CHAPTER 45

Granger clicked on his cell and called Tiberius. "JJ's missing. Cammie and Lydia are heading to the farm. I'm staying here until I find him. His girlfriend turned on us and may have been a Pepper operative all along. She and Paulukaitis have him somewhere, but I don't know where. And McDonald is missing, as well."

"Gabby heard from Pepper and I'm headed out to meet Marc at the fishing spot. I'll contact you when I get there." The call ended as Granger thought about Allenby in custody in Everett and Wilkins, Rivers, and Gonzales locked up in Seattle. He wondered where Pepper was hiding and how he was contacting the remnants of his organization. Another twist screwed plans again.

At the office he spoke with Detective Michael Kensington and waved at another person to come in. "Mike and I were talking about the latest news regarding Pepper."

"Pepper escaped from custody because of Jose and this case is in turmoil." He placed hands on hips and asked, "Have you any idea where JJ is right now?"

"No, but since he left with Deputy Jose from our gathering, he may be in trouble. Do you know where they might have gone?"

"I can't be sure, but I'll try his place and then hers. If McDonald is with them, I'm pretty sure Paulukaitis will be, as well. Regina could be in danger, also."

"At least she has leverage since Paulukaitis's mother is in custody in Vancouver."

"Unless she doesn't care." Kensington and Granger stared at the other man. They understood the gravity of the situation. The sheriff's office had more bad seed than previously known. "Is Orwell still on our side?"

Granger frowned. "He's been the backbone to my investigation."

"Did he suspect Jose?"

"None of us suspected her. She hadn't been on the job long enough for any distrust. She played us and your son. I really thought she like him and all she did was gather information from him."

"He's a smart kid but the brain goes dead around a pretty woman."

"Get Orwell and find him. And McDonald. They have to be together since I've not heard from either since last night." Mike wagged his head and the two men left to gather Lincoln for a game of hide and seek.

At the front desk he asked to be connected with Sergeant Orwell. "Linc, where are you right now?"

"I'm arresting a drunk driver with an outstanding warrant. Whatcha need?"

"Meet me at the station when you get done or I can meet you where you are."

"I'll turn this over to Jose who just arrived."

"Lincoln, don't do it. She aided in Peppers' escape last night and should be detained. Be careful. She knows we're on to her."

The call ended and they decided to track down Orwell's position.

"Sarge, where did Orwell call in from? I need to meet him before he leaves."

"He's at the corner of Rucker and 32nd in the post office parking lot. He hasn't called in a departure. Want me to have him wait?"

"Yes." The two men entered an unmarked car and drove away. The man's cell chimed. Checking the name, he wrinkled his brow. "Why does Fellington want me?" he thought. He clicked open the call. "Yes."

"Marc asked me call Granger, but something else has happened. His cell phone is on and he is talking with Andrew Pepper. It appears he's a hostage and they're heading for the fishing spot. Contact Tiberius and warn him."

"What about Joan and the kids?"

"They're here at the station. Marc sent them before he was to meet with Tiberius. I thought Pepper was in custody?"

"Pepper escaped with the help of another dirty deputy." The call ended and he punched in Tiberius's number as they drove to Orwell.

Tiberius's cell went to message. He left one explaining the collusion in play at the moment. Approaching Rucker Avenue, they turned into the parking area and slowed as they neared the two patrol cars and one beat up Chevy Nova. Two people stood near a man who sat on the ground with handcuffs on.

Both looked at the approaching car which stopped nearby. The two men exited to join them. "She doesn't think we know what she did," he thought. "I sure am glad to find you two. Pepper escaped custody and is on the run."

Deputy Jose's eyes flitted and peered at the newcomers. Before she could get the edge, they pulled revolvers and pointed them at her. Orwell removed his and pointed at her, as well.

"Samantha, you are under arrest for abetting in the escape of a known criminal and the possible kidnapping of two other officers of the law." Mike turned her around and placed handcuffs on her wrists. She did not resist.

"Lincoln, why aren't you helping me? They're wrong about me." Orwell read her the Miranda and smiled as he holstered his weapon. He removed her gun before any problems could occur.

"Sam, I've known about your involvement with Helene and her using you for information about JJ and the rest of the department. I've been undercover for Granger for two years. I wouldn't say too much."

The man's eyes blazed as he spoke. "Where's JJ and McDonald. Does Paulukaitis have them?" She remained quiet. "Tell me or I'll be sure you never get to see the inside of a prison." Lincoln placed an arm on his shoulder. He shook it off. "Where's JJ? Did you ever love him or was he a mark for you to use to further your own agenda?" He shook her and then walked away. "Get her out of here." Lincoln placed her in the backseat of his cruiser with the surprised driver of the Nova.

Clicking on his cell, he punched in a number which went to message. He clicked off leaving no message. Driving to his JJ's apartment, they expected to find no one home and were not disappointed. Samantha's place was next on the agenda, but they didn't have her address. Calling the precinct Mike procured the street and house number. Back up seemed prudent but they decided to go alone. No fanfare of sirens and lights which could be a death sentence for JJ and Ginny, should they be hostages.

Mike slowed his speed and checked the front of the house as he drove by. The curtains were closed and no activity showed. JJ's car was not in the driveway or on the street. With the car parked nearby, they left and walked back to the house. Approaching the driveway and checking to see if curtains moved or a door opened made time crawl as they worked their way to a window of a detached garage and peered in.

Darkness made it difficult to see, but a tarp covered a vehicle. A fold in the covering hinted at an antenna of a patrol car. Mike found the door locked and they decided to enter the house, instead.

At the back door a movement inside caught their attention. Helene was in the kitchen. Withdrawing weapons and leaning against the wall of the house, the man strode to the door and tried it. The knob moved and the latch retreated.

As quiet and patient as a hunting tiger, he opened the door and they slipped in. A mud room next to the kitchen separated them from their prey. They waited for her to leave the room before following her. In the living room she sat next to a dark skinned man, recognized as a member of Pepper's cartel.

Backing into the kitchen, another door led to a dining area. Another of Pepper's men was seated at a table writing. Mike switched to his Taser, jolting the man to unconsciousness. The noise attracted attention of the other man who came in through the kitchen.

As he entered to investigate, he saw his cohort slumped forward on the table. Before he could react a gun touched his temple. "Don't move or you're a dead man," a voice whispered. "Down on your knees and hands on your head." The surprised man did as told. With cuffs clicked on him the butt of a pistol slugged him in the head. The man slouched to the floor.

Slipping into a hallway between the living and dining areas of the house, they listened for any more noises. Before moving in on Helene, another person started down the stairs to their left. They slinked back into the dining room.

"Where's Carson?" The voice spoke to Helene.

"He thought he heard a noise in the kitchen," she answered. "He went to check it out." The man entered the dining room to find two bodies and a gun pointing at him. He raised his hands and then turned to run. One bullet dropped the man in the hall.

Helene screamed at the reverberation and ran in to discover what happened. "Please place your hands on your head and get on your knees." The man beside her squirmed in pain from the wound in his back. "Where are JJ and Ginny?" Her eyes followed the staircase.

Taking out plastic restrains, he locked them on the wounded man and onto Helene who guided them up the stairs. "Anyone else in the house?" Her head rocked sideways.

At the top landing, she nodded toward a door. They entered to find JJ and Ginny bound together back to back. "Sit down on the bed." Taking a knife from his belt, Mike cut the bindings and released the two officers.

"Boy, am I glad to see you." JJ hugged the man after which Ginny smacked his lips with a long passionate kiss. JJ looked at her in wonderment. "Something going on between you two?" They laughed.

The man spoke, "What happened?" Looking at Helene, he continued, "I thought you were on our side." Tears welled up in her eyes and spilled over her cheeks. She related a story as unbelievable as any concoction by storytellers.

"Pepper's men surprised us before we could return to JJ's place so he could change his clothes. They sent Sam in to get Pepper out and held us as hostages." The tears abated and sniffling began.

JJ said, "That's pretty much the story. They warned Sam that Helene would be raped and murdered and that we were to be cut into little pieces if she didn't comply. She left here last night and somehow got him out of the lockup without anyone knowing."

Mike interrupted. "She was seen on surveillance tapes leading Pepper out to a waiting Lincoln Town car. She then disappeared into the night."

"She came back here to report her success, but the men didn't release us. They sent her out today to find Orwell and bring him back here."

"Do they know he worked undercover?" JJ shook his head and looked at Ginny.

"They wanted him to get them out of the county. He had the escape route mapped out for them."

Jerry studied Helene. Something seemed out of place. "What's your story in this? Why weren't you trussed up like JJ and Ginny?"

CHAPTER 46

Tiberius waited in a hidden area of the meeting spot. King County sheriffs escorted Gabby away to a safe place. Several officers from Seattle and the county waited for the meeting to occur. No one showed as expected and he began to worry something had happened to his son.

A call to Marc's phone went to voice mail. He had to believe the phone was not yet discovered. Was he still coming, or dead? Another few minutes passed as several messages were transmitted between the officers. Nothing happened. He walked toward his vehicle to leave the scene when a black Lincoln Town car arrived.

He walked toward the car as it stopped and a door opened. The man who stepped out was unfamiliar, dressed in black suit and coat. His dark complexion made for an eerie countenance. "Are you Tiberius Jefferson?"

"Who wants to know?"

"I have a message for you from my employer." Tiberius folded his arms across his chest. "You are to accompany me to meet with your son. At that time a decision about your future will be made."

"And if I refuse, I suppose I get my son back in pieces." Tiberius closed the gap between them.

"Don't do anything stupid. I must report back that I have you or else." He stuck out a hand. "Now, if you please, hand me your cell phone and your weapon." Tiberius did as instructed. "In the car please."

As he sat in the front passenger seat he clicked on the tracking device embedded in his belt. Waiting for the man to contact Pepper, Tiberius stared at the copse of trees across the lot. A nod of his head signaled the waiting officers to follow. When the man entered and sat, he asked, "Where are we heading?" One glance told him to be quiet. He raised his hands in surrender.

As the car departed the area, an unmarked car preceded them onto Highway 18. The tracking device registered on the map controlled by the Seattle officer in passenger seat. A second car pulled onto the highway behind the Lincoln. A third car trailed behind to become the next in line to deflect any suspicion.

Tiberius asked again, "Where are we heading?"

"You talk too much." The drive was short; only a few miles. The front car had turned off Highway 18 in Auburn awaiting a movement off the road. The following car came off the same exit. As the third trailer made its way, the first car came up the ramp to become the trailer.

After a five minute drive they turned off onto highway 167 and parked in a vacant area by West Valley Way South. Tiberius wondered about the exposed location. Another car waited along with Marcus's car, empty of people. "Where's my son?"

One of the unmarked cars passed as he was commanded to change vehicles. "Patience. We have to be sure you are alone. Your son is safe for now."

"And when I arrive? Are we both going to be safe or is your boss planning to eliminate us?"

"It would serve you right. Everything was just fine until you and your son meddled. Now, you must help us to escape to safety and then you will get your son back." Tiberius sat in the older model Ford Taurus quiet as a mouse hiding from a cat, resigned to letting things play out. The driver swung the car around and headed south on the road. They were alone except for the one car which passed by earlier. The police frequencies crackled to life as the man turned on the scanner in the car.

The frequency being used to follow him was outside the usual range of registered police and CenCom messaging. He hoped Pepper wasn't listening to higher frequencies.

After a short ride, they pulled into a parking area of a warehouse and entered one of the freight doors. Tiberius clicked off the tracker as a signal to his whereabouts.

His patience had run out. He slipped an undetected knife from his shoe, slipping it into his sleeve, securing it to the Velcro strap attached to the shirt. He was glad for the suggestions from County deputies about the belt and the knife. His next move was going to be dangerous and bloody if any harm had befallen Marcus.

As he exited the car, another person appeared from a room off to the left side. It was Andrew Pepper.

"You have been a pain in my side, Mr. Jefferson. Now you will pay for your insolence."

"Oh, now comes the threat of death. Will it be slow and painful or quick? Maybe I should start begging."

Pepper grinned as he said, "Humor. Great, I needed that. Now here is what's going to happen. I'm going to shoot your son in a nonfatal part of his body as an example of why you should cooperate. Then I'm going collect from you the help for me to extricate myself from this state. I do hope you understand."

Tiberius folded his arms across his chest and sneered. "I have yet to see my son, so any plans you have for me are not happening."

"Okay, I'll shoot you and have your son do the task. How is that for you?" Tiberius dropped his arms, crossing his wrists.

"Just let me see him and I'll do what you want." He reached into the sleeve, touching the hilt of the knife.

Pepper looked toward the room and bobbed his head. A few seconds passed until the door opened and Marcus was shoved out, followed by another man with a sneer on his lips. Tiberius noticed the blood trail above the left eye. His son staggered.

Moving toward him, Tiberius reached him before he fell to the floor. "You beat him before I got here. I'll be sure and see you in Hell first." Pepper laughed and waved to the two men who placed arms under Marcus and lifted him to his feet.

"So now you see what I'm capable of doing. You need more incentives?" He gestured for them to place him in a chair. Tiberius pushed his way to his son. A gun butt crashed on his head.

CHAPTER 47

The tires on Mike's unmarked car squealed around the corner of the highway exit, following the state patrol trailblazer via lights and siren. After leaving the highway exit from Interstate 5 to State Highway 18, lights remained but sound warning ended.

They were minutes from the warehouse, the last known location of Tiberius. Two years to clear the scourge in Snohomish County and now the escape of their nemesis appeared imminent. The other passenger, RCMP Regina McDonald, said, "I'll hunt and hurt him myself if we don't find Tiberius and Marcus."

Coming down the hill to the valley exit, the state patrol car slowed as others moved aside to let them pass. Arriving at the assemblage point. The three of them reported to the lead investigator. "What do we have in the warehouse?"

"As far as we can tell, nothing is moving. We can't be sure anyone is still there." The man spun around slamming his right hand into his left.

"He doesn't know it, but he wants me. Let me go up there and confront him. I'll keep my cell phone on so you can listen and be the cavalry when needed."

The Seattle captain in charge held a hand against his shoulder. "That's suicide."

"I've already done that so I won't be doing it again. McDonald, you follow around the other side of the building. Stay on the windowless side." She dipped her head. Staying out of sight for the first hundred yards, the two approached until no cover stood between them and the warehouse.

Emboldened by a sense of finality to the years old dilemma, he straightened his back and walked to the door. A voice inside recalled days of fostering a persona which wanted to cripple an organization which had tried to cripple his family. He listened to the commands barked out to an unknown accomplice for the dismantling of bodies and disposal of the parts.

He whispered into his phone, "I'm going in. Give me three minutes and then break down everything." He pulled his semiautomatic from his holster and turned the knob. Pushing the door, a slight creak announced its opening. He stopped and waited for the talking to cease.

From the back of the building another sound drew attention away from him. McDonald had found another entrance and moved in. He shoved the door open and low rolled into the darkness. Gunshots alerted everyone that three minutes was too much time.

Sirens blared and cars raced into the lot. As doors opened and officers positioned for a siege, two more shots rang out. The silence heard next scared him. Had his brother and nephew been the recipients or had Ginny used her skill to silence their enemy? He found cover behind a large crate and peered around the corner.

Tiberius lay on the ground, not moving. Marcus slumped in a chair tied to the arms and legs. A man lay nearby, unmoved by the commotion. Jerry did not see the blood running from his body. Another man wriggled as if crawling to a safer place was an option. One leg dragged as he moved.

Jerry then saw Andrew Pepper place a gun to Marc's head, as he yelled, "Come out or he's a dead man." He was not looking toward Jerry but to a doorway at the back of the building.

The chance for a surprise lasted only a moment as the door opened and Ginny bold as mind allowed marched into the space with her hands held high. Jerry made his move.

"Hey, Andrew, remember me? I have arisen from the dead to haunt your life." Pepper spun around as Jerry squeezed the trigger.

The roar of the weapon in the room deafened him for a moment. Another boom sounded as Pepper's face registered the impact of one bullet and then another. He fell on his back, his pistol flipping out of his hand on impact.

It was over. Jerry raced to his family members as doors crashed in from the onslaught of state, county, and city officers entering from various spots.

"About time you got here," Marcus groaned. "Check Dad. They hit him pretty hard."

Ginny removed a pocket knife from her jacket and sliced the bindings holding him to the chair." You've been hit." She signaled for paramedics to attend his wounds.

"Not shot, thanks to you and your abilities. Those two had no chance. They wanted Dad to see what they could do to me, so I got a beating and a cut above my eye." He reached down to his uncle who held an unconscious brother.

Sitting on the floor, Marcus put an arm around Jerry. Paramedics worked on Tiberius and placed him on a gurney for a run to Harborview. Another young female swabbed and medicated the cut before bandaging Marc's head.

Other officers secured the scene and checked on the three bodies which comprised the last of Andrew Pepper's operations. The coroner who accompanied the team of policemen and women declared them deceased. Jerry relaxed with his nephew, whom he trusted with the case and his life. Sacrifice had come at a price which nearly cost him his brother and two nephews, a daughter and a son. Two years away from the calamity which he created, motivated him to ruin a man who attempted to ruin his family.

CHAPTER 48

Hospitals are not the best place for family reunions. The food is not catered and the music isn't upbeat and raucous. The environment is drab, undecorated, and smells of medications and body waste. Today's reunion was better than most, however.

Marcus, bandaged and checked out, stood near his father's unconscious body while his mother, Gabrielle, sat in a chair holding his hand. Antonio's release from Providence in Everett and Jerry's return from the dead filled in missing parts.

Lydia, JJ, and Cammie stood in the corner of the large room as machines monitored Tiberius. Joan, Sarah, Marcus Junior, and James remained in the hallway for lack of space. But the family was again intact. The trauma created by a crafty sergeant and supported by wife and friends provided the end result.

As the conversations waned, Marcus pulled his Uncle Jerry out of the room. They strolled down the corridor, away from prying ears. "How much trust did you have in us that you left us out of the loop? You never gave in to Pepper, but leaving me to believe you a coward hurt me. And Dad? He kept on pushing for more because Collins asked him to be a party to your scheme. And yet, he didn't know you were alive. Your children, my children, my brother all missing you. Why?"

"I had to make it real. Involving anyone in the family would ultimately build suspicion and wreak havoc with the materials being gathered. The fewer involved the better."

"Did you know about JJ's girlfriend, Sam, and Helene being sisters?"

"That was a surprise. Jorge Gonzalez working for the same organization as his daughter and not knowing another one worked for law enforcement is a bit ironic. Helene turned on him because her mother ratted him out in Vancouver. Sam's mother kept her secret for twenty six years."

They walked back to the room when Marc's cell chimed. "Tom, what's up?" He listened and clicked off. "Tim, didn't make it. He died about an hour ago." Tears formed in Jerry's eyes.

"He and I had a great relationship. He didn't deserve to die. I thought he might get better." Marc placed an arm around him as Joan and the kids wondered about the news.

"Uncle Jerry, since Collins knew everything, how come he didn't bust Allenby or Rivers? He must have had enough evidence to go after Pepper."

"He wasn't convinced Orwell was being straight with him, so he waited and watched."

"After two years Aunt Lydia follows the plan and contacts me so the remaining evidence could be added. How did Tim McDonald know about me?"

Jerry smiled as he cleared a falling tear. "Using a coded message, Granger was asked to find Tim and ask him to get involved. I knew your dander would be raised and keep you on the case."

Marc returned the smile. "You always did know me well. Okay, so you sent him to entice me and scare the hell out of Joan. She left the house with the kids because she wasn't sure about staying with me. Thanks a lot." He retraced his steps to his family, and then left with them for home.

Tiberius remained in the hospital for another week before he woke from the coma and spoke his first words. "Is that son-of-a-bitch dead?" Gabby shrieked. Jerry, who had stopped by to check up on his progress, laughed aloud.

"He's looking for a tall cool drink to quench his hellish thirst." He watched his sister-in-law embrace her husband as he reached out a hand to clasp his brother.

"Sorry I wasn't able to get him for you. He was going to kill Marcus and he was pissed you still lived."

"I know. He indicated as much, just before he died." Jerry held tight to his brother, not wanting to lose another friend and companion.

A nurse appeared at the door. "Welcome back, Mr. Jefferson. I'll get the doctor." The grin on her face spoke volumes. Staff members wagered the day of Tiberius's awakening, disappointing many whose day had passed and unexpectedly ruining the rest save one, who left to find the doctor.

Marcus and Joan completed their preparations for the Alaskan cruise no longer threatened with a delay or loss. The world was again right and those people who turned away from evil and toward the light began new existences without fear of reprisals from former employers.

Regina McDonald returned to Vancouver to bring Laila Jearene Paulukaitis to her daughter and to see the young deputy, the son of the man who changed her life. Samantha Jose was arraigned on charges of aiding the escape of a known criminal and was released from the Snohomish Sheriff's office. The disclosure of her paternity prompted a breakup with JJ.

Yes, all was again right with the world.

EPILOGUE

"As I understand this," Tiberius growled at Granger, "you and my brother conspired together without including us, leaving us with the impression a suicide had occurred."

Jerry interrupted, "I am sorry about the deception, but I needed the time to collect the remaining evidence. It worked. So I guess all is well again." He sat with Tiberius, Marcus, JJ and Tom Knudson, across the restaurant table from Lydia, Joan, Gabrielle, and Regina. Granger Collins, Lincoln Orwell, and Thomas Eric Beaumont completed the meeting of the intrepid force of officers and their companions. The celebration of Tiberius' recovery and the completion of the investigation offered time to gather the force which fouled Andrew Pepper and his cartel. A tale ensued as creative as any conjured from the minds of crazy people.

"Jerry has not yet heard all of the details of what happened to him. Although, I guess Lydia filled in as much as she could." Thomas Beaumont said. "Jerry asked me about ways to appear dead and yet still be alive. I thought he had lost his mind, but as he explained his plan, I realized the possibilities. I went to work reading about poisons, toxins, and neuro-inhibitors which have the ability to suppress normal bodily functions. I found one which presented the best options."

Jerry cut in. "I wanted to be dead without it being fatal." Laughter filled the air. So much had transformed this crowd in the last few days no one wanted to keep somber or maudlin.

Marc asked another pertinent question which ate at him for two years. "Why? Why suicide?"

"I had to die and control who knew it was a sham. Granger bought in, as did Bentley. So I constructed a play of sorts and put it into action. Suicide seemed the best way to make the enemy relax."

JJ spoke next, "Dad, you left Cammie and me."

"Your mother had full knowledge of my operation and designed the mask I wore to simulate a bullet wound. You both were in good hands." Thomas raised his hand.

"Let me continue. I decided the best toxin was tetradotoxin from the puffer fish. It would give the desired effect and I could revive him as we moved to the morgue. So I obtained 5 milligrams from a University friend with an explanation of using it for research in a case I caught. Or course, the case was Jerry."

Thomas Eric Beaumont continued his tale as fanciful and unbelievable as possible in creative minds. Jerry smirked as the account began.

———— ✦ ————

Jerry, Lydia, and he met in a secluded room of an out-of-the-way motel in Marysville. He brought with him the necessary equipment and toxins to complete the plan. Training to use the materials included Lydia who sat in a chair with them. Next to her was Pharris Blakemore, the mortician who had responsibility for the care of Jerry's body after the program was finished.

"I think you are out of your mind. This is as dangerous an undertaking as anyone can do. I cannot help you if timing is off even a few minutes. This poison can work quickly and unexpectedly in your system."

Lydia said to Jerry, "Must you do this? I can't stomach the idea of anything happening to you."

"I know, dear, but in order to complete what I want to do and to keep you and the children safe, this needs to happen." He held her hand as the instructions commenced.

Listening to each step of the plan, no notes were scribbled for fear of written material falling into unsavory hands. Memory was the safest. Thomas continued.

"After Lydia prepares you for the scene you will have only a few moments to steady nerves if we stick to the time table outlined for this. How will you get GSR on your hands?"

"I plan on firing my weapon using a blank cartridge. After which I will install a spent cartridge and dispose of the blank. Some of the GSR will be rubbed on the wound as well. Lydia is helping with this as she will remove the cartridge from the house when she leaves with a deputy."

"Are you going to have enough time to do this and take the toxin?" Tom asked.

"I'm sure of it. The only concern is whether the neighbors should hear the gunshot and report it or if it doesn't matter."

"It won't matter. Lydia calls Granger who reports it to Bentley who responds with others to find a body which I come to inspect. I remove the body to the morgue doing what must be done during the transfer. As we progress through this play, we have to be unquestionable that each act, each scene, each line is given an impactful performance."

The remainder of the meeting filled out the final details for each person and each act. Jerry and Lydia bid goodbyes and left Tom and Pharris to work out the last moments of his life. Their drive home involved little interaction as each of them churned the concepts in their brains. Lydia doubted the process. Jerry uncovered no other option.

As days passed toward the fateful finality of life as they experienced it, second thoughts invaded his persona. Depression shouldn't precede suicide when the final decision has been made. One is supposed to be tranquil and at peace. This moment contained other revelations for him, however. He had to become history and be gone from the family he loved. He had to protect them and this was the way.

Lydia accepted the change in her life and the situation her children would live in without a second parent. She continued practicing creating the mask for the fateful day, using materials she garnered from a stage make-up artist friend. Her story of wanting to learn the art for local theater satisfied the person who trained her for a week and did not question her intent.

Jerry continued to gather all of the materials for Marcus to use when the two years elapsed. He agonized about telling him his plan, but concluded this way was best. Better to be gone and history to his extended family than to cause possible retribution.

He and Lydia traveled to Vancouver the week before the play commenced, spending the night in an upscale inn as a palliative for her torments which his action was sure to initiate.

The meeting with the Royal Canadian Mounted Police, as odd and unorthodox as it was, settled the final details for his final resting place. The deal was struck and the play was written. The director, actor, playwright, producer, and initiator relaxed as he and his accepting wife arrived back in Everett for a final time together.

"Jerry, I must ask one more time," Lydia said. "Does this suicide have to be completed as planned? Can't we do something less horrendous to you and terrifying to those of us left behind?"

"I know you and others are questioning my motives, but I embrace what must be done for the resolution of this terrible tragedy which befell me and exacerbated your life. It must be as planned." She hugged him and they made love for the last time before his fateful day.

All of the ingredients were placed for his death and no more debate ensued as the minor actors sorted through their various roles to perform an Oscar worthy tragedy. Whatever detail could unhinge the stage on which the characters acted was unknown and disregarded.

Regina smiled as the crowd listened to the various aspects. Marcus observed her and asked, "What made you decide to participate? After all, you played my father and me for chumps in Vancouver. You were so cool, I never suspected your involvement."

"I do apologize, but your uncle's story was compelling and our problem in Vancouver was serious. We figured a little subterfuge was appropriate. By the way, the truck which followed us when we were returning our prisoners to the district office was your uncle. I recognized him."

"Great, Just great. Uncle Jerry, I must say. You pulled off one of the best scams ever." Marc's head swung back and forth.

Jerry cut in. "Thanks, but I want to hear what Thomas has to say about the time after I was put in the ambulance. What happened to me?"

Tom continued the story. "I came in to your house to find you slumped in a chair, your semiautomatic lying on the floor next to you. You moved your eyes, so I whispered for you to close them and let the toxin work. My assistant asked me why I was talking to you. I said I was saying 'goodbye' to an old dear friend. She began shooting pictures of the scene as others came into the room. Bentley came with them and I directed him to have one of the officers relocate Lydia." She smiled and nodded her agreement with the tale.

"As I fussed with you, I declared you dead and had the paras come in and take you to the wagon. They placed you in a bag on the gurney and left. I followed. By this time I figured you had maybe twenty or thirty minutes before serious damage would occur or death."

Tiberius interrupted, "He could have died? Jerry, you're an idiot, but I guess we don't have to worry now." He closed his mouth and pointed at Beaumont. "Please continue."

"I had equipped the wagon with the proper materials for resuscitation and made sure the right guys came with it. They didn't know you were still alive, Jerry, and I made sure they were never to know. That said, they arrived with the correct unit which included an AED with voice monitoring deactivated. That's an automatic external defibrillator. When we departed your property, I hit you with a dose of epinephrine and a shot of dopamine. I couldn't risk I.V.s since that would look suspicious to the crew in the cab. As we drove to my lab, it seemed interminably slow but lasted only a few minutes." Thomas paused and drank some water from a glass on the table.

JJ asked the question all of them wanted to ask. "Did Dad die? I mean, in the real sense of not having a pulse or the ability to breathe. Did he?"

"I guess one could say he was dead. The guys on the gurney were sure of it. He was cool to the touch and unresponsive, even stiffening as if he had rigor mortis."

"And you? Were you suspecting he was dead?"

"JJ, let me continue and I think I will answer your question." He glance around the table at the many pairs of eyes expecting his next words.

"When the guys put Jerry on the table, I asked them for some privacy so I could say a proper goodbye for my friend and cohort. They left me alone with him. Time was passing and I needed to shock him and put him on artificial breathing so he could recover. But I needed the place secured before anyone came to see him on the slab. I pounded his chest to wake up the heart and hit him with the portable AED from the wagon. I thought I had a rhythm started but I could not find a pulse. A noise alerted me to other people coming into the building. I administered another epinephrine and a milli-gram of atropine." He paused and looked at Granger.

"I was sure someone without knowledge of our play was about to interrupt me. And you, Jerry, just lying there dead to the world. I had no idea if you were alive or already past resuscitation. I stopped working on you as Granger came in with Bentley and Lydia. I nearly had a heart attack."

"Yeah, you kind of paled when we came in." Granger smirked as he spoke. "I asked about Jerry but the look on your face wasn't promising."

"No and I was sure Lydia was going to want my hide for not fulfilling my part of the bargain. I checked our victim with a stethoscope and heard a faint beating. He still wasn't breathing so I hooked up a respirator and pumped air into the lungs. If his heart was moving the blood, then his cells would be fed."

Jerry laughed. "I don't remember any of this. So what happened to me must have been traumatic. All I recalled was feeling like I had been slammed by a truck. My chest hurt. My head ached and nothing wanted to move. I do remember trying to sit up and having to be told to lie down and act dead. It was not easy to lie still on that cold table."

Thomas Beaumont nodded. "I was afraid of the next possibility. You dying of hypothermia. I checked your temp which was down close to 96. I had to warm you. Hard to do in a room kept at 68 degrees."

Lydia watched as the tale was unfolding. She was a witness and said nothing as if the event was too traumatic to accept. Thomas continued, "Lydia then applied the next round of makeup to assure people I had done the proper autopsy. He now had the incisions and stitching on his chest as though I had cut him open. Tox screens using blood from earlier withdrawals was sent to the labs to help with the realism. I had recovered a spent bullet from the skull of a pig and sent it to ballistics. It had been fired into the head to give it the proper amount of damage."

"And then you jammed me with something to make me sleep. I remember waking in the bag in your locker. That was spooky, but I was warm because of the blanket wrapped around me."

"We had to wait twenty four hours for Pharris to show and take you to the mortuary. I needed you in a place which looked legitimate." Turning to Lydia he said, "Your makeup job held up well."

"Thank you."

"As Jerry said, he remained in my custody and in a locker. It was better to have him asleep and dead rather than have the enemy discover the deception."

"As the evening progressed, I feared the invasion of my space by those who wanted assurance of Jerry's death. And I was not disappointed. Allenby and Orwell entered the lab as I placed him in the locker. They wanted to see the results of my autopsy. So I showed them. They left satisfied."

"I'm guessing the report got back to Pepper." Marcus's comment created a murmur amongst the group. "Now that he's gone, we can finish the dismantling of his business and get back to being a family."

"I know I planted the bullet in his head, but I have to see the body, to be sure, to be really sure." Jerry squirmed, holding Lydia's hand.

Tiberius interposed, "Thomas, finish your story. What happened after they left the lab?"

"I checked his vitals and nothing was measuring. I figured the toxins were still working against what I had used to undo the effects. He was comatose and had only minutes left. My lab isn't set up for resuscitation, but I keep the needed supplies in my locker, just in case." He paused and each person leaned in to encourage continuance. "I retrieved my bag of tricks and pumped air into the lungs and massaged his chest to get the heart to respond. The ambulance crew came in and got the AED back on the ambulance which had left. So I had to improvise. I shocked him with the ends of the wires of a lamp I had in the room. Not the best way to help, but he's here."

Jerry's head rocked a slow rhythm against the tide of heads staring at him. "That explains the burn scars on my chest."

"Sorry for the inconvenience. I figured you'd accept an apology at a later date. I got a faint beat and monitored you until the toxin effect waned. Then Lydia signed the papers to have you shipped to Blakemore."

"I remember so little of that time period."

"You spent much of it recovering from the effects of the toxin. I sedated you to keep you from yelling and ruining your plan. The side effects of my shocking you and the epinephrine would not be the easiest to endure. Anyway, I made the decision to keep you quiet so you could recover. Blakemore finished the ruse and here you are." Thomas grinned as the Cheshire cat did when he spoke with Alice in Wonderland.

"So now we know how you died, but you convinced people to participate. How?" Marcus flailed hands out to his side.

"Fair question." Jerry explained his part in the scheme.

He sat quiet as mouse on Christmas Eve as Lydia transformed him from living being to corpse. The practice session produced an eerie effect on the observers in the room.

Granger Collins examined her techniques for flaws which could scuttle the plot. He found nothing. Bentley Zacharias stood at a distance of ten feet to be sure nothing suspicious evidenced itself. He gave a thumbs up.

Jerry spoke as his wife stepped back to admire her handiwork. "Does this really convey the idea? Or am I blowing wind out of my ass?"

Lydia spoke first, "I think you're out of your mind. No one is going to believe your corpse image is real. If you want to be dead, you need to be dead. And I, personally, don't want you dead."

"Jerry, as your friend, I have to agree with Lydia. You aren't in fact going to commit an act as heinous as what you propose. So Bentley may be able to keep others at bay, but someone will examine you closely to find out you're a fake."

"Alright, I get that. I'm investigating alternative plans for making this work, but they are dangerous and deadly, which defeats the purpose."

Bentley chimed in, "If the medical examiner has a say, you won't get too far."

"Tom's on board. He's doing the actual research and should get back to me before the end of the week. He has a plan which has risk but will provide the needed features you claim will scuttle my plot."

"After the medical examiner certifies, what about the next step Lydia has to take?" Granger peered at the wound in Jerry's head as he spoke. "You know, the one where she claims the body and we have a ceremony to honor our fallen comrade in arms. What happens then?"

Stepping in to examine her craftsmanship Bentley said, "Jerry, we can only do so much to make it happen. We need to be sure all the right people are on board and accepting your motives for pulling off the greatest con I've ever witnessed."

"Thomas spoke with a friend who is a mortician. I get cremated so no one gets a chance to determine my actual success or failure. When I asked him to help, he just stared at me, guffawing until his face was red. But he agreed to participate. All I want is for you three to agree."

"What can you do to get around the people who are coming in to investigate the scene?" Granger understood his role as the detective of record but wanted clarity about other officers.

"You and Ben should be the only ones allowed near the body, along with Tom. His assistant will take pictures but must not be allowed to touch it. If anyone suspects the body is not a real dead body then the sham is rejected. Tom will guide that part of this."

Ben asked, "What about other deputies?"

"They are to provide outside crowd control and to take care of Lydia and get her away from the scene. They can question her and accumulate evidence as planted but not about the body."

"How is Tom going to determine the body as dead when he has to do an autopsy and certify death? How is it your body will be dead?"

"I don't know what he has for me, but I trust it will work. He knows what he's doing and he's researching this in depth."

"I don't think this is a good idea. What if something terrible goes wrong and the body is dead?"

"Then carry on as if I was still here and make the bastards pay for their atrocities against the good people of Snohomish County. But most important I want those bastards to pay for what they did to Camilla. They took a beautiful, innocent girl and made her into someone who suffered indignities no one should suffer."

"Enough," Lydia interrupted. "Jerry, we are done here. Get cleaned up." After he left she continued speaking to the other men. "My Jerry is doing something I find difficult to accept, but he has been a rock for me and me for him. So I will stand by him and support him. You must do the same."

Granger and Bentley nodded heads in unison. He had been a rock for them, as well. The plan was to be implemented and followed to a successful conclusion, even if it took another year or two.

On the day of reckoning Lydia worked without rest or complaint as she applied the needed disguise. Jerry sat quiet as a mouse when a cat is near, the anxiety of the chase looming large in his head as he wrote the note to be left with her explaining his reasons for the rash action soon to unfold.

"Lydia, thank you for everything. This is going to be hard on you. I know. JJ and Cammie will need the strength you have supplied to me for these many years."

"If you'd let me, or rather, the justice system, I'd just shoot them all and get it finished."

"I agree, but vigilantism flies in the face of what we stand for in life." He signed his letter and handed to her. "Will this do?"

She read it and nodded. "It says what it has to say. The right people will see it and believe it."

"I'll leave it on the table by the chair I'll sit in." She handed him a mirror. "This is the best one yet. Practice has made perfect. Where's the cartridge?"

She reached in her pocket, retrieving the lethal item. He loaded it into his service weapon, a gift from the department when he retired. "Alright then, let's do it. Make sure you call Granger right away." She remained silent wagging her head to assure him of her answer.

He stood from the kitchen chair as Lydia cleared the room of her make-up components and the mess of preparing Jerry for the play about to commence. Sitting in the den in the proper form for suicide, he pulled the gun from his pocket, loaded the blank and locked the clip into the handle. He figured he had one chance to make it right and one chance to finish the job he started many months ago.

After this it was up to Tiberius and Marcus to complete the investigation and round up the usual suspects, to dismantle the scourge desecrating Snohomish County. Granger and Bentley offered the best help to accomplish the task. He trusted them as much as he distrusted the others in the department he suspected of maleficence.

"Are you ready," he asked his wife of twenty nine years. He married the first girl he ever trusted with his heart and entered the academy to become a cop. She supported him throughout the good times and the bad, his being wounded in a gunfight with a murderer who died from the injury inflicted by Jerry. She faced the fact that any day was his last and she loved him the more as a result. Now his last day arrived without ceremony, without pomp, without honor. A day of necessity. A day of restructuring lives.

Jerry ingested the potion Thomas Beaumont created which contained the tetradotoxin, waiting for the first indications of the poison taking affect. "Do you have the spent cartridge ready?" he asked.

She held it out for him and he took it, placing it on the edge of the chair. "How are you feeling?" she asked.

"I can't feel my lips. I better fire the blank."

He cocked the weapon, shifting the bullet into the chamber. All was set. Pulling the trigger in a confined room creates echoes which deafen the living, ignoring the dead. Lydia left the room to avoid the noise and waited for the occurrence. As the noise abated, he changed out the blank fumbling as fingers failed to hold tight. "Lydia, I need your help." His voice slurred.

She entered the room discovering his challenge. Although touching the weapon was not planned, she picked up the spent blank which was to leave with her. He struggled with the replacement cartridge but final managed to load and cock it.

"Did you rub some of the gun powder on the wound?" He nodded and then groaned.

———

Tiberius asked a pertinent question. "With your body reacting to the toxin what happened before the arrival of other players?"

Lydia continued the story.

———

"I can't feel my eyeballs. It's time." Words fell out of his mouth without clarity. He slumped backward, gun falling to the floor. His body no longer capable of moving, breathing coming to a halt. She lifted the wall phone from its cradle and dialed the number mentally written for the script of the play now being performed.

"He's done it." Her conversation short and meaningful. She awaited the convergence of forces different and allied. She waited for the belief of others as to the effect of the action undertaken.

Within ten minutes Bentley Zacharias stormed in, sirens blaring, lights grilling the neighborhood for evidence of their acknowledgement. He knocked on the door as Granger's car arrived with lights illuminating bushes and trees, reflecting off windows which now had faces.

Lydia stepped aside for them to do the needed tasks and continue Act 2 of Jerry's Death, a play in three Acts. Bentley returned to the outside as another squad car arrived. He directed the deputy to tape the area and restrict movement of the uninvolved but rubbernecking flock assembling near the front lawn.

As if a magician conjured the next being from air, Medical Examiner Thomas Eric Beaumont and an assistant drove up in a van equipped with the latest equipment.

Bentley directed them to enter the house as he placed names and times of personnel on the record sheet he carried with him. Three people would see the body of Jeremais Jefferson as it resided in the house. Others would receive the photos taken at the scene.

Beaumont reviewed in his mind the steps they had written for the actions taken on this sunny afternoon. It provided light for pictures as well as a clear summary of what happened.

Granger spoke with Lydia. "I want you to go to the station and wait for me there. I'll see to it Jerry is correctly taken care of. Nobody's messing with this plan of his." He called Bentley on his radio to send an officer in to escort her to a car and transport her to his office. The deputy was the sole witness of the tragedy playing out on the stage of Jefferson Theater who did not have a prescreened part. His task performed with aplomb added to the belief structure of the author.

Mortician Pharris Blakemore prepared the coffin for transport to Vancouver, British Columbia. Lydia had come to say goodbye to

Jerry. His journey, as unusual as it was to be, played out the last scene of this odd staging of an end of life.

She was not traveling with him and arranged with Regina McDonald to meet the van carrying the coffin. Arrangements for crossing the border had been preset by the Royal Mounties. Their placement of the casket in the tomb ended the play.

Lydia accepted the urn which worked as her reminder of Jerry's end and was to be the symbol to others of his final act.

JJ's curiosity compelled another question. "After we attended a memorial service with other members of the family and friends. Those of you who had participated in the play and knew the truth, performed their roles well. The next two years contained far more expectations than originally outlined. Somebody explain to me why an investigation continued without Uncle Marcus or me?"

Tiberius smiled as he spoke. "Granger said we should meet as soon as possible. I asked him about what and he explained"

"Jerry wanted us to continue his work, on the sly." Granger scanned the room. "He had almost everything he needed to finish but lost it because of the corruption in the department."

"Do you know who's rotten?"

"Not yet, but I have some ideas of how to uncover them. We can watch and wait, as Jerry outlined his plan. Are you up for it?"

Tiberius rocked his head and smiled. "Marcus can know nothing if this. He has enough to do in Kitsap. By the way, are you thinking of taking over the top job if Kastner leaves?"

"Maybe, but others are interested and an election has expenses I don't have."

"You'd be the best candidate." Granger shrugged his shoulders. "Think about this for a moment. You would be in the driver's seat to ferret out the corruption."

"I guess but we need to concentrate on the goal Jerry left us. He wants us to dismantle Pepper's group. The rest will fall with him." Tiberius dipped his head in recognition.

───※───

"Uncle Jerry, what about the trip to Vancouver?" Marcus interjected in Tiberius's story. "How did you get there?"

"I guess I have a part of this tale to relate," Regina smirked. "We waited at the border with a truck and instructions from Granger, sent by messenger.

───※───

The van arrived at the Blaine Arches north of Bellingham at the prescribed time. Officer Regina McDonald of the Royal Canadian Mounted Police waited at the border crossing office of the United States. Her assignment was simple. Pick up a coffin.

"Sir," she said to Deputy Chief Arlen Landrensen of the US border patrol, "thank you for helping with this move. We will take control of the item and be on our way."

"This is a different sort of request, but I understand Buell supports it. So knock yourself out."

She repeated her thank you and with the help of two other Mounties removed the casket from the van to an enclosed truck with a medical crew present.

After driving for fifteen minutes the team of officers and medics pulled to a side street building which housed a business run by one of the people involved in the transfer of Jeremais Jefferson to a safe house in North Vancouver. The casket was opened and the body inside removed. The medics revived the sedated person.

As he awakened, Regina spoke in calm words. "Welcome to Canada. I do hope your scheme worked as planned." Jerry grinned and blinked his eyes.

"Have I arrived? Is it over?"

"Yes sir. You are now in the care of the Royal Mounties and safe from any threats. We will need to move you into the house we have for you, but all is as it should be." He sat up next to the box which contained oxygen and lights in case of a premature awakening.

"Has the code been sent?"

"Not yet. It will be transmitted as soon as you are settled in Vancouver." Her voice soothed his angst.

"These people are trustworthy, I presume. Can't play this too safely, you know."

His paranoia had merit. "They are the best and quite to be trusted."

He moved with deliberate steps to the car designated as his vehicle. One of the deputies was assigned to finish the trip to the house. Jerry closed his eyes and breathed a slow intake of air. Releasing it, he stood and moved with steadier legs toward the young beauty he'd convinced to trust in an outrageous plot.

"I could kiss you, but that would be a breach of etiquette. I am grateful to you and your colleagues for participating in this outlandish scam."

"You need to get settled in the house and then we can talk about how the rest of this plot plays out." He nodded and left with the assigned person, another young and talented officer. Canada had the best police force in North America as far as he was concerned.

At the small cabin in North Vancouver, he surveyed the supplies required to make a home for the next two years. If Andrew Pepper knew the extent to which the $50,000 had bought time for Jerry, no one would have been safe in Snohomish. His life was modest at best. His only regret was leaving Lydia and lying to his children and extended family.

The ruse had to work. Everyone thought him to have committed suicide and now things could settle down in Everett until the proper pieces were quietly placed in the puzzle and the investigation concluded. The plan incorporated the assistance of outside forces, which had problems of a nature that tied them to his own area.

After showering and changing into new clothes arranged in the drawers and closet of the bedroom, he sat with the folder of materials sent to Vancouver. His studies began anew.

Without being a problem for the other officers or his own family, he now wanted to plot revenge he would exact on the group which dishonored and despoiled his daughter. Directly killing anyone was not in the plan, but his mind concocted scenarios of physical harm leading to lethal wounds.

He could be the one person who could carry out the elimination without consequences. As long as Tiberius was not aware and Bentley and Granger gathered intelligence, he had a chance. Dismissing the ideas of killing Pepper, he returned to the plan as he outlined it.

Jerry smirked. The danger of using a neurotoxin to simulate his death penetrated even his own sanity. But the con had worked and he had become a memory for the people who wanted to con him. M.E. Thomas Eric Beaumont had the greatest medical knowledge of anyone he knew and his idea of using Puffer fish tetradotoxin to still his beating heart for the 45 minutes required to get him out of the house and to the morgue had functioned as smooth as whipped cream on strawberry shortcake.

"For a period of time, I was like the zombies of Haitian legend. Alive and dead. Living and not breathing. Having a heart not beating. I took a cold water bath which prepared my skin for the proper feel when touched. Lydia's makeup created the illusion of a bullet entering my skull. Collins, Zacharias, Beaumont, and Blakemore agreed to instill the proper protocol for any uninitiated person to believe the unbelievable. I questioned whether I could survive for two years, but I had to since everything and everyone depended on this scam and its success.

"Lydia visited irregularly to keep our relationship moving through turmoil's enigmas. Regina acted as the intermediary. Little or nothing was recorded on any medium which could compromise the plan. Granger used untraceable cell phones which changed week to week to stay in touch.

"As days became weeks and weeks turned into months, I directed the investigation through Granger Collins and Bentley Zacharias. Lincoln Orwell played the game and kept tabs on Robert Allenby. Tiberius worked with Granger and Lincoln to gather material to complete the work needed to take apart the gang. Neither he nor Orwell were included in the intelligence about me which Granger carried.

"Ginny and I kept in touch uncovering the connection between Vancouver's drug gangs and the Snohomish group. As the pile of information grew, we hatched another plot to remove the export of material to Washington State through the crossings along the border."

"One day I said to Ginny, the two years is up and Lydia will be sending the note to my nephew. Keep an eye on the locker and let me know when he comes to get the suitcase."

"And I responded with yes sir, Mr. Jefferson. The choice of working with you has been far greater training than any I had at the academy. You are one of the smartest people I have ever met. It was my pleasure to assist your nephew. I imagined he was as brilliant. And now I know."

"He knows his way around an investigation." They clasp each other in the embrace of a parent for a child but the next action had waited for the proper moment.

"Alright, young lady, I said a long time ago that I could kiss you for what you did for me those two years." He framed her face in his hands and kissed her. Not on the mouth but on her forehead. Releasing her he watched as eyes welled up with tears. All of the others smiled and Lydia embraced her Canadian friend.

He offered a tissue which she used to daub the wetness. "Thanks." She looked at JJ. "Funny thing I said to your dad. I said, now about that son you keep telling me is available. I'm not going to have an opportunity to meet him if I don't get to Everett when the investigation blows open."

"And I said, I'll see to it you're part of the team." She left with JJ to play her part in the next act. A part suited to her youth and vibrancy. A part for a person desiring to be another member of the cast of the family which crafted inexplicable mayhem on evil.

Jerry had contacted Granger at the prescribed time, using the secret code he and Tiberius concocted as children, being sure to include his friend at the State Patrol. Bennie Goodman had been informed of the appearance of one Marcus Jefferson and to stop him before he left Everett. A message was delivered about the open investigation of Andrew Pepper by the Patrol.

As the crowd dissipated leaving family members as the remnants of the party, Marcus watched the others wondering why his uncle had been so callus about his life. Suicide. The truth had been uncovered about what really happened. Jerry was a smart person and dedicated to honest work. The corruption by him had been a focused action of his investigation.

He and Joan gathered the children and said their goodbyes to Lydia and Cammie. Tiberius and Gabrielle hugged and promised to have them for dinner soon. Antonio and his girlfriend left without much said.

On the ferry to Kingston, Joan asked Marc if he was convinced his Uncle Jerry had done the right thing. "This investigation almost poisoned our relationship with you trying to prove something which wasn't true. If someone had killed him, it wouldn't have brought him back."

He looked at her and then out the window. "I know. It just seemed wrong, like something was out of kilter."

Joan worried another investigation might commence before their scheduled Alaskan cruise. His job involved odd times, odd people, and odd situations. She feared the loss of her husband to criminal pursuits leaving her and the family to their own pursuits.

ACKNOWLEDGEMENTS

THIS BOOK HAS BEEN A FUN RIDE THROUGH MY IMAGINATION. AS I CREATED the story arc I had a dilemma as to how to end the story. My wife, Sandy, and I discussed what the goal of my story should be. As ideas percolated the surprise ending boiled to the top and became the cornerstone for the development of the entire book.

While I wrote I wanted to read it to Sandy who insisted I finish the manuscript first, and then she would read it in one shot. I had others who read early drafts and related the same information to me about the twist of the story. It came too soon. Rewriting required the removal of several chapters which ended up in the epilogue.

Tovi Andrews, Rebecca Bauer, Maggie Scott, and Susan Wall, as well as, Sandy read my manuscript and related that this work was my best writing so far. I accepted the compliments as endorsements of my improvement in sentence structure, story development, dialogue, character description and interaction, scene setting, and pace.

Sheila Curwen used her editing skills to find and correct my boners in writing a great novel. She realized the need for certain changes to build drama and suspense, giving readers a book which is hard to put down. The final line editing uncovered a few more anomalies which were corrected. Now it will be up to readers to find anything missed by the many eyes which have perused the manuscript.

David Smith, pharmacist extraordinaire and friend, provided the answer to my question of how to kill someone without it being fatal. I had researched the toxins available and had chosen puffer fish poison. So my question to him dealt with the recovery process for anyone who had ingested the tetradotoxin. He provided the needed steps for survival and the realization that it was painful and potentially unquiet. So I created the need of sedation which had its own dangers.

I need to thank my friends, Robert Dugoni, Jeff Ayers, Terry Persun, and Mike Lawson for providing blurbs. I respect each of them for their teaching me about writing a better book and hanging in there when it comes to staying the course and publishing stories.

I charged ahead with making my own cover for the book, a daunting task for anyone. After creating several versions which I showed to friends, the current cover became the leading candidate and with a few tweaks, I finalized it.

Marsha Slomowitz formatted the interior for printing, a job she had done for Motivations. Epicenter Press/Aftershock Media provided the bids for printing the paperback versions of the book. With Partners West warehousing them, the sales staff markets my books to stores across the country.

Smashwords formatted the e-books and sent them to the various marketing venues. Now for the work—marketing. As each of you readers enjoy what I have created, I ask for you to share your experience with family and friends. I also want to have you review my books on line at Amazon and other venues so that many can share the fun of reading.

BIOGRAPHY

PETER STOCKWELL IS A NORTHWEST NATIVE, BORN IN IDAHO AND RAISED IN Washington State. He spent three years attending Shattuck School in Minnesota for his high school years and graduated from Washington State University with a Bachelors' degree in Education. He holds a Masters' degree in Special Education from Seattle Pacific University.

He spent 32 years teaching middle school in Kitsap County, first in Central Kitsap Schools and then in Bremerton School District. He retired in 2010 and began the pursuit of writing a book.

Learning the craft of writing by attending conferences in Seattle, Cincinnati, and New York City and listening from premier, world-renown authors, he independently published his first book, Motive, in 2013. A second book, Motivations, came out in spring of 2015. Each book has received accolades from people who have read them.

He lives in Silverdale, Washington with his wife, Sandy, two cats, and his special needs son, David. He can be contacted at stockwellpa@ wavecable.com. Follow him on Facebook at www. facebook.com/ pastockwell and on Twitter @pastockwell.

OTHER WORKS
BY PETER STOCKWELL

ADULT FICTION

Motive Series

Motive
Motivations

Historical

Jesus and the Rich Man
(Coming soon)

MIDDLE GRADE BOOKS

Puddle Jumper Series

(Coming soon)

Off to New York
Seattle is Home
San Francisco Rocks

NONFICTION

Stormin' Norman –
The Sermons of an Episcopal Priest

Blog
www.wordpress.com/peter.stockwell